I0534514

ONE NIGHT WITH THE BRIDAL PARTY

By

SARA DANIEL

Includes:

One Night With the Bride
One Night With the Bridesmaid
One Night With the Groom
One Night With the Best Man
One Night With her Husband
One Night With his Wife

ೠ

Decadent Publishing
www.decadentpublishing.com

The unauthorized reproduction or distribution of a copyrighted work is illegal. Criminal This book is a work of fiction. Names, characters, places, and incidents are the products of the author's imagination or used fictitiously. Any resemblance to actual events, locales or persons, living or dead, is entirely coincidental.

One Night With The Bridal Party Box Set
Copyright 2015 by Sara Daniel
ISBN: 978-1-61333-876-6
Cover art by Tibbs Designs

All rights reserved. Except for use in any review, the reproduction or utilization of this work, in whole or in part, in any form by any electronic, mechanical or other means now known or hereafter invented, is forbidden without the written permission of the publisher.

Published by Decadent Publishing Company
www.decadentpublishing.com

Printed in the United States of America

ONE NIGHT WITH THE BRIDE

A 1Night Stand Story

By
Sara Daniel

~Dedication~

For David. For better or worse, richer or poorer, I'll always be your bride.

Chapter One

"It's a week before my wedding, and you're giving me what?" Surely no one would consider such a crass idea an appropriate prenuptial gift. Caroline Sunburst turned to her best friend, Sabrina, who appeared just as shocked.

"A one-night stand," her mother repeated, patting a plastic card into Caroline's hand as if the gifts were perfectly natural, expected even. "And one for your maid of honor, too. Sabrina, you need some excitement to spice up your boring life."

Although too well-trained to make a scene in the crowded, elegant restaurant frequented by the society ladies of San Diego, Caroline would not accept the gift. Faithfulness and trust were her top requirements—she didn't want a relationship like her parents had.

"Mother, I'm committed to being faithful. Blake and I agreed we won't have affairs or cheat on each other."

"How noble of you." Her mother sniffed her displeasure. "You have a week to squeeze in a lifetime of passion. Lord knows there's not a speck of it to be found between you and Mr. Stuffed Shirt."

Needing support, she glanced at her friend again, but Sabrina seemed too caught up in her own shock over receiving such an inappropriate gift from an impeccable, proper society matron.

"You like Blake."

"Sure, I do. He's the future of Sunburst Hotels and knows how to make a business profitable."

Caroline squeezed the card until the edges dug into her flesh. She'd been brought up to manage every aspect of the hotel business and her competence exceeded that of the other executives, even though her contributions were denied equal consideration by her family and corporate management.

"However," her mother continued, "I have a hunch you and Blake have as much fun in bed as your father and I do, which is to say none. When we do have sex together."

Ugh. "I do not need to hear this."

"Actually, since you are following in our footsteps, you do."

Caroline tapped the gift card against the restaurant table. Once, long ago, she'd experienced passion. Or maybe it being first love and her not knowing better caused her to imagine so. Anyway, it didn't matter. Weighted by her father's strong disapproval, she and her lover had gone their separate ways.

"The match has been set up through Madame Eve and paid for in advance, but the gift card will pay for any extras you want at the Alvarado Ranch."

She lurched, bumping the table with her knee and sloshing the water in their glasses. "Where?"

"I couldn't exactly book a room at a Sunburst property, now could I? You need to go someplace far enough away no one will recognize you. I suggested this location, and Madame Eve immediately agreed."

The logo on the plastic card came into focus, teasing her eyes. *The Alvarado Ranch Resort.* The Google alerts about Javier Alvarado and his Montana business came regularly. Despite having no money for horses of his own, he'd shown a natural affinity for the animals as a stable hand where she practiced for equestrian competitions in high school.

Together, they concocted elaborate plans to combine their love of horses and her destiny as an hotelier. The resulting fantasy resort allowed people to pretend to be ranchers for a week while enjoying all the comforts of an upscale life. They even envisioned the house they'd build on the grounds, designing it right down to the "Home is Where My Horse is" craft sign hanging on the front door.

But she'd bowed to her family's pressure, while he built their dream alone.

Her mother hadn't stood up to her father when he'd forbidden all contact with Javier. Surely, she wouldn't have set Caroline up to have a final fling him. No, the one-night stand was simply scheduled to take place at his location. He might have knowledge of such setups but would hardly arrange one for himself where his employees might get wind of it.

She'd go to his resort, satisfy her curiosity over what he'd become, and spend the night alone. When she returned home, she would delete the Google alert and marry Mr. Stuffed Shirt…er, Blake…without a single hesitation over what might have been.

Pulling out her phone, she texted Blake to tell him about the trip, but saw no reason to mention the one-night stand. She would absolutely not sleep with anyone besides her soon-to-be husband.

ය

Javier Alvarado ducked out of the way of the spirited stallion's hooves and grasped the reins, whispering in Spanish to the agitated animal. A moment later, the hum of a helicopter cut through the stillness of the afternoon, and he squinted at the object arriving from the southwest.

So, Mr. Pallson, the latest applicant for the president of operations position, came for his interview after all. Six hours late.

"Can you believe I'm going to offer this inconsiderate ass an incentive bonus to move here?" he muttered, stroking the horse's velvet muzzle.

The proud animal snorted and shook its head.

Javier smiled in spite of his frustration and dug a sugar cube out of his pocket. Breaking wild horses kept him sane. He needed to fill the administrative job before throwing in the towel on the entire venture and working as a simple ranch hand with no other responsibilities. He no longer remembered or cared who he'd been trying to prove himself to when he started.

After brushing down the stallion and mucking out the stall, he took his time settling the animal, then checked his phone to see if his assistant, Alberto, thought the interviewee's excuse worthy of Javier's time. The only text came not from an employee but from Madame Eve.

Your one-night stand has been scheduled. Tonight. Room 1502.

What the hell? Dust caked his skin and clothes; he smelled like horseflesh and sweat and ached from head to toe. He'd be lucky to muster enough energy to clean up, and if he did, a mountain of urgent paperwork waited on his desk. Getting lucky in any other sense didn't figure into his plans.

He'd once dreamed of the fun diversion. Not long after The Alvarado Ranch Resort opened, Madame Eve contacted him, needing to use his ranch to accommodate a 1Night Stand request. His personal life sorely neglected and his sex life nonexistent, Javier half-joked he wanted a complimentary one-night stand in return.

She promised to set him up, but when she didn't deliver immediately or in the following months, he eventually forgot about it.

No way. No woman will want me the way I smell right now, he texted back.

She'll want you. And you'll thank me later. Eight o'clock. Don't be late.

⑃

Caroline thanked the pilot and stepped from the helicopter, the hot wind swirling her hair around her face.

"Ma'am, allow me to take your bag." A portly man in a three-piece suit rushed forward. "Mr. Pallson failed to mention a companion."

She repeated the unfamiliar name. "Mr. Pallson?" If he was her one-night stand, he would be quite disappointed. She should have contacted Madame Eve to clarify she wouldn't have sex with anyone.

"The interviewee." He looked beyond her to the helicopter as if expecting someone else to emerge.

"I came here alone. I'm Caroline Sunburst." Flying to a resort in the middle of nowhere a week before her wedding while a million tiny details waited to be dealt with at home was foolish enough. *All for the possibility of a glimpse of Javier.*

The man gaped at her.

She winced. Way to blow her chance of anonymity. The Sunburst hotel chain's upscale reputation preceded her everywhere.

He clasped her hand and pumped it enthusiastically. "Ms. Sunburst, we are honored to have you apply for the position. Come, I will give you a tour before the interview."

Her mind whirled with confusion. Madame Eve's service surely didn't expect her to interview for the one-night stand. "I'm not—"

"Actually, Alberto, I'll do the honors of the grounds tour," a male voice with a faint Spanish accent announced. Javier stood before her in the flesh—dirtier, more disheveled, and unfortunately a bit smellier than the Internet images led her to believe.

"Very good, sir. I look forward to meeting you again later, Ms. Sunburst." Alberto bowed and disappeared, leaving her alone in the blinding Montana sun with the man who'd once asked her to cast her family and privileged life aside to live with him and everything he owned in the back of his pickup truck.

His gaze swept over her, giving away nothing, not contempt, not lust, not regret. "You're not here to interview for the president of operations position."

"No." Her father had been right to forbid her to exchange her plush bedroom for the bed of Javier's truck. She would have forever regretted her decision and blamed him, leading them to self-destruct. But good gracious, if they'd survived those early years, her dream job would be hers. And so would Javier.

Instead, she'd let her family talk her into resigning her VP position with Sunburst Hotels to focus on her new role as society wife to the man who won the coveted promotion she'd worked her whole life for. "I'm here as a guest, but I would still love a tour."

"Come with me." He offered a dirty hand but immediately pulled it back. "Sorry. I refused to clean up for some asshole who couldn't respect my people and my time enough to show up for the interview when he promised. I've been breaking a horse while I waited."

"You sure he hasn't been breaking you?"

Laughter cut through his solemn expression, and white teeth gleamed in his handsome brown face.

She trained her gaze on the flat expanse of land around them, steeling herself not to give in to the inevitable attraction. Thank goodness the sweat and dirt caked on him kept her from wrapping her arms around him and kissing him the way she longed to.

They'd had their chance together and lost. In a week, she would marry someone else. She ought to return to the helicopter and demand the pilot take her straight home.

Chapter Two

*T*he helicopter took off without Caroline while she fell into step with her former lover. He walked her around the outside of the hotel. When they came to a line of employee golf carts, he climbed into one and gestured for her to join him.

She did so, eager to learn the bad along with the sugar-coated press releases. She'd left Javier for a reason.

They circled the premises for an hour as he explained the workings of the resort, the chores the guests could help with, and the available activities. In between fun, games, and pampering, he'd created a real working ranch, regardless of whether the customers discerned a difference.

While she debated throwing her name into the hat of candidates for the president of operations position, he stopped the cart in front of a bar disguised as a wooden ranch house. The large rocking chairs on the front porch served as outdoor seating, giving patrons a full view of the stables.

"I need to run home and shower, so I can at least shake your hand. The bar is air-conditioned, if you don't mind waiting here." He spoke to her with the polite distance of an acquaintance.

"Sounds perfect." Yet, disappointment plagued her as she followed him across the smooth wooden planks to the front door. This man meant so much more to her than a colleague or congenial stranger. She missed the intimate connection they'd once shared.

Pulling the door open, he called across the room, "Mac, the lady can have whatever she wants."

"Anything?" the burly bartender asked with a raised eyebrow.

"Anything," he repeated with absolute certainty, pinning her with his gaze. Her disillusionment vanished, and she shivered with anticipation. For her conscience's sake, she should have worked her engagement into their earlier small talk.

A traitorous part of her never wanted him to know.

"What would you like?" the bartender asked, as Javier left her alone.

Strolling over, she sat on a stool. "Iced tea, please. Have you worked here long, Mac?"

"Since the boss opened the doors."

A loyal employee. Caroline smiled. "He's created an amazing place."

"He envisioned combining a working man's world with high class luxury." The barman handed her a tall glass with a lemon wedged on the rim. "To tell you the truth, I didn't think it would work, but he proved me wrong."

She squeezed the lemon into the glass, grateful to have something to occupy her hands as second guessing invaded her thoughts. Would he have made their relationship work against the odds, too? Wondering how far away he was at the moment, she changed the subject. "So where do you all live? Is there a town close by?"

"Twenty miles. A lot of us live there. Some commute farther. My wife and I live in the country. A few ranch hands stay on the premises."

"Javier is one of them?" She still knew him well enough to be confident he'd live on site, despite his responsibilities extending beyond those of a simple ranch hand.

"He has his own place, two buildings over. Don't even think about going there," Mac warned. "In all the time I've been here, he's never taken anyone inside with him—no employees, not his friends, nor a single girlfriend."

She bit her tongue to keep from asking about his current girlfriend status. None of her business. Anyway, having never invited her to his house, a relationship couldn't be serious.

She shifted uncomfortably on the stool. Despite welcoming Blake in her physical house, their relationship cruised on a superficial level. She never let him inside her psyche, and he showed no interest in checking it out. Yet the pending wedding pointed to a more serious relationship. If she critiqued Javier's intimacy levels, she needed to examine her own.

A family entered through the front door, pulling her from her uneasy musings. The parents ordered drinks and snacks, and Caroline chatted with the kids. From the East Coast, they'd enjoyed their ranch vacation so much the previous year, they'd returned as repeat customers.

The kids' contagious enthusiasm combined with their parents' high praise for the staff sent her into another spiral of wishful thinking. If only she'd been part of building her and Javier's dream destination from the ground up.

The mentality at Sunburst Hotels shunned big dreams. Her innovations had been stifled from the start. Life with Blake would be little more than an exercise in maintaining the status quo.

After the family took their food to the porch, another couple came in and ordered margaritas.

"We're on our honeymoon," the lady announced. Her husband splayed his hand across her ass, and she kissed him fully on the lips then straddled him on the bar stool.

Their public display of affection stabbed Caroline with longing. In a week, she, too, would be on her honeymoon but couldn't imagine acting so unrestrained with Blake, even in private.

"You know, we're going to take a rain check on those drinks." The groom lifted his giggling bride in his arms and staggered for the door.

"Newlyweds," Mac muttered, more amused than annoyed, pushing the couple's abandoned cocktails toward her. "On the house."

"No thanks." Raising the iced tea to her lips, she tried to remember acting so embarrassingly lovesick. Memories flashed so swiftly and vividly, she reached for the nearest margarita to blur them.

Javier came into focus anyway. He strode into the bar, radiating his ever-present aura of raw sexuality. Freshly showered, with dark, wet hair curling around his ears and broad shoulders stretching his clean cowboy shirt, he epitomized everything she found irresistible in a man.

Arriving in the helicopter, she'd looked down over the oasis created in an endless plain of land and sky, and fallen in love. After an hour touring the grounds, her affection had cemented into a need to make herself one with the place, and she'd considered interviewing for the top job to run the resort. But working for Javier would never be just a job. And living so close to him, she'd never remain faithful to anyone else.

His exhaustion hadn't left him too tired to respond to a woman. The purely feminine appreciation in Caroline's eyes as he walked toward her stirred his awareness and long-suppressed need. Unfortunately, Madame Eve had picked the worst time to set him up with a one-night stand. No matter how perfect the date he had yet to meet, he only wanted the woman who'd stolen his teenage heart.

He offered his right hand. "I'm finally presentable enough for a handshake."

Curling her fingers around his, she flooded him with heat until he damn near forgot what he planned to interrogate her about.

"Thanks for keeping me company, Mac." She tipped her head toward his bartender then rose from her stool, leaving her drinks behind with a folded bill discretely tucked under one coaster.

People didn't end up sipping frou-frou drinks at his resort because they were passing through and needed a place to crash for the night. No, she'd shown up deliberately and very much alone in her fancy-schmancy helicopter, clueless about the job opening.

Was she trying to rub her wealth in his face? He immediately discarded the notion and not because his worth had surpassed her parents'. She'd never put stock in riches and social status, even when everyone else, including him, believed she could do better than him.

He led her to the seclusion of the stable then spun to face her. "Are you buttering up my employees to gather secrets about my resort so you can undermine my success and create your own for Sunburst Hotels?"

She blinked, her blue eyes owlish and innocent. "You think I arrived in a helicopter and announced my presence to the entire county to engage in corporate espionage? Granted, I don't have any prior experience, but I think I'd take the under-the-radar approach. Arrive in a rental car and check in anonymously. Maybe apply for a job as a janitor."

Okay, so he'd accused before thinking the idea through. Her closeness rendered him temporarily insane. He gripped her upper arms. "What are you doing then?"

"For Sunburst Hotels? Absolutely nothing. I quit my job a month ago."

"You want to apply as my private janitor? I'm only in my office at night, and if you came in I guarantee you wouldn't be emptying garbage cans."

Her eyes grew even more luminous. "What would I be doing?"

"Stripping, so I could take you on my desk."

Her lips parted, as if the image turned her on.

The hell with the desk. He pulled her flush to his body, wanting her immediately—in the stable, on his real turf.

"Wait." She pushed against his chest. "We can't just pick up where we left off fifteen years ago."

"Why not? We're two consenting, unattached adults."

Of course, they had issues from the past to work through. But when they'd been together, she understood him the way no one else ever had.

"Um." Her gaze dropped away from his. "Actually, I'm not unattached. I'm engaged."

Oh. Fuck.

Chapter Three

She'd finally admitted what she should have said the moment she stepped out of the helicopter and came face to face with her former lover. Not expecting any congratulations, Caroline waited for his shocked betrayal to penetrate enough for him to speak.

Indeed, he snatched her left hand off his chest and lifted it in front of his face. "Where's your ring?"

"I left it at home. I don't wear it unless I have to."

"So you can screw around on him?"

She yanked her hand away, stung he saw her actions as a purposeful attempt to deceive him. "I have no intention of screwing around with anyone. I'm going to be faithful."

"When? After the wedding?"

Her stomach twisted. She'd been true to Blake and always intended to. Her only expectation from a partner was fidelity. Yet, hadn't she traveled to the resort on the prospect of a one-night stand?

Having no intention of going through with the meaningless hookup didn't excuse her. Despite knowing the odds were good she would run into the only man she'd ever loved, she'd never asked Blake to accompany her or considered introducing the two men. And within an hour, her litany of what if's had flamed into raging desire, leaving her aching to betray her principles and jump into the sack.

"When we kiss, are you going to think about your fiancé?"

Javier's deep brown eyes filled with pain.

Hating herself for causing it, she lifted her hand to his cheek. "I'm not going to kiss you."

He intercepted her fingers and batted them away. "Don't try your seduction tricks on me."

"I'm not seducing you. I came here to close this chapter of my life."

"You closed it long ago then reopened it today when you stepped out of your pretentious helicopter." Bridging the distance between them, he pressed his lips hard and furious against hers, thrusting his tongue into her mouth, taking possession.

His fury and frustration tasted too delicious to push away, and she welcomed his domination, kissing him back with the same wild desperation.

Every exhilarating, explosive kiss from his sensuous mouth melted away the intervening years, reviving the components of their past relationship—quiet discussions, camaraderie, and instant passion.

Until a horse snorted. No longer accustomed to the smells and sounds of a barn, Caroline jerked and turned toward the closest stall.

Javier shoved away and stalked over to soothe the animal. "What's your fiancé's name?" he demanded, not glancing at her.

She stared at him stupidly, her lips swollen and tingling. Every nerve screamed for his touch, leaving her wanting him with such longing nothing else mattered, including her own name, or what it would soon become.

Finally, he met her gaze, glaring with such patent disgust, her haze of lust disintegrated. "I won't be your dirty, cheap thrill this time, Caroline."

"You never were." The specialness of their past connection had brought her to his resort. Discovering it still existed both complicated her life and excited her. She reached out to touch him, but he sidestepped and stormed out of the stable, swearing in Spanish and leaving her alone with impatient, prancing horses. Several of them lifted their heads over the stall doors to snort at her in disapproval.

The dim, unfamiliar environment spooked her enough to keep her from dissolving into a puddle of tears. She crossed her arms over her chest and hurried out of the barn into the glare of a pink and orange sunset.

Javier had disappeared, along with the rest of the resort staff and guests, leaving her alone.

She pulled out her phone and dialed Blake's number, hating the cruelty of the message she needed to leave. But the truth couldn't wait for an appropriate opening.

Instead of voicemail, he answered in person, and her stomach twisted.

"I can't marry you," she blurted, then cringed. If etiquette for breaking an engagement over the phone existed, surely the first rule would be to break the news gently.

"Caroline? Are you okay?"

"Yes. No. I just kissed another man, a man I've been in love with since I was sixteen. I would have slept with him, too, if he'd allowed the kiss to continue." She pressed her fingers to her trembling lips, still swollen and aching. "I'm sorry." Not sorry for kissing Javier, just sorry for breaking her vow to Blake.

Sorry for hurting him and her parents and inconveniencing all their guests with travel plans for the wedding weekend. She doubled over, imagining what they—people who liked her, who she called friends—would say about her. "I'm so sorry. I'll make all the calls. I'll tell everyone it's my fault. I never meant to hurt you."

Her stomach twisted with nausea. If she felt that way, her revelation had to be killing Blake.

"You only kissed him." His voice remained calm, even a bit distracted. "Nothing serious. You don't have to call everything off over a kiss. Why don't you talk it over with Sabrina? She and I are meeting with the florist this evening. She can bring me up to speed then."

Announcing she was in love with Javier and wanted to sleep with him didn't count as serious? Her actions exploded, terminated, destroyed their relationship. Her maid of honor might be handling a lot of the wedding details, but Caroline needed to clean up her own mess. "There's nothing to discuss. I can't marry you. I won't go through with a sham relationship like my parents have. I want the real thing."

"And the guy you kissed is the one to give it to you?" He sounded dubious.

Only Javier could. They'd discovered true love as teenagers, and she'd thrown it away. He might not give her another chance, but she couldn't stay with Blake and pretend their halfhearted attempt was good enough.

"I know you and I don't have it." Admitting so eased her stomach cramps and allowed her to draw a deep breath.

"Well, this is damn inconvenient." An exasperated sigh gusted through the phone. "I already booked vacation time for the honeymoon. I've been putting in extra hours to get ahead of schedule while I'm out of the office. Honestly, Caroline, this isn't like you at all. You're usually so dependable."

She leaned against the wooden fence of a dusty corral while he complained about the inconvenience and her unreliability. Really? Not even a tiny bit of heartbreak? She didn't want him to cry over her, but his lack of emotion compared to Javier's fury sealed her decision.

"I'm sorry," she said again. "But this is the right choice for both of us."

She clicked off the phone and closed her eyes. When she opened them, Alberto—the well-dressed man who'd greeted her at the helicopter—was approaching.

"Would you like a tour of the inside of the resort, Ms. Sunburst?"

Had Javier sent him, or did the assistant still consider her a viable job candidate? She straightened. As a matter of fact, the position did interest her. Her father was bound to freeze her out when he discovered her broken engagement to his chosen heir. She needed a job and a change of scenery.

"Actually, I'd like to check into my room and relax this evening. Could I possibly meet with you tomorrow to talk about the president of operations position? I really like what I've seen so far. And I need a job. I'm definitely interested."

"Tomorrow it is," Alberto said, leading her across the grounds. "This resort needs an executive with your experience. Since you arrived, I've buried myself in Internet searches, uncovering what you've done at Sunburst Hotels."

"Not nearly as much as I envisioned," she admitted. She'd let others talk her out of her grand dreams and into settling for ho-hum—in both her professional and personal lives. Well, not anymore.

She didn't have to pacify her father or tiptoe around family tradition and executives who remembered her back when she wore diapers and still treated her with the same indulgent condescension.

Free of a fiancé who barely noticed her existence, she could search for a man who would love her right—well, except for the man of her past and future dreams. His standards exceeded the disloyal, shady kisses she offered. His rejection stung far more than her broken engagement.

She squared her shoulders, resolving not to dwell on either man. Fated with a one-night stand at her disposal, she had the freedom to indulge guilt free.

Why not? She and Blake didn't exactly burn up the sheets, and if she ever slept with Javier again, he would no doubt ruin her for anyone else.

戃

Engaged. Javier still couldn't believe it, not when she kissed him like he completed her soul. He rubbed his chest and picked up a supplier contract overdue for a final decision.

The shift of paper unburied the face of the clock on his desk. 8:00 p.m.

After hearing of Madame Eve's uncanny predictions, he experienced it firsthand. Blowing off steam on a one-night stand might be the only solution to keep his sanity. The matchmaking service paired him with someone who'd signed up for a no-strings fling, which gave him a free pass for a mindless fuck with no guilt. He didn't care what his date wanted from him, as long as she got his mind off Caroline. Madame Eve was a genius.

After filling his pockets with condoms, he took the elevator to her room and slid his master keycard in the lock. Turning the handle, he opened the door. Caroline sat on the couch, studying the screen of her phone. Her somber gaze lifted, and the phone slipped from her fingers to the floor.

Hell, somehow he'd ended up in the wrong room—the worst possible room. Perhaps the details had changed and he hadn't received Madame Eve's updated information. He definitely should have knocked.

"You're my one-night stand?" the former love of his life whispered.

Madame Eve hadn't provided him with the wrong information. Caroline flat-out tricked him, intending to have a fling with him while engaged to someone else. Like a sucker, he'd given her a tour of the resort built from their teenage dreams. While he bared his heart and soul, she pretended interest, toying with him as if she didn't have her own hotel chain at her disposal.

His chest ached, and with trembling hands he closed the door and secured the lock. He should leave before she used him to satisfy her itch. But damn, with his dream of holding her in his arms one more time within reach, he didn't have the saintly willpower to pass up the opportunity.

He waited until his hands were steady then turned to her. "Let me guess. You snuck out on your parents to relive the old thrill before you settled into your perfect life with a man they approve of."

"My mother—never mind. That's not important right now." A smirk almost broke through her pale, strained face.

Yep, she came to use him. He didn't have the strength to push her away as he had in the stable. He might not be able to deny her, but he would take charge in bed. "I assume you have a position in mind that your fiancé won't agree to."

"He's not my fiancé anymore. We broke up." She met his gaze. "I broke up with him."

His cock swelled, eager to claim her. If Javier dared to trust her words, nothing kept them from being together.

He didn't dare. She'd held out on him the entire time they'd toured the resort. If she really had broken up with her fiancé, she could just as easily have more ugly secrets. He wouldn't become one of them. "Don't lie. I don't care if you're engaged. If you want to cheat with me, do it. I only want tonight. I don't care who you'll be with tomorrow."

The lie tasted like acid on his tongue. He cared and always would. Heartbreak exacted a steep price to hold her in his arms again. Even knowing he'd regret the decision later, he placed his chips all in.

Standing, she stepped toward him. "I want to be with you, Javier. Will you listen to me? I broke up with him because you're the only one I belong with."

Her sweet voice seeped under his skin. His hands started shaking again with the need to believe her. Maybe she had belonged to him before, but the connection hadn't been strong enough to stop her from turning away from him and the future they'd dreamed of together.

No matter what she said, her family would draw her back under its control, and she'd leave him. He would only allow a purely physical encounter. Anything more, and he wouldn't get over her a second time.

Chapter Four

Caroline had tried to be honest with Blake, with Javier, and herself. After trying so hard to be a faithful partner and a good daughter, she'd thrown away the stability she'd built with her fiancé. Worse, from Javier's words, it seemed she'd destroyed the possibility of cultivating a trusting relationship with the man she still loved.

Her only chance to break through to Javier virtually guaranteed heartbreak. By expressing her feelings physically, she hoped the connection would translate emotionally to him.

She lifted her hand and caressed his neck from his hairline to the inside of his collar, then touched her lips to his jaw.

His head snapped back, his expression full of banked fury and another emotion she couldn't pinpoint. "Be careful what you start. You might get more than you bargained for."

"You can't give me more than I want." *Not when I want it all.*

"Wanna bet?" He dared her with his eyes and grasped the opening of her silk shirt.

"Yes."

With a yank, he shredded the fabric, buttons pinging across the room.

She gasped. "You're ripping my clothes!"

His lips curled into a sexy, aroused smile, and the hard edge in his gaze melted away. "Yeah. Having second thoughts?"

Not a single one. No man ever wanted her so much that he ripped her clothes to get to her body. Javier elevated her from mere woman to sex goddess. "I'm hot, and I'm wet. I'm shaking because I want you so much. Touch me, please."

He groaned, his erection pulsing. Only Caroline could turn him into a quivering mass with just words. Only *she* could issue a royal decree in just such a way.

"Touch you like this?" He tugged the black lacy cups of her bra down until her nipples peeked over the top, then squeezed one pink areola between his thumb and forefinger.

She moaned and reached for the buttons of his shirt, carefully working them open.

"Or like this?" Embarrassed he'd ripped her clothes in an out-of-control frenzy and, doubly determined to bring her to the same state, he bent his head and took her nipple into his mouth, sucking the sensitive bud. She writhed and arched in response, forcing him to press her into the back of the couch to pin her movements and preserve his own control.

"Yes." She slid her fingers inside his shirt, clutching his shoulders. Raising her leg, she curled it around his waist, still gyrating her body against his.

He'd imagined Caroline willing, begging for him and surrounding him so many times. But he hadn't anticipated being reduced to begging, too. Lifting his head, he braced shaky arms on the sofa on either side of her. "I'm doing you. Got it? We're having sex my way."

With parted lips and blue eyes glazed with passion, she nodded. "Just touch me again. I need you so much. You complete me."

He slammed his mouth back over hers but couldn't undo the fatal mistake of allowing her to say what his soul longed to hear. She might have forgotten they were engaging in a purely physical one-night stand. He wouldn't forget.

Peeling her leg from around his waist, he worked open the zipper to her tailored suit pants and shoved them down her hips. He couldn't let her repeat how much she wanted him, and kept his mouth sealed to hers. But she didn't need to say a word to let him know exactly how much she liked what he did to her. The pounding of her heart and her enthusiasm as she tangled her tongue with his gave her away.

So she wanted him, but how far would she go before she retreated to her safe, comfortable life? The sooner he discovered the answer, the sooner he could separate his fantasies from reality and prove only the fantasy appealed to him.

Raising his head, he demanded, "Lift your leg."

She settled hands on his shoulders, meeting his gaze without hesitation.

Feeling the balance of control slipping toward her, he pushed her slacks and panties off one ankle, leaving them hanging from her other leg. Then he shifted her to the end of the couch, guiding her foot up to the armrest.

She stared at him, her creamy skin flushed, her face as vulnerable as her body.

He pressed one finger inside her, inching into her slick, hot tightness, memories of the past sweeping through him. Keeping the encounter completely physical might have worked if he'd been able to break eye contact. Instead, he trembled, needing her to believe he'd honor the trust she'd placed in him by allowing him to touch her.

He shifted, trying not to let her body's sweetness dissolve him into a quivering mass.

"Don't stop. Please."

"I don't intend to. I'm going to make you come, then keep touching you until you come again." Focusing exclusively on her pleasure, he added a second finger.

Eyes glazed, she moaned, surrendering her body to him. "Please, oh please yes." Her hips jerked, and she convulsed, drowning him with her passion.

His own muscles lurched in response, and he yanked his hand away. Despite his pledge, he couldn't give her a second orgasm without coming in his jeans.

Limp, she leaned into the couch armrest. "Come back inside me. I want everything you promised."

The longing on her face squeezed his heart. They were supposed to be engaging in sex. Only sex, no emotion. Instead, he wanted to promise her forever, to offer her a glittery ring she'd be proud to wear. "This armrest has potential. Let's see what else we can do here."

After considering the furniture for a moment, she stood and looped her arms around his neck, nipping at his lower lip. "I can sit on it and wrap my legs around you. But you still need to take your pants off, you know."

He ached to give her what she wanted. Unfortunately, if he continued to stare into her face, he'd fall head-first in love, a love she didn't reciprocate with the same devotion. "I want you on your knees on the armrest, your ass facing me."

Her teasing grin fell into uncertainty.

While he was doing those things, he would stay in control—of the situation, of his body, of his emotions. "I'm going to take care of you and give you what you want, I promise."

Caressing his cheek with her fingertips, she immediately threatened every ounce of that control. "I know you will." She dropped her hand and turned her back on him, tucking her knees under her on the armrest.

"Javier." She tipped her head to the side, her blonde hair falling over her cheek. "Please do me."

She lifted her hips, raising her ass to him.

He swallowed, amazed at the gift of trust, afraid he wouldn't be able to live up to the experience she deserved. Her smooth skin contrasted with his calloused hands. He swept his thumbs across her wet pussy then into her hot sex.

She bucked and moaned. "Yes, more. Deeper."

Even writhing with need, she still issued orders. He wanted to follow each one to the letter, giving her exactly what she wanted. Easing his thumbs out, he cupped her round cheeks. He hoped her trembling was a sign she needed him—just as his shaking hands gave away how much he needed her.

Releasing her before she noticed his weakness, he unbuckled and opened his pants. The need was only physical. Sex wouldn't give them a lasting connection. Desperate to achieve that connection nonetheless, he ripped open the condom, rolling it on his rock hard erection.

She reached back and dug her fingers into his thigh. "I missed you so much."

Grasping her hips, he glided inside her ready pussy. He squeezed his eyes closed and couldn't stop the moan torn from his throat. "You are so damn wet and tight. Fricking amazing. I didn't want it to be as good as I remembered."

Hell, he sucked at impersonal one-night stand stuff.

"It's not like before," she said, roaming her fingers along the back of his leg. "It's better."

Unable to allow her to touch him for fear of combusting, he pulled her hand away and extended it forward on the couch. He leaned over her smooth back, brushing his chin on the thin, lacy bra he had yet to remove. When she accepted him deeper, bliss overcame him.

Need built too fast and strong to corral. He tried pulling back but hurtled closer to the brink. "I can't wait. You have to come now."

"Yes. I want it," she promised.

Leaving her less than completely satisfied when he did orgasm wasn't an option. The building release would be every bit as earthshattering for her as it promised to be for him. He palmed her ass again and massaged his thumb along the crevice between the cheeks.

She bucked her hips, smacking his pelvis, and his control disintegrated. Pulling her tight to the base of his shaft, he fingered her clitoris.

Spasming around his cock, she screamed his name.

He squeezed his eyes closed and bent over her, releasing into her. He'd found the missing part of his soul. His past and his future collided, completing his life.

Except, she'd just used him for a freaking one-night stand.

"Sex with you is amazing," Caroline whispered, still shaking but safe and treasured, spooned in his arms. "You are amazing, Javier Alvarado." She turned her head to meet his gaze.

For a moment, he appeared to return the sentiment, before his expression hardened. "I hope you remember tonight every time you have boring, vanilla sex with your husband." Releasing her, he stepped back.

Nearly whimpering at the loss, she rolled on her back then sat up. The sex had changed her, connecting her to him on an elemental level. Surely, he felt it, too, and would believe the truth she spoke from her heart.

"I told you, I'm not marrying anyone. I couldn't when I never stopped loving you."

He fumbled in the process of fastening his belt buckle. "This has nothing to do with love, *querida*."

"Then what is it?" Throwing her words back in her face chilled her, but a small part of her thrilled at his use of her old nickname. Even if he didn't recognize it, she emotionally engaged him.

"A one-night stand where we used each other to get a good fuck." He strode toward the exit.

Despite his intention to shock her, she prayed he didn't believe his own words. "Javier, wait."

Damn it, he'd stayed dressed, while her bra sat at a crooked angle over her breasts and her pants hung around one ankle. He paused and glanced over his shoulder. His gaze raked her, revealing no hint of emotion or tenderness under his stone mask. "I got what I wanted, and I don't ever want to see you again." He slammed the door behind him.

Caroline stared at it for a moment then sank back on the sofa. Opening her body and her heart, she'd given him everything she had. He took what he wanted, nothing more, nothing less. Making the same mistake as millions of women throughout history, she'd believed she could reach him emotionally through physical expression. And she failed.

Too late to reverse the evening's strategy, she resolved to make better choices going forward. Starting with eradicating reminders of the night, she removed the twisted bra and pants then gathered the remains of her shirt and stuffed everything in the garbage.

Flipping the security lock in place, she stumbled to the bathroom, indulging in a long cry and a longer hot bath. She loved Javier, always had. She'd been foolish and wrong to come so close to marrying someone else, and even more so to imagine sex would convince the man she loved to return her feelings.

Using her business degree and résumé of solid experience, she had to create her own life apart from the father she'd tried so hard to please and even further from the love of her life.

Despite having no plans to meet anyone and no one to impress, she dressed in a business pant suit with a full blazer. Her image and her pride were the only things within her control. With precious little of either one to fall back on, she intended to preserve what she did have.

Picking up the phone, she took a deep breath and dialed. No one answered, hardly a surprise considering the time, so she waited for the tone to leave a message.

"Alberto, this is Caroline Sunburst. Thank you for offering me the opportunity to interview with your beautiful resort. The position is and will always remain my dream job, but unfortunately, I need to remove my name from consideration. Thank you for your wonderful hospitality." She paused and swallowed hard, but didn't lower the receiver. After burning her bridges at Sunburst Hotels by abruptly calling off the wedding and embarrassing her family, she couldn't afford to turn her back on any business contacts. "I do have an unusual request," she continued, her long cry earlier allowing her to keep her voice even. "If you hear of any similar positions open at other resorts, would you be so kind as to pass my name on to them? I'm willing to go anywhere."

The farther away the better, she added silently, replacing the phone. With trembling fingers she shouldered her purse, grabbed the handle of her rolling suitcase, and walked into the empty hall.

Moments later, she checked out at the registration desk and requested a cab to take her somewhere to start over—far away from her broken heart and tattered dreams.

Chapter Five

*J*avier listened to the message Alberto had forwarded to him, every word from Caroline drenched with sincerity and heartbreak. She'd given her name as an interview candidate, considering building her life near him.

His brain turned, remembering the words she'd spoken in an effort to get through to him.

He's not my fiancé anymore. We broke up. I broke up with him.

I want to be with you, Javier.

You're the only one I belong with.

You complete me.

I told you, I'm not marrying anyone. I couldn't when I never stopped loving you.

He flinched at the memory of his heartless response. Loving him, Caroline opened her heart and offered him everything. She'd seen the possibilities of them partnering in work and in life. Meanwhile, he selfishly took her body, using her, hurting her. Of course she would leave him after his efforts to prove he didn't care.

Sprinting from his office, he took the stairs two at a time to the fifteenth floor. "Caroline!" He pounded on her door, his heart thundering and not from the race up to her room. "*Querida*, I have to talk to you."

No answer.

He pulled a master key from his pocket and entered. After a cursory glance, he ran back to the bedroom. The bedspread didn't have a single wrinkle. The bathroom at least appeared used, with wet towels hanging on the rack and a tip for the housekeeping staff on the marble countertop.

Returning to the sitting room, he paused. He lifted her ripped shirt from the wastebasket, and his stomach twisted. Reaching in again, he pulled out her bra, then her pants and underwear, no longer a symbol of the evening's passion but evidence of something foul and disgusting.

He'd deliberately hurt Caroline, the only woman he'd ever loved. The only woman who'd ever loved him. *Dios*, what had he done?

He dashed from the room and punched the elevator button. When the doors didn't immediately open, he ran for the stairwell and down to the lobby.

"Stop the helicopter," he shouted to a security guard before spinning toward the girl at the front desk. "Did she check out? Which way did she go?"

"Who, sir?"

Who? How many people could possibly have checked out in the past ten minutes? He didn't waste time answering but strode out the front door just as a taxi pulled to a halt in front of the building.

And he found her, standing next to Alberto. She started to shake his assistant's hand then wrapped him in a hug. "Thank you. You've been wonderful," she murmured.

Stepping back, her gaze locked on Javier, and the air seemed to whoosh out of her. Just for a moment. Then her shoulders straightened, and she turned toward the cab, as if he were beneath her notice.

The driver reached for her bag.

Javier darted forward, grabbing it first. "Don't go."

"I have wedding plans to make and other guys to screw. I don't have time for you," she said in a flat tone, her gaze fixed vacantly beyond him.

Stupidly believing so, he'd proved what an ass he was. While his assistant immediately recognized the truth, Javier had been too scared she would break his heart again, turning his Caroline into a woman as heartless as he'd treated her. *"Por favor, querida*, I want you to stay with me. I'm asking."

Tracing his finger along her cheek, he ached to draw a response from her. She didn't lean into him or flinch from his touch. Any reaction would have been better than none. *I've already lost her.*

"Ma'am, do you want me to take your suitcase?" the cab driver asked.

"Please, Caroline," Javier said again. "I was wrong. Give me a chance to make it up to you. *Por favor.*"

Caroline dug her fingernails into her palms, trying to forget he only lapsed into Spanish when overcome with emotion. She didn't have the will to move away from him, but the ache in her throat also prevented her from saying anything to push him away.

"Ms. Sunburst, what can I do to help?" Alberto asked, his voice full of genuine concern.

Tears blurred her vision.

Javier uncurled her fingers. With a hissed breath, he lifted her hand and pressed his lips to each indent created by her nails. *"Lo siento, querida*. This is all my fault. You told me the truth, I didn't listen, and I hurt you. Give me a chance to fix it."

With an achingly sweet swipe of his thumb, he whisked her tears away while Alberto slipped quietly into the building.

Javier lowered his voice to the barest of whispers. "Let me make love to you the way you were meant to be loved. If you still want to leave in the morning, I'll send Alberto to personally escort you wherever you want to go."

As much as she wanted to believe him, she wouldn't let him cast her aside after sex again. "You don't trust me."

"I do trust you. I didn't trust what I felt for you. My feelings for you scared me and I feared if I allowed them to take over, I would end up hurt. But I love you and I don't want to lose you again."

Desperate to hear those words, she didn't trust her own ears. "Say it again. In Spanish."

He repeated in his native tongue the words she longed for but had stopped believing she'd ever hear, and she knew he spoke the truth.

She wrapped her arms around his neck and held him close, needing to soak in the rapid changes and allow the emotional roller coaster to glide to a stop.

After a moment, he pulled back, meeting her gaze again. "I want to show you my house. Will you come with me?"

Shock rippled through her. He'd invited her to his house, the one that he didn't allow others inside. With anyone else, the intimacy might have happened too quickly, but her need and love for Javier had been building and simmering her whole life. She didn't hesitate.

"Yes. I'd be honored."

"So, you don't need a taxi ride?" the driver demanded.

"We do need one," Javier said. "Fast as you can, down the employee path, over the dirt road, along the fence line, and behind the corral. A hundred bucks if you can do it in less than three minutes."

Two minutes later, they arrived.

The cab sped away, a thin layer of dust covering Caroline and her suitcase. The oversized front porch and the whimsical ranch design loomed instantly recognizable despite being encased in darkness offset only by the light of the moon.

"This is our house," she whispered.

Beginning as a cheesy high school class assignment, they'd worked on the plans together until perfecting their dream house down to the children's bedrooms and the colors of the towels in the bathrooms.

"I need you to make it a home. Can I take you inside?" He shifted, the moonlight reflecting the vulnerability in his brown eyes.

She nodded and looped her arms around his neck. "Please."

He scooped her up in his arms. More than simply bringing her to his house, it seemed he intended to sweep her off her feet to carry her over the threshold. She hugged him tighter and kissed his neck, delighted by the romance and the emotion behind it.

Carrying her up the front porch, he kicked the front door open. The sign, "Home is Where My Horse is," tilted to one side. She tried to adjust it, but he didn't pause. Neither did he stop as he strode through the living room, kitchen, and down the hall, not giving her time to take everything in.

"This is not how you give a tour."

He paused in the doorway to the bedroom. "Is that what you want? A tour?"

Lifting her gaze to his face, she knew whatever she requested he'd move heaven and earth to provide it for her. At the same time, material possessions ceased to matter. She didn't care if they lived in the bed of a pickup truck.

"I want to make love. I want to create an equal partnership. I want us both to believe our love will last forever." She touched her forehead to his.

"*Sí*, I want those things, too." He lowered her to her feet, sucking her lower lip between his.

Her eyes drifted closed, savoring the sweetness of the gesture. She caressed his sculpted cheek, then skimmed her tongue over his mouth, sighing as he opened, welcoming her.

He took his time unbuttoning her blazer before sliding it from her shoulders. Pressing his lips to the hollow of her throat, he repeated the process with her blouse, massaging and exploring each inch of skin he uncovered. As tenderly as if he was unwrapping the most precious of gifts, he unhooked and peeled away the lace of her bra.

She opened his well-worn cowboy shirt, exploring his muscled chest as reverently as he'd touched hers before tugging the cuffs from his wrists. Encircling him with her arms, she fit against him, reveling in the warmth of their half-naked bodies together, his heart beating steadily in time with hers.

Reaching between them, she pushed his jeans down his thighs, filling her hand with his hot erection. He gasped then moaned as she stroked his impressive length.

He laid her back on the bed, removing her slacks with tender care. Returning to her chest, he lavished attention on each breast, trailing kisses down to her navel.

For a moment she closed her eyes, savoring his touch, but she wanted him to be with her, a part of her. Half rising from her prone position, she tugged him next to her on the bed. "I don't want things to be one-sided this time. I'm going to give to you, too."

"I didn't give last time," he said, regret etched in the small lines at the corners of his sensuous mouth. "I took. This time I'm going to give. Let me show you how much I love you." He shifted to kneel between her thighs, kissing and licking her to the brink of orgasm.

Oh, yes. He'd pledged his love in English and Spanish. Her doubts melted away at his words. She rose to a sitting position and helped him shift his legs so he sat as well. As much as she could have lain savoring every drop of pleasure he wrung from her, she wanted something else. "I want us to come together."

She straddled him, wrapping her legs around his waist. Threading her fingers with his, she sank onto his straining cock. They sat unmoving, palm to palm, chest to chest, bodies pulsing, hearts pumping in unison.

Staring into his soulful brown eyes, she connected more deeply and completely than she'd dreamed possible. "I love you, Javier Alvarado. I always have."

His cock lurched inside her. "*Dios, querida.* I never stopped loving you. God knows I tried, but I couldn't."

She trembled and shuddered around him when he came in a hot burst of passion, filling her, sealing their love.

They stayed together long after the last moments of orgasm shuddered through them.

Finally, Javier gathered her in his arms and shifted until they lay together, still intimately joined. "Home isn't where the horse is. It's where you are, Caroline."

She snuggled contentedly. "Even though I won't be leaving, you can welcome me home like this anytime."

ONE NIGHT WITH THE BRIDESMAID

A 1Night Stand Story

By
Sara Daniel

~DEDICATION~

For Lisbeth

Chapter One

"You must be new here. The staff never comes in the front door. Do it again, and you're fired." The hostess of one of San Diego's finest dining establishments blocked Sabrina Lopez from taking another step.

Of course, an overweight, inner-city schoolteacher didn't belong, and in any other circumstance, Sabrina would have made an excuse to skip the luncheon with her best friend and her friend's society matron mother. But she had a laundry list of last minute wedding details she needed their approval to go ahead with before the big day next week.

"Sabrina, oh good, you're finally here. Mother and I already have a table." Caroline Sunburst strolled through the entry and linked arms with her, as the red-faced hostess backed away, stammering an apology.

When they arrived at the table, Sabrina gave Mrs. Sunburst the requisite air-kiss and slipped into an open chair. "I'm sorry I'm late. I stopped to check on the flowers on the way over. I'm planning to meet Blake at the caterer's this afternoon to make sure they understand we wanted the filet mignon, not T-bone steak." She pulled her planner out of her purse, only to have the waiter cover it with a menu.

"I don't want to see anyone gnawing on bones at my daughter's wedding." Mrs. Sunburst shuddered. "On a happier note, I've picked up a gift for each of you girls."

"I'm not the one getting married," Sabrina reminded her, setting the menu aside. Even the side salad was beyond her budget. Regardless of the Sunburst family's wealth, she could not accept any more outlandish gifts.

"Don't be silly. You've done more wedding preparations than Blake and Caroline put together."

She couldn't argue with that. "I'm happy to help." Okay, maybe she was living life vicariously through her friend because she had no life of her own. But she had yet to meet a man who brought any excitement into her bed.

"So," Mrs. Sunburst continued, "I booked a one-night stand for each of you through Madame Eve's elite, highly recommended service."

Sabrina's head spun. A spa treatment or a too-expensive piece of jewelry wouldn't have surprised her, but a one-night stand?

"A week before my wedding, you're giving me what?" Caroline, who never raised her voice, exploded.

"A one-night stand pre-wedding gift," Mrs. Sunburst repeated, patting a plastic card into Caroline's hand. "And one for your maid of honor, too."

Mrs. Sunburst pushed a stack of papers fastened with a metal clasp in Sabrina's direction. Unable to make eye contact with the others, she stared at the packet. Walking in the front door of this restaurant paled in comparison to how out-of-place she felt now. Questions about her occupation, food preferences, sleeping habits, and secret dreams jumped out at her. She flipped to the second page. *What is your ideal liaison?*

Sabrina flattened the questionnaire. She spent her weekends grading homework, not hooking up at the nightclubs.

Not that she was a virgin. She knew what to do on a technical level. *Insert slot A into tab B. Shove back and forth approximately six to eight times.* The experience didn't come close to satisfying her, so she'd stopped bothering.

This could be her ticket to hook up with a man she'd never have the nerve to approach in real life, someone who considered a woman's pleasure integral to the sexual experience, who wanted more than a few thrusts in the missionary position under the covers in a dark room.

Excitement and arousal stirred inside her. A real man who could fulfill her desires had to exist somewhere, even if she'd only found him in Rob Wellington movies and through her vibrator. With any luck, Madame Eve could help her discover where the real men were hiding.

CS

"What do you mean the wedding's off?" Rob Wellington had planned his movie production schedule around his little brother's wedding and had busted his ass, along with every speed zone between LA and San Diego to get here in time for the rehearsal dinner.

"Caroline called it off a couple days ago. She told me she'd take care of canceling everything and letting everyone know."

"Apparently, she thought you might want to tell your brother yourself." Or the message was buried in the stack on his desk that had become so dauntingly high he preferred to ignore the fact that he had an office to return to after wrapping for the day.

Rob stepped inside Blake's home, decorated with too much stainless steel, mahogany, and uncomfortable furniture to be used for actual living.

"Sorry I don't have any food to offer. I was working all day and just got home myself."

"You still went to the office this week? If I were you, I'd have headed to Mexico to drown my sorrows in as much debauchery as I could legally get away with."

"I worked too hard to become CEO of her family's hotel chain to have her defection put my job at risk."

Rob had never been married. But underneath his hard-won Hollywood cynicism, he remained idealistic enough to insist marriage be for no other reason but pure, simple love. "So she didn't break your heart when she dumped you."

"Of course, I'm upset," Blake said.

"You're frustrated. That's different from brokenhearted."

"I'm pissed at how much time I've wasted over the past six

months. Every moment I haven't been working, Sabrina and I have been picking out flowers, tasting the caterer's menu, and pouring over music playlists. All for nothing, as it turns out."

"I thought you were marrying Caroline," Rob said. Had he mistaken the bride's name? Clearly, he and his brother had drifted too far apart. He'd rectify that tonight. He set down the whiskey bottle he'd intended for the bachelor party and began searching the cabinets for shot glasses.

"Sabrina is her maid of honor. She's been filling in when Caroline's too busy."

A woman too busy for her own wedding? Yeah, right. More likely, Sabrina had an agenda of her own, with Blake at the top of her to-do list. "This maid of honor doesn't have a speck of honor in her. Did you sleep with her?"

"Of course not. She's like a sister to me."

Sister. Like hell. Blake might be tucked away in his corner office, oblivious to the people using his hotel beds to cheat on their significant others, but Rob was not. Every day, he dealt with women who coveted the bigger, better role of another actress and would stop at nothing to get it. Jealous, scheming Sabrina wanted Blake for herself and had convinced her friend to call off the wedding so she could have him. "What you need is some hot, dirty sex to forget you ever met these backstabbing women."

Blake laughed, the sound devoid of humor. "Caroline agrees with you. She left me after reuniting with a long-lost love through Madame Eve's 1Night Stand service. She found the experience so rewarding that as her breakup apology to me, she gave me a date from the same service."

"She gave you a prostitute? Now that's a gift I can appreciate. No wonder you're not happy to see me. You have better plans than drinking your way to oblivion."

"Not a prostitute. Madame Eve runs a high-end matchmaking service." Blake tossed a multi-page form across the room at him. "Take a look. I haven't filled it out yet, and I'm not planning to cash in the certificate tonight or anytime soon. In fact, why don't you use it instead? This application asks so many lifestyle and personality questions, I get the impression Madame Eve wants to connect people for a long-term relationship. That's the last thing I'm interested in right now."

Rob turned his attention from the paperwork to the whiskey shots. "Judging by the name of the business, they're not promoting long-term relationships. Sounds like the perfect way to spend your wedding night."

"I'm not ready," Blake insisted. "Anyway, Sabrina offered to hang out and keep me company."

I'll bet she did. Rob's first girlfriend after he'd moved to Hollywood had used him for his wealth and fame then dumped him for someone with more of both. As a brand new CEO, Blake was on the cusp of experiencing the harsh reality of mixing love and money. "On the bright side, you'll have sex on your wedding night either way."

Blake glared at him. "Shut up. I told you, I'm not sleeping with her. She and Caroline have been friends since elementary school."

Friendships meant nothing when money and power were at stake, but people tended to be idealistic until they experienced it firsthand. Rob passed his brother a glass. "Back to Plan A then. I'll help you fill out the application."

Blake downed the first shot. "What the hell. Let's do it."

"That's the spirit." Rob raised his glass with one hand and refilled Blake's empty one with the other.

A half-dozen refills later, they abandoned the glasses and swigged straight from the source. "So, we've decided you want a woman—" Rob squinted at his chicken scratches on the paper. "With double-Ds and a big, sweet ass, preferably a contortionist with a mouth like—"

"Hell, yeah. Send it off." Blake hoisted the bottle as he stumbled around his desk, powering up every electronic in sight.

Rob scanned the form, attaching it to a blank e-mail. "I should write a cover letter." He took the whiskey from his brother and lifted it to his lips. "Definitely need to mark this sucker as urgent, since you need the match to happen in…." He glanced at the blurry clock on the wall. Hell, they'd been at this all night. "Less than twelve hours."

He and Blake finished off the last of the alcohol as they debated the wording of the e-mail. In the end, short and sweet won because they were both too drunk to write anything more complicated.

Dear Madame Eve, Attached is my brother Blake's application. He needs his date for tonight to make him forget it's his wedding day. Your service sounds so awesome, I'd like a date for myself, too. Rob Wellington

He sent the e-mail while Blake went to the bathroom to puke. Twelve hours later, his brother was still sleeping off his hangover when the reply came. Rob's head throbbed as he fumbled to bring it up on his phone.

"One-night stand," he muttered, squinting at the screen. "Tonight…with Sabrina Lopez. Oh, hell no."

The pounding in his head no longer came from a hangover but from the conniving woman determined to put her claws into his brother. Rob tucked away his phone and frowned at Blake's snoring form.

He wouldn't be surprised if Madame Eve's service wasn't a scam set up by Sabrina herself to get her hands on his brother. Well, she was in for a surprise. Blake wouldn't be waiting for her in the hotel room. Instead, she'd have to deal with someone she couldn't fool.

Chapter Two

Sabrina stood in front of the closed door, biting her lip. Knock or let herself in? Knock. She didn't want to get off on the wrong foot by barging in on a stranger. If he chose not to answer, she'd let herself in.

She shifted her feet in their high-heeled sandals. A moment later, the door flew open. Rob Wellington stood before her, taller in the flesh than his tabloid pictures had led her to believe. The ice blue eyes and curling brown hair were the same. Instead of the red-carpet tuxedo she was accustomed to from the entertainment news clips, he wore jeans and a blue button-down shirt with the sleeves rolled to the elbows.

Regardless of whether anything she'd read or heard about Hollywood's hottest movie director were true, never in a million years would he have given bland, overweight Sabrina a second look. A few hours ago, when Madame Eve confirmed he was her date, she'd been so terrified, she'd picked up the phone three separate times to cancel. But the thought of spending the night with him left her too intrigued and aroused to follow through.

Madame Eve had provided her with the exciting man she'd said she wanted. She had to take the next step to break out of her shell and bring sexual fulfillment to her safe, boring life.

"Hi. I'm Sabrina." She forced a tremulous smile but didn't offer a handshake for fear of drawing attention to her wobbly limbs. If only she had the nerve to dive straight in for a hug or, better yet, a French kiss. That would have established her as his confident, sophisticated equal.

She smoothed her sweaty palms over her yellow sundress. Caroline was not going to rush to her aid this time. She needed to prove she was worthy of his presence on her own.

His contemptuous gaze followed her movements.

Her cheeks heated. If the women who posed in photos with him were any indication, her thighs might well be the largest he'd ever encountered. She lowered her hands so not to repulse him further.

"Rob Wellington, Blake's brother." He stepped back to allow her inside.

"Yes, I know." She crossed the threshold, trying not to betray her nerves. He brushed her shoulder as he closed the door in her wake, and her nipples beaded beneath her dress. The man exuded sexuality the way most of her dates reeked of garlic.

She wracked her short-circuiting brain for a safe conversation topic. "How is Blake? I offered to stay with him tonight, but he assured me he preferred to be alone."

"So, you went to Madame Eve and convinced her to hook you up instead," Rob said, his sensual lips curving in a knowing smirk.

Her cheeks burned hotter. He made her sound so shallow, so slutty. He'd asked for this hookup, too, hadn't he? Why should she be held to a different standard because of her gender? "Well, no. I did request a weekend, since I work during the week, but I didn't expect her to set me up *this* weekend."

"Enough games," Rob snapped. "You admitted you wanted to spend tonight with Blake, and you thought Madame Eve would deliver him to this hotel room. You didn't count on me seeing through your plan, did you?"

"Plan?" The last time Sabrina had concocted a plan to snag a man had been in junior high. She'd begged Caroline to ask a boy to dance with her. He'd laughed so hard he'd been unable to reply, and Sabrina had never scoured up the courage to initiate a flirtation again.

"Yes, your plan." Rob stepped toward her, settling his fingers on her cheek then skimming them down to her jawline.

She stood frozen, enveloped in sensuality.

"Did you think I wouldn't put two and two together?" he asked, skating a single finger down the side of her neck. "You picked out flowers, music, and food for Blake's wedding. You were available when the bride called off the wedding. How long did it take you to convince her not to marry him?"

She jerked away from his touch. "You think I broke up your brother's wedding because I wanted him for myself?" The idea was so ludicrous she might have laughed if Rob's glower hadn't proved his seriousness. "Caroline is my best friend. I helped her with *her* wedding plans. Do you know how many hours and weeks I wasted planning a wedding that never happened?"

"But your efforts paid off, didn't they, because now you have Blake all to yourself." Rob leaned so close, his lips brushed hers as he spoke.

Did that count as a kiss? Her skin tingled more than she could remember feeling from any "true" kiss. "I came here to spend the night with you. I can understand if you don't find me attractive, but don't make offensive insinuations about my relationship with Blake. He's like a brother to me, and I would never come between him and my best friend."

ଔ

The façade had gone on too long, and Rob intended to end it. He slanted his lips across hers. In a moment, she would shove him away and announce she wanted Blake, not him, confirming everything he'd accused her of. The sooner, the better because he hadn't predicted the wave of physical attraction making him itch to explore her lush body and claim her as his own.

She shivered beneath him but didn't break the contact. Instead, she moaned, curling her hands around the back of his neck. Her sweet taste and eager touch threw him off his game. She disguised her calculations so well, he couldn't anticipate her next move.

He backed her against the wall, not taking his lips off hers. If she tested him on how far he would take this, she would lose. The more he kissed her, the more he wanted to immerse himself in her amazing curves and powder fresh scent while dumping his grand plan to strip her down to her intentions.

He slid her dress strap from her left shoulder and rubbed his palm over her full breast. Her nipple tightened, and her breathing hitched with each stroke of his fingers. Hell, he was hard and throbbing, as if this was a real seduction.

He tore his lips away from hers before he forgot the reason he'd chosen to meet her. "How dare you break up my brother's wedding, trick him into a one-night stand with you, and then kiss me like I'm the only man who matters to you right now."

"You are. I came here to be with you, Rob, not Blake." She pulled his hand off her breast and yanked her strap back up, crossing her arms over her chest.

"You came here to meet me?" The possibility hadn't entered his mind. Now the fantasy bloomed to life. He wanted nothing more than to peel the yellow dress off her, run his hands over her light brown skin, and bury his face in her curves. But his only goal was to warn her away from his hurting, vulnerable brother.

"Yes, but not to let you bully and belittle me," Sabrina said. "If you're going to treat me that way, you can leave."

"I can leave?" Was this another tactic to throw him off? If so, it was definitely working. People took orders from him, not the other way around.

"Yes, you." Her voice rang with authority. "I thought Madame Eve vetted her clients and their intentions, but she slipped up on your file. If you believe I'm here to take advantage of Blake, why are you kissing me? As punishment? Warning?"

"Something like that." He was no longer sure. She made him feel ashamed of his noble and righteous actions.

"My fault, I suppose." She gave a humorless laugh, the sparkle in her brown eyes extinguished. "I put too much emphasis on adventure and excitement on my application when I should have stressed how important trust, honesty, and straightforwardness mean to me. Will you please leave, so I can salvage the evening enjoying room service at a place I'll never be able to afford on my teaching salary?"

She was kicking him out. Rob stood rooted to the floor. If she wasn't looking to take advantage of his brother, then she deserved to have her request granted. But he didn't want to leave.

"Please," she said again. "Blake told me who you are. Even if he hadn't, I'd have recognized you from the celebrity magazines. I know you have the money to enjoy a hotel like this any time you want. I can't."

She knew who he was. Yet she wasn't throwing herself at him, trying to get some of that money and fame to rub off on her. A niggle of suspicion raised its head. "How do I know you're not kicking me out just to convince my brother to join you?"

A defeated sigh escaped her lips. She dug into her purse and extracted a folded piece of paper. "I don't know why you think your brother should be here instead of you, but read this. Maybe then you'll believe I expected to spend the night with you, no one else. Again, I'm sorry about the mix-up."

At a loss for words, Rob took the paper but continued to stare at Sabrina. She opened the hotel door behind her and waved him through. Having no reason to stay, he took a step toward both her and the exit.

She hooked an arm around his neck and pulled him toward her. Her full, soft lips slammed against his. Her tongue thrust into his mouth. The force of unsophisticated passion stunned him. Arousal strummed through him, demanding he claim her for himself.

Before he could lift a hand to draw her closer or push her away, she pulled back. With both hands, she shoved him out the door, then shut it in his face.

Chapter Three

*F*rom the other side, he heard the safety flip over the lock. His key card wouldn't get him back in. Either she'd kicked him out because he wasn't Blake or because he'd acted like a self-righteous ass. Either way, he had to give her kudos for playing her cards so well.

His cock strained at his zipper. Damn, he wanted her. To distract himself from jerking off in a hotel hallway and from begging through the closed door, both of which the paparazzi would have a field day with, he unfolded the paper she'd given him. A quick glance revealed a series of e-mail exchanges, so he began to read from the bottom up to put them in chronological order.

Dear Sabrina, I've reviewed your application and have matched you up for a one-night stand tonight at the Castillo Hotel San Diego. Sincerely, Madame Eve.

Dear Madame Eve, Is it possible to change the date? Tonight was supposed to be my friend Blake Wellington's wedding, and I promised not to leave him alone. Blake has been like a brother to me, and without Caroline's connection, I'm afraid I will lose his friendship. Sabrina

Sabrina, My sources tell me Blake feels the same way for you, and your friendship will endure despite his broken engagement. But forgive me for pointing out that a man does not want to spend what should have been his wedding night in the arms of his sister. Tonight is for you to have the romance and excitement sadly lacking in your life, and Rob Wellington is just the man to fulfill your needs. Come to the Castillo Hotel tonight. You won't regret it. Madame Eve

Rob Wellington? Blake's brother? The famous movie director? The guy who has a different woman on his arm every night of the week? My fingers are trembling so much I can barely type. I don't think I have the nerve to do this.

Yes, that Rob. No need for nerves. He'll be as nervous as you are.

Rob lowered the paper. He did not have a different woman on his arm every night of the week, despite what the tabloids reported. He'd become so cynical and jaded that even a once-a-month date wasn't worth the effort.

Sabrina might not have all her facts straight about him, but Madame Eve hit the bull's eye. He was a jangle of nerves. He had to convince Sabrina to let him return so he could retract the accusations he'd hurtled and make the evening right for her.

In his haste to defend his brother from female deception, games, and power plays, he hadn't taken her feelings into consideration. He'd believed the worst about her based on his own prejudices. In his world, everyone wanted something from him, but no one had any intention of telling him straight out what they wanted.

Sabrina had.

If he didn't fix what he'd done, he'd be responsible for making her as cynical as he'd become.

As much as he'd been attracted to her smooth skin, ripe breasts and generous hips before, knowing she'd been open with him from the beginning made every physical feature infinitely more enticing.

As he leaned against the wall, debating the best course of action to regain her trust and make the evening as pleasurable as possible for both of them, the elevator opened. A waiter pushing a silver cart emerged. To avoid making eye contact, Rob pulled out his phone and scrolled through his own emails. He paused on the one that had come early this morning.

Dear Rob, Your requested one-night stand has been set up....

His requested one-night stand, not Blake's. Because he hadn't expected Madame Eve to take his drunken interest in her service as a legitimate request, he'd jumped to conclusions and humiliated Sabrina in the process.

The waiter stopped in front of her door and knocked. "Room service."

The door opened. Sabrina's smile for the uniformed man faded as soon as her gaze met his in the background.

The serviceman glanced at him warily. "I'll page Security, ma'am."

"No, um—" She chewed on her lip. "He just stepped out and must have forgotten his key."

Rob couldn't believe his ears. She was covering for him after she'd kicked him out. By all rights, she should enjoy watching Security and the paparazzi swarm around him. They could take a stalker angle or spurned jealous lover, feeding for days off the possible ways to humiliate him.

"You can put the food on the table by the kitchenette," Sabrina instructed the deliveryman, allowing him to enter.

As she raised her gaze to his, Rob drew a steadying breath, doing his best to rein in his nerves and sound casual as he held up the page of e-mails. "I believe you. Can I come in? I'd like to start over."

She hesitated then gave a small nod. Despite her agreement, she turned her back on him and went to deal with the food. The waiter spoke to her in furtive tones, shooting him nasty glances. Sabrina shook her head, tipped the man, and escorted him out.

Rob stepped toward the kitchenette to check out the spread.

After locking the door again, Sabrina joined him. Her breasts rose as she took a deep breath. "I really thought you'd left. I never considered you might come back. If I had, I would have ordered something besides deluxe nachos and a Corona."

He bit back a relieved laugh. Instead of holding a grudge against him for the way he'd treated her or being embarrassed for kissing him earlier, she was self-conscious about the food. He lifted the silver lid from the platter. She had indeed ordered a single bottle of beer and a large plate of nachos drenched in cheese and jalapeños. Thank goodness she wasn't one of those women who freaked out over the number of calories in a single leaf of lettuce. "You're going to need more than one beer if you intend to eat all that."

Her cheeks flushed. "I'm not a big drinker. I figured I'd better switch to water after I finished the beer."

Rob grinned, aching to take her in his arms. But he'd returned to the room on her terms. He wanted her to continue to feel like she had the upper hand. He didn't intend to screw up the second chance she'd given him. "Are you going invite me to share your beer and nachos, or do I have to watch you eat?"

"Oh, yeah, I mean, no, you don't have to watch. Help yourself." She practically shoved the Corona into his hands.

He held the bottle he didn't want. He wanted her, but, as Madame Eve had predicted, nerves had destroyed his ability to risk rejection. "What do you want, Sabrina?"

She fiddled with the fabric of her dress, but he was pleased the shine had returned to her luminous brown eyes. "I came here to make love to you. I still want that."

He dropped the beer.

She lunged and caught the bottle before it could shatter on the floor. Straightening, she set it on the table and turned to him, her thick, dark hair falling in disheveled waves across her face. "Sorry. I should have rephrased that to sound subtle and enticing."

"No. You said it just right." He adored how she didn't toy with him but said what she meant. He draped his hand along her neck, pushing her hair over her shoulder. Her pulse jackhammered beneath his thumb. He leaned in and brushed his lips over hers.

Her fingers quivered as she settled them on his cheek and returned his kiss with a gentle one of her own. The sweetness and sincerity of the gesture blew his mind.

A new concern took hold. "You have had a one-night stand before, right?"

The flush that had almost disappeared from her cheeks returned in full force. "Well, no, but a girl has to start somewhere. I mean, I've had sex before. I just have to make the first time good with you because I won't get a second chance."

He'd done nothing to deserve the honor of initiating her, but he wouldn't let her regret that he was the one. "You might be surprised by how many second chances we can cram into a single evening."

But even knowing how many condoms they could use in a few hours, he couldn't shake the certainty that one night wouldn't be enough for everything he wanted to do to her.

Chapter Four

"*We* better get started so you can show me." Sabrina hoped her smile radiated confidence. In reality, she was in so far over her head she had no hope of reaching the surface before she drowned. She tugged her dress straps down her arms before she lost her nerve.

Rob groaned, threading his fingers through hers and halting her awkward attempt at a strip tease. "Let me undress you."

"Am I doing it wrong?"

"Wrong?" Disbelief echoed in his voice. "Of course not, but this should be about your pleasure." He pressed his lips to her bare shoulder and tasted his way along her collarbone to the opposite side.

"What about yours?" His kisses left her both vulnerable and treasured in equal measure. She didn't know how to steer the encounter to give him what he wanted.

"All my pleasure comes from you. If you like it, I'm hard, and I want more."

She tipped her head back, craving the connected arousal he promised. She'd signed up for excitement and new positions, not weakness and a need so great she was ready to beg. But she couldn't deny what he offered exceeded her own fantasies.

He kissed her exposed neck, exploring the hollow at the base of her throat with his tongue.

Bolts of desire shot through her body, straight between her legs. Her knees threatened to buckle. If his desire fed off hers like he claimed, he had to be on the verge of coming. Good grief, they were still in the kitchenette, across the sitting room from the bedroom door. She needed to start thinking instead of just feeling. "I left my purse on the couch. I have condoms in there."

"I have condoms right here." He pulled two packets from his pocket to show her. "But we're not ready for them yet."

"We're not?" Dismay filled her as the foil squares disappeared back into his pocket. Her trembling body couldn't wait. If he felt the same as her, he wouldn't want to wait either. Her need for this man already exceeded anything she'd experienced, making her overeager. "I mean, of course not, we're still dressed."

He kissed the swell of her breast at her dress line. "I like how your responsible mind works. But we have a lot of exploring to do without a condom first."

"Like what?"

"Like this." He ran his hands from her shoulders all the way down to her knees, then back up again, pressing against her breasts and between her thighs. Before she could do more than gasp, his mouth covered her cleavage, heating her with his breath, lapping her with tongue.

Desire clouded her brain, and she needed something to steady her. She ran her fingers over his hair but couldn't use this man who dated actresses and directed A-list movies as an anchor. "I can't keep standing, Rob."

"What do you want to do?"

"Lie down, I guess." So much for not appearing overeager. She could have suggested leaning against the counter or sitting on the chair. But how would she be able to deliver a satisfying sexual encounter for him from those unfamiliar positions?

"Your wish is my command." He slipped an arm under her knees and another behind her back, scooping her into his arms.

"I'm too heavy," she whispered, mortified. She'd never allowed a man to lift her before. She wouldn't have this time if she'd realized his intention.

"You are not," he declared without gasping. He also didn't stumble or stagger, as he strode into the bedroom. He laid her across the bed with the gentle care of one dealing with fragile glass.

Taking a deep breath, she regained her equilibrium. She cupped his cheeks, pulling his face down until she could kiss him hard enough to convince him she wouldn't break.

He kissed her back until she stopped trying to anticipate what she needed to do next. He tugged her dress down, baring her breasts, then covered them with his hands. Desire drummed through her, leaving her panting.

He massaged her breasts, gliding his hands beneath them, supporting their weight, as he scooted down the bed bringing his face level with them. He kissed the swell and along her sternum, abrading her nipples with his whiskers every time he turned his head.

Sparks shot through her body, and she lifted her back, soaking in the crazy, intense pleasure that still didn't come close to satisfying her. "Suck me, Rob."

She couldn't believe those wanton words had come from her mouth, but he didn't question her command as he drew her nipple into his mouth. Every nerve in her body sprang awake, aching for him. She squirmed with needs that threatened to overwhelm her, needs beyond her ability to articulate.

Rob seemed to understand, stripping her dress down her hips and taking her panties with it. The garments slithered off her ankles to the floor, leaving her naked. Any thoughts of modesty or self-consciousness fled as he glided his palm over her mound.

She arched her hips. He had to believe she was ready now. Her heat and wetness beckoned him. The urge to scream built like a tsunami wave ready to crash over her and Rob hadn't even entered her yet.

He still didn't. Instead, he removed the marvelous heat of his hand from her pelvis and lavished attention on her breasts, kissing one while massaging the other. When she couldn't bear another moment, he switched sides, bringing her need to a higher pitch. At last, his hands stroked lower, down to her navel.

She sucked in her stomach and held her breath, hoping he'd return to her breasts or move down between her legs. Of course, he'd been attracted to her big breasts. What man wasn't? But a plump, jiggling stomach didn't hold any of the same enticing qualities.

He paused, his fingers spread wide across her skin, his chin resting against her belly button. "What's wrong?"

"Nothing." Her stomach expanded with the act of speaking, forcing her to take a breath. She blinked back tears. How could he feel any desire for her with his face surrounded by fat? Damn it, why hadn't she thought to turn out the lights? "Just skip this part and keep going lower."

"Skip it?" His tone turned ominous. "I'm not going to skip it. This is you, Sabrina. I'm bringing pleasure to your entire body, and I intend to enjoy every inch, not just your boobs and pussy. Don't insult me by insinuating that's all I'm after."

"I didn't insult you," she whispered.

"Don't insult yourself, either because I take that as a personal insult."

Sabrina wiped her eyes, so she could see him. This famous man didn't have an inch of fat on him. He worked with size-zero actresses on a daily basis. Yet, his blue eyes weren't icy with the disgust she'd glimpsed earlier. He wanted her to embrace her curves. Heck, he'd been completely into them in a good way until she'd freaked out.

He stroked his fingertips over her skin from her shoulder down her thighs, then repeated the stroke with a light scrape of his fingernails. With his tongue, he lapped the underside of her breasts, then swirled circles across her stomach, tasting her belly button, then lower, gliding over her clit.

"Rob." She tried to lift her hips, but his hands pressed against her soft stomach, holding her down.

He returned his mouth to her navel. "Do you want more?"

"Yes." Of course, yes. She died a million deaths from wanting him.

"Say 'I'm naked, and I'm beautiful.'"

He was heart-stoppingly gorgeous, not her. "Rob, don't—"

He lifted his face away from her.

"I'm naked, and I'm...beautiful." She stumbled on the word but managed to force it out.

He licked his way down, gliding inside her again.

She gasped and reached for his head, desperate to hold him in to bring her to completion.

Gripping his hair wasn't enough. He started to draw out.

"I am beautiful," she cried.

He plunged into her again, the sweetest affirmation she'd ever received.

She circled her arms around his back, holding him as close to her as possible. The heat and hardness of his body through his clothes intensified the ache inside her. "Oh, Rob, you make me feel so beautiful. No one's made me feel like this before. Please make love to me. I can't stand it anymore. Please."

He lifted his head, fire in his gaze. "Are you sure?"

"Yes." She'd never wanted anything more.

He pushed down his pants, pulled a foil packet from the pocket, and tossed the clothing aside. She lifted her head to watch him roll the condom on his impressive erection. Something in her eyes must have given him pause because the heat in his gaze tempered with tenderness. "You can still back out, Sabrina. You don't have to do anything you're not ready for."

"I want every inch of you inside me."

Desire flaring from the depths of his blue eyes again, he hooked his arms behind her knees, positioning himself at her entrance. He panted as he lifted his head with one final questioning look, but she had no reservations.

"I'm so ready. For you, Rob." She grasped his hips, pulling him into her. He slid inside as promised, locking in a custom fit. The beauty of the man and the sheer pleasure of their connection took her breath away.

He bent his head, touching his lips to hers. The tenderness of the gesture threatened to unravel her. He pulsed within her, bringing her closer to the edge. With a moan, his kiss turned feverish, and she responded with every ounce of her own desperation.

Despite his constant throb of need, he didn't shift his body at all. Keeping her thighs pinned up and his hips pressing her into the bed, he prevented her from rocking against him. Regardless, her muscles clenched. Her body shook, coming apart from his very presence.

He thrust, filling her once, twice, a third delicious time. She convulsed with a pleasure so amazing, and she screamed his name. Her entire world belonged to Rob.

She dug her fingers into his buttocks as he pumped against her, harder, faster, pushing her higher, giving her more pleasure than she thought possible from any position, let alone the missionary. Then he came in a torrent of hot sweetness.

"Sabrina," he groaned. The single word from his lips sent her soaring again. He released her legs to cup her face with his hands, kissing her with the same depth and sweetness he employed when he'd made love to her.

Sabrina had come here for excitement, and oh man, had Rob ever delivered. Who knew excitement could be so transforming? At the moment, she felt invincible. Everywhere, except in her heart, which suddenly felt vulnerable and exposed.

Chapter Five

Rob lifted his head. His heart rate and breathing had almost returned to normal, although he no longer had any grasp of what constituted normal. Reconsidering his original assumption that Sabrina had broken up his brother's nuptials, he couldn't understand why Blake hadn't fallen head over heels for her. How could any man have eyes for anyone else?

"You're still wearing your shirt," she said, her lips tilting into a frown.

"That can be remedied." He lifted himself off her, eager to please. But the condom demanded his attention first. By the time he removed it and cleaned himself, Sabrina had her thong panties back on and was reaching for her dress.

He grabbed the dress before she could. "You shouldn't be putting your clothes on while I'm still taking mine off."

"Yeah, but we already…." She gestured to the bed.

"Made love? Yes, we did. Are you going to toss me aside after one time? The night's far from over."

Her hands trembled as she reached for him and unbuttoned his shirt. "No one in their right mind would toss you aside, Rob."

In that case, he'd met a lot of people who weren't in their right mind. They no longer mattered. Only Sabrina did. "Will you still feel that way when I tell you I want to take you against the wall and on the kitchen table?"

Her eyes widened and her nostrils flared, due either to his words or the fact that she'd peeled his shirt off and was perusing his chest. "Can I make a request, too?"

"Of course." He immediately hardened, wanting to fulfill her fantasy, regardless of what it entailed.

She concentrated on slipping her arms into his shirtsleeves. "Will you take me doggie style? I always wanted to try it, but if I'm being too weird, we don't have to."

He stared at her as she buttoned the middle two buttons on the shirt, leaving the rest open. Good God, he had no idea his clothes had the potential to look that hot on anyone. "There is nothing weird about any suggestion, especially doggie style. The angle of penetration rocks a heck of an orgasm."

Her cheeks flushed crimson, reminding him how naïve and sheltered she was. No one had ever trusted him half as much as she did, despite knowing him for only a few hours. He wished he had a way of proving he'd never hurt her.

He dropped his gaze. That kind of proof involved deep emotions, the type he was too cynical to believe existed outside of the movie screen.

The tantalizing view of her cleavage drove his mind and body back to the familiar ground of lust. The lace thong cupping her pubic region peeked from beneath the tails of his shirt, bringing him to a state of full arousal. "Another thing for the night's bucket list: I want to take you in that shirt. Do you realize I'm never going to be able to wear my own clothes again without getting a hard-on thinking of you?"

Sabrina giggled. "Wow. Walking the red carpet is sure going to be awkward—whether you do it with clothes on or not."

Her delight flowed over him. He was so happy in her presence, he couldn't have cared less if he ever walked the red carpet again. He draped his hands inside the shirt collar, cupping her shoulders and tugging her closer. The moment his lips touched hers, she melted against him. He gathered her hair in his hands and blew softly across her exposed neck.

She shivered and rubbed her hands down his bare back, urging him closer.

Despite what should have been the perfect opportunity explore her body while his own recovered, his cock ached with the need to bury itself inside her again.

She palmed his ass.

"I had plans to take our time," he gritted.

"I have plans to give you a lap dance in that chair," she said, nodding at the one across from the bed.

"You win." He'd bet his Oscar she'd never given a lap dance in her life. He couldn't wait to be her first. He pulled her with him, stumbling backward until he bumped into the armrest. The chair teetered but didn't tip over.

Sabrina laughed, pushing him into the seat. She swiveled her hips in front of him, brushing against his enthusiastic erection. But then her expression shifted to consternation. "Aren't I supposed to straddle you? How do I do that with these big cushioned armrests?"

"We'll have to improvise, maybe save the lap dance for a different piece of furniture later." Like when he was sated enough not to come the moment she sank down on him. He stood and traced his tongue over her parted lips, then thrust it against them. Not coming close to expressing the depth of his desire, he twisted them both around, nudging Sabrina into his seat. He leaned over her, tangling his tongue with hers, then pulling back and plunging against her mouth.

She grasped his shoulders, her nails digging into his skin. Immediately, her grip slackened. "Sorry," she whispered. "I didn't mean to hurt you."

"I want you to scratch me up because you need me so much. Make your mark on me, Sabrina." He braced one hand on the back of the chair behind her head, leaving his other free to wander her lush body, making the most of the gaping opening below the closed buttons of his shirt.

She grazed her nails up his bare chest, catching his nipples.

He gasped at the unexpected need coursing through him. He'd never thought of his chest as sensitive, but it was proving to be a main erogenous zone.

She blew air across his aching nipples, and just when he thought he couldn't take anymore, she ran her fingertips over his skin again, standing up to reach him everywhere.

The loss of her weight on the furniture, coupled with his hand pushing on the backrest caused it to tip backward. Off-balance, he fell with it into Sabrina. He wrapped her in his arms and turned, falling on his side on the floor. She sprawled on top of him, her luscious body tempting him even in the middle of an accident.

"Are you hurt?" she asked.

He considered his shoulder for a moment. He'd feel it for a few days, but with or without the reminder, he wouldn't forget anything about tonight. "No, you?"

She laughed in answer, then teased her thigh over his full erection. "We knocked a chair over during sexual foreplay. Doesn't that turn you on?" Her voice was a mixture of awe and desire.

He grinned. "Everything about you turns me on."

Sitting up, he hooked her left leg over his shoulder, exposing her bare skin and the lacy thong at the juncture of her thighs. Then he skated his fingers from the back of her knee down her thigh, cresting at her buttocks.

"Oh Rob, talk about turning me on."

He repeated the motion, loving the way she squirmed. "You like that? Or would you like this more?" Shimmying his index finger inside her scrap of panty lace, he sank into her warm, moist depth. Oh yeah, he was turned on. He was addicted to her. He wanted to explore and claim every inch.

"Deeper," she demanded.

"Or maybe not." He started to pull out, wanting to tease, wanting to make the foreplay last, even if it destroyed his own tenuous control.

Her ass pressed down on his hand so his finger slid back where she wanted it as she sat up straight. "Yes, I want you inside me."

Rob laughed, loving the demands he was certain she'd never made on any other man. He grasped a condom that had fallen from his pants pocket onto the floor. "If you want it, stand up."

She hesitated, and he started to withdraw. Quickly, breathing hard, she complied.

He kept his hand connected to her hot, slick pussy as he also stood. Raising his head to look over her shoulder, he checked out the path behind her through the bedroom doorway. "Walk backwards. It's a straight shot from here to the breakfast table."

She took a step and gasped. With the second step, she clung to his neck for balance. "Oh God, Rob, walking with you inside me is so hot."

She wasn't kidding about the hotness. Her pussy rubbing his hand drove him over the edge. He thumbed her clit, and she stumbled.

Unable to stand another second, Rob lifted her in his arms, carrying her until he could set her against the edge of the table.

Hands quivering, she took the condom from him and attempted to rip the foil. Beyond ready to roll it on and plunge into her, he concentrated on bringing her pleasure with his hands. Positioning a second finger at her slippery opening, he pressed them both inside her.

Sabrina bucked against him. "Rob! Yes."

"Yes," he echoed, loving the glaze over her eyes and the fluttering pulse at her neck. He plunged his fingers in and out in time to her breathing and then wrapped his pinkie around the string of her thong, tightening it to stroke against her sensitive flesh.

"More, Rob. Oh yes." She flung her arm out, connecting with the Corona bottle. It crashed to the floor with a loud crack, but she continued to lift her hips and call his name without pause.

Holy moly, she was so crazy for him she didn't notice a bottle breaking. Desire coursed through him so strong, he couldn't wait another second. He lifted her in his arms again and strode toward the front door, away from the shattered glass and spilled beer. He kissed her against the wall, then released her to roll on the condom.

Sabrina's knees buckled, and she sank down the wall, until her mouth was level with his cock.

The thought of her sucking him was more than he could handle. "Another time. And I will collect. But right now, I need to be inside you. Let me show you how good doggie style is."

She shifted onto her hands and knees, presenting him with her ass. "Like this?"

"Perfect. You are perfect." He caressed her cheeks, amazed at her lack of hesitation, her complete trust in him. He dipped his finger inside her, making sure she was still ready for him. Her heat and wetness erased any doubt.

"Don't tease me. I want you now." Her voice vibrated.

"Okay." He readied himself at her entrance, prepared to inch inside, giving her time to adjust to him.

"All of you at once. All the way. Please." What had sounded like an order at first turned into a plea, and giving her anything and everything she wanted became his single goal.

He gripped her cheeks and drove himself into her with one sure thrust. Heaven welcomed him and, for a moment, the sheer pleasure paralyzed him. "Sabrina."

"You're not going to come yet. I've never done it this way before, and I want my first time to be good." She reached back and cupped his balls.

Pleasure so great it bordered on pain slammed into him. He pulled back and thrust, finding a fast and deep rhythm.

Sabrina met him stroke for stroke, intensifying each pulse of their bodies.

He reached in front of her and massaged her clit.

She gasped his name, lifting her ass higher.

"Sabrina," he shouted. He came hard and fast, clinging to her as a lifeline. And still, he couldn't stop pumping. "Oh, Sabrina."

Beneath him, her muscles contorted. She screamed his name as she convulsed.

Rob's body shook. He had no control. As impossible as he would have thought, he poured himself into her a second time.

He collapsed, rolling to the side and taking her with him, so they stayed connected yet he didn't hurt her. "Damn. Sex with you makes a helluva one-night stand."

Sex with you makes a helluva one-night stand.

Rob's words echoed in Sabrina's brain, leaving her more and more frenzied as the night went on. With each passing hour, their time together came closer to an end.

As the sun crested the sky, they soaked their sore, sated bodies in the suite's luxurious hot tub. Back in the bedroom, she pushed him onto his back and rode him hard, drinking in his moans and gasps. For her. She'd made Rob Wellington desire her.

When he shouted his ecstasy, she lay across his chest, pressing her lips to the rapid beat of his heart until it slowed and every muscle in his body relaxed.

She eased off him and found her dress, slipping it over her head. "Thank you for the wonderful one-night stand."

He rose onto his elbows. "You're leaving?"

Desperation not to humiliate herself created a force of will stronger than she imagined existed inside her. "It's morning, almost checkout time."

"When can I see you again?"

She could invite him back to her apartment and not have to end their time together. But that would prolong the illusion that she had something to offer him, that their relationship was based on more than sex. She wasn't stupid. She'd gone into this encounter with her eyes wide open. If her throat ached now and she wanted something different than she had when she'd knocked on the door yesterday evening, she had to work through those issues on her own. "That's not how a one-night stand works."

"You don't want to see me again?"

She looked him in the eye, hoping her face didn't betray how much she wanted exactly that. Despite the fantasy night they'd shared, she hadn't forgotten he was a famous movie director with an unending supply of both money and women. Meanwhile, she remained a poor inner-city schoolteacher.

The best way she could thank him for the massive sexual awakening he'd given her was to not throw herself at him. She wouldn't act pathetic and needy. She wouldn't let on how she imagined she'd fallen in love with him.

"No, I don't," she said with conviction.

Chapter Six

"*I* have some ideas on how we can enhance my role." The bombshell actress methodically peeled open her shirt one buttonhole at a time, expanding her cleavage down to her navel.

Her less than subtle offer didn't tempt Rob. In the two months since his one-night stand with Sabrina, he couldn't even look at another woman on a personal level. He worked, of course. Like his brother, he had a robust workaholic gene, but where he had once been passionate about the films he brought to life, feeling strongly about anything hurt too much. Going through the motions took all his effort.

No matter how many roles he enhanced or cut altogether, the movie would be a massive flop. He'd created a technical masterpiece packaged in a flat production with no heart. As a jaded cynic before he met Sabrina, he'd been able to fake the emotions needed to reach his audience. Now he was too raw to put any emotion on display. He'd once accused her of ruining his brother's wedding. He never imagined she'd be responsible for destroying his career.

He left the set and the frustrated actress behind. Since they'd been shooting near the San Diego coast, he detoured to Blake's office instead of going home.

"You look worse than I did when my fiancée ran off on me the week before my wedding," Blake said, not looking surprised to see him. "What's up?"

"Sabrina. I can't stop thinking about her." The admission caused another pang, but he felt lighter speaking the truth aloud.

"Then call her. Don't come whining to me."

He wished the solution was that simple. "She didn't give me her number. She didn't want to see me again."

Blake rolled his eyes. "Of course she fed you that line. She signed up for a night of exciting sex with someone so far out of her league you wouldn't have noticed she existed in any other situation. She believed you wouldn't want to see her again but might be too polite to say so. Like most of us, she didn't want to get her heart stomped on."

"How do you know?" Sabrina had told him no. It hadn't occurred to him she hadn't been honest with him. She was the most straightforward person he'd ever met.

"I'm her friend, aren't I?" Blake said. "She's the one person who can talk me out of the office once a week for dinner. Speaking of which, it's Wednesday, and I'm late."

"You're supposed to meet her now?" Rob demanded. He'd come here needing the commiseration of Blake's company and a bottle of whiskey. But Sabrina was waiting somewhere, and he could only hope her eyes would fill with pleasure at the sight of him.

"In fifteen minutes, at this little café across town." Blake glanced at the papers piled on his desk. "But I have too much to do here. I'll call her and cancel."

"Don't cancel," Rob ordered, desperate not to let the opportunity slip through his fingers.

"You want to take my place?" Blake guessed.

"Text the address to my phone," he called, sprinting from the office, hope pulsing through him for the first time in weeks.

☃

Blake was late, as was his MO. Sabrina didn't mind. In fact, she preferred it. Every time she sat across from him staring into blue eyes so startlingly like Rob's, it became harder to face him. She'd thought as time passed she'd become used to the reminders, that she'd be left with pleasant memories—okay, smoking hot memories but good ones, nonetheless, not this painful knife to the heart.

Friends and fellow teachers had offered to set her up on dates, but Sabrina had made excuses. She didn't want staid conversations and lackluster sex. She wanted the heart-stopping, scream out loud, go at it until you can no longer move variety of sex. And she wanted love, too. Yep, she wanted everything—the happily ever after fairy tale and sexual satisfaction rolled into one.

She sipped from her water glass and opened the file folder of papers to grade while she waited for Blake to arrive. Halfway through the stack, she felt him slip into the booth across from her. "I knew you'd get here eventually," she murmured without glancing at him.

"Did you?"

Her head snapped up at the familiar voice. Instead of Blake facing her, the guarded blue eyes, the Hollywood handsome face, the husky voice, and the rock solid body belonged to the man who had haunted her dreams for the past two months.

"Rob." She dropped her red pen and stared in shock.

"I don't want a one-night stand," he said, leaning forward and placing both elbows on the table.

She swallowed, trying to form words or thoughts. But she was paralyzed between hope and heartbreak.

The waitress arrived at their table, but Sabrina simply shook her head, unable to make even the simplest decision of what to eat.

Rob consulted with the server and ordered for both of them. After she walked away, he turned the full force of his attention on Sabrina again. "Look, I know you told me to stay away, and I tried, but—"

"I don't want you to stay away," she whispered. There, she'd admitted it.

He reached across the table and took her hand in his. "Then why did you tell me to?"

His touch warmed her, allowing her to risk embarrassing herself enough to admit, "I thought I was supposed to say that. I thought a one-night stand was supposed to end after the night was over. I didn't want to be one of those clingy ladies who humiliate themselves by not knowing when to step back and accept the truth of the situation."

"What truth?"

"I'm far more attracted to you than you could ever feel for me."

He scooted around the end of the booth to join her on her bench, wrapping an arm around her shoulders. "That's the old, insecure Sabrina talking, not the siren I spent the night with."

"They're both me," she said, leaning into his warmth. She'd missed him so much. The hot sex was wonderful, but she could spend every evening cuddled against him with his arm around her shoulder and be in heaven.

"I'm crazy about all the complexities of your personality, among other things."

The hope she hadn't dared to allow in stampeded past her defenses. "What other things?"

He smiled. "You're going to have to go out with me to find out. What can I do to talk you into visiting a movie set this weekend? I need to find the heart of this film so I can fix it."

"If you take me to your movie set, other people might see me with you," she pointed out. Even if she wrapped her head around the possibility that he wanted to see her again, she hadn't expected he'd want anyone other than Blake to be the wiser for it.

"Honey, if I have my way, we'll be joined at the hip, and everyone will see us together everywhere we go."

Her cheeks heated at all the ways they had joined at the hip during their night together and how much she wanted to do it again. "You're talking about dating."

"Only because I'm afraid you'll think I'm insane if I pledge my heart and my life after a one-night stand."

Maybe she should have thought so, but she didn't. She was ready to pledge hers, too. Of course, they needed a few dates and heartfelt conversations before they did. But, in the meantime, she wouldn't push him away due to her own fears and insecurities. If he could accept her, she could accept him for who he was and accept herself too.

The waitress returned with their platters of food.

"This counts as a date, right?" she asked Rob.

"You bet. The first of many. Well, the second of many. We can count Madame Eve's night as our first." He lowered his lips to hers.

She wrapped her arms around his neck. "This second date has a lot to live up to. We better get our food to go."

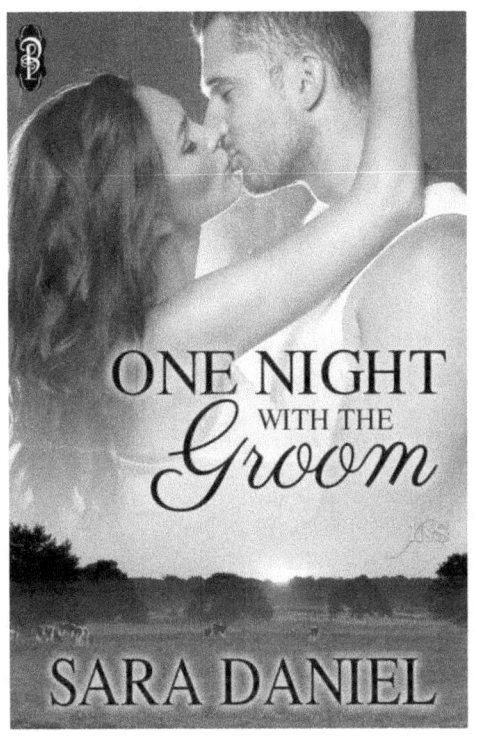

ONE NIGHT WITH THE GROOM

A 1Night Stand Story

By
Sara Daniel

~Dedication~

For everyone who holds special memories of The Farm, especially David, Mary, Michael, and Amy.

Chapter One

*L*uciana Cortez stared into the empty envelope, willing the cash to materialize. Of course, it didn't. Rifling through her labeled manila envelopes in the scarred oak desk, she prayed the mortgage money had simply been misplaced.

Her pleas went unanswered.

Heart pounding, she gazed out the front window at the windblown pastures and cornfields. Only the meager funds she'd scraped together for her meeting with the hospital billing department in two days remained. She needed a miracle before then, or she'd be forced to choose between saving the farm and her mother's health.

A maroon pickup raised a cloud of dust as it turned from the gravel road into the rutted drive.

Mama would tell her to say a rosary to find the missing funds. If Papa were alive, he would have told her to work harder to make up for it. And her brother, Alejandro, borrowing her ancient Chevy Silverado while on leave from the Marines, would concoct a ridiculous moneymaking scheme.

She shoved her chair back and slammed out of the house to confront him. Bracing her hands on her hips in the middle of the driveway, she waited for the vehicle to stop.

The rusted bumper coasted inches from her legs, but she refused to flinch.

"You'd make a hell of a Marine," he called through the open window. "Most soldiers would have dived for cover." He shifted into park and ran his fingers through his military-short haircut. Guilty.

Luciana stormed to the door and yanked it open. "God damn it, Alejandro. What'd you do with the money?"

"Don't get mad. I can explain."

"Did you use it to pay the mortgage?" She clung to her last hope everything would turn out all right.

"No."

A lump swelled in her throat, but she ignored it along with the tears filling her eyes. "How could you? I trusted you."

"Since we weren't going to have enough this month, just like we didn't last month or the one before, I came up with another plan."

"The bank knows I'm making a good faith effort. Paying something is better than nothing."

"The threatening letters they're sending make it clear they're not going to settle for 'something' and 'good faith.' Not to mention, the bank president enjoys being an ass rather than cutting anyone any slack. Every penny I have is tied up in a new investment that hasn't paid out yet. Since I don't have anything to loan you, I used the mortgage money to buy you a one-night stand."

Her jaw dropped, and her stomach plummeted. "You did what?"

"I found this company called 1Night Stand. The proprietor, Madame Eve, will match you up. I explained our goal is for you to meet someone with too much cash who's looking for a place to unload it so our troubles will be over."

Mama didn't have to worry about her baby boy dying in a war zone because Luciana would kill him with her bare hands. He didn't even have the decency to squander her hard-earned money on a get-rich scheme with a conceivable chance of paying off. "You want me to sell my body to save the farm?"

"Of course not. Madame Eve isn't sleazy. I have some buddies who met their wives through her. Hang on. I brought a brochure that explains the service." He reached across the seat to the glove box.

She grabbed his ear and twisted, yanking him out of the vehicle.

"Ow." He pulled his head free of her grip and blinked, rubbing his ear. "Stop using torture techniques that violate the Geneva Convention."

"Then don't start a family war. I don't want a brochure. I don't want a sleazy one-night stand, or an upscale one for that matter, regardless of what's been promised in return. I want my mortgage money back. All of it."

He jutted his chin. "Madame Eve takes into account more than just sexual needs when she matches people. The guy she finds will be our best chance."

"How can you think a matchmaker, or whatever you call someone who hooks people up for one night, is the answer to our money problems? She *took* all our money."

"Listen, if it doesn't work out, then I'll call and ask for a refund. *No problemo.*" He shrugged.

Oh yeah, no problemo getting cash back from a scammer. "Damn it, Alejandro. What were you thinking?"

"I thought you were so worried about the farm you didn't have time for a date, so this could kill two birds with one stone."

She gritted her teeth. She wouldn't really commit violence against her brother, just hit him hard enough to knock some sense into him. "Not interested. I don't need a man to fix my life."

"I also figured if it works out, you can gift me with a 1Night Stand when I'm best man at your wedding."

She swung her arm to smack him. He chuckled and ducked back into the truck, avoiding her, then shifted into reverse and gunned down the driveway. If she'd had Papa's shotgun handy, she would have shot out the tires.

Most of the time, she treasured Alejandro's presence, his antics brightening her routine of drudgery and responsibility. Papa's life goal had been to be an organic dairy farmer. Her own dreams of love and family had died years ago, leaving her no other purpose but to take over his plans and attempt to honor him and provide for her mother.

She pulled her hair back as the wind whipped it around her face then watched the Silverado turn the corner, vanishing behind a hill. At least her brother had been smart enough to cut his losses and drive away, instead of attempting to drag her to the ridiculous one-night stand.

Chores and the evening milking awaited her, so she marched to the barn to tackle the never-ending workload. At the end of the day, she didn't have the energy to pick up her vibrator, let alone find a man. Despite her frustration, a tiny part of her filled with disappointment that the night ahead held the same tedium and exhaustion as every other one.

03

Denver held a lot of promise as an expansion site for Sunburst Hotels. Omaha, not so much. Anticipating the situation, Blake Wellington had sent the rest of his team straight from Denver to the next potential location in Des Moines while he'd made a quick side trip through Omaha, confirmed his analysis, and hopped on another flight. Exiting the plane and striding through the Des Moines airport, he texted his estimated time to rejoin the group.

Sidestepping a father trying to corral a toddler in full meltdown mode, he dialed his boss who'd elected to sit out the trip. "Mr. Sunburst, the team will arrive home late this evening. If you want to schedule a meeting for first thing in the morning, I'll update you on everything before we make our recommendation to the board."

"Tomorrow? Are you trying to keep me out of the loop, boy? My schedule is wide open tonight."

Blake might be CEO of Sunburst Hotels, but Mr. Sunburst didn't let him forget who owned the company. "Ten o'clock tonight is the earliest I can expect to be back."

"Ten, it is. Don't keep me waiting. And stay away from Caroline's place. We're not competing with my daughter."

No way would he go near his ex-fiancée's ranch resort in Montana. Mr. Sunburst had been easy to please when he'd been Blake's future father-in-law. However, Caroline's defection a week before their wedding had turned Blake's dream job into a minefield. He constantly walked a tightrope of trying to satisfy his boss without stifling the innovations and changes he wanted to bring to the company.

He sank into the seat of the waiting limousine and began setting up the spreadsheets with the preliminary findings on the first two sites, so he could begin working on the presentation he'd thought he would have all night to perfect.

Keying information into his laptop, he phoned his assistant to glean what she'd already learned about the Des Moines location. He needed the distraction. Although he might be a tolerable distance from his ex-fiancée, anywhere in the state of Iowa put him way too close to the town where he'd grown up, where he'd left behind the girl who'd owned his heart.

"What did you say? You're cutting in and out," Marcia complained.

He frowned. "You'd think the biggest city in the state would have better cell service. Research their capabilities for me, please. I can't invest in a hotel where my guests aren't going to be able to use their phones and electronics to their satisfaction."

"Speaking of which, where are you? We've been expecting you for the past half hour."

"I'm on my way from the airport."

"I know. That's why I expected you to be here already."

He lifted his head, surprised to see fields of corn and pastures instead of city streets. "Driver, where are we going?"

"Where my instructions said to take you, sir." The man slowed and turned the vehicle down a gravel road.

In other words, he'd gotten lost and needed to turn around. Blake refocused on his notes and ran some projections through the spreadsheet. "Marcia, e-mail me all the Des Moines information."

No response. Dammit.

He typed his analysis of the first two locations, not looking up until the driver opened the door. "We're here, sir."

Perfect. He'd get the figures he needed, and if a better communications infrastructure wasn't coming down the pike, the location would be axed from consideration. Gathering his laptop and notes, he stepped out of the car. The wind rustled the loose papers, threatening to yank them from his grasp.

"Enjoy your evening, sir." The driver closed the door, bowed, returned to his seat, and pulled away.

Before the wind left him scrambling like an idiot to retrieve his notes, Blake zipped everything in his laptop case. Straightening, he studied the landscape, familiar for all the wrong reasons.

Farmhouse, barn, silo, cows mooing in the distance.

His team wasn't waiting for him. He'd never consider replacing the farm in front of him with a hotel. In fact, the last time he'd been on the property, Luciana's father had shot out the taillights of his truck. Nobody would roll out a welcome mat if he knocked on the door.

Waving his arm, he attempted to hail the limo driver, but the car continued down the road, scattering dust across the fields.

The meeting with Mr. Sunburst looming, he needed to spend an hour or two at the potential Des Moines site before the flight home. He held up his phone to maximize any signal, so he could contact Marcia.

A buzz announced a text message. *Enjoy your one-night stand. Madame Eve*

"What one-night stand? Who are you? What are you talking about?" Before he could type any of those questions, *no service* lit the display. He pocketed the useless phone while down the road the limo disappeared from view.

Caroline had given him a breakup gift of a one-night stand. His brother then "helped" him fill out the application during a pathetic bachelor pity-party. Whether Madame Eve intended for his hookup to happen on a dilapidated farm or at his own hotel in San Diego, he had no idea. The text hadn't given him details, but regardless of the impression from his drunken questionnaire, he would never engage in anything so crass on company time.

The scent of fresh hay mixed with a faint whiff of manure, and the moos of cattle in the distance blasted him both back to the present and deeper into the past. Another glance at the house sent his heart thundering. Luciana. Despite blocking her image for the past fifteen years, his heart ached at the crystal-clear memories.

He squared his shoulders and calculated the odds she still lived there. Slim, and the chances were even smaller that she'd let him borrow her landline before her father took another shot at him.

Chapter Two

*L*uciana released the final cow from its milking stall, finished cleaning off the machinery then traipsed outside. The gusty wind whipped the barn door from her grasp, slamming it against the side of the building. She reached for it then paused as a male silhouette strode into view from around the front of the house. Alejandro had had a change of heart. He'd better have gotten their money back.

The man marched closer. Not her brother. She laid her palm over her stomach. Holy Mother, the stress had finally cracked her. After giving up hope that he would ever return for her, she'd conjured up an all-too-real hallucination of him striding across the grass lot.

"Hello, Luciana." His voice rang out a shade deeper than she remembered, his shoulders broader. He dressed like he'd never set foot on a farm in his life—three-piece charcoal suit, maroon tie. She lifted her head before he caught her inspecting any lower. His arresting blue eyes captivated her.

"Blake." Her heart bled as if she'd stabbed it with a pitchfork. She dropped her hand from her stomach to her side. "What are you doing here?"

"I haven't the foggiest idea." His lips curved in a crooked smile.

Aching to wrap her arms around him, to kiss his sexy mouth, to soak in his presence while grinning at him like a fool, she took a step back. She might not be hallucinating, but his sudden appearance had the power to drive her over the edge of insanity and longing. Her heel caught on the threshold at the opening of the barn, and she stumbled.

He reached for her, but she steadied herself on the doorframe, holding out her other palm to ward him away. She couldn't handle seeing him, let alone skin-on-skin contact.

"Give me a minute," she begged. "I'm kind of shocked to see you." *Kind of, ha.* Completely would have been an understatement.

His smile faded. "Good shocked or bad shocked?"

"I don't know yet." The dead tree beside the barn creaked in the wind. She'd let her fear over it falling on the barn or, worse, in the other direction keep her from cutting it down, but the nasty gusts made her regret the decision.

"Keep me posted on which way it goes. I'm already skittish about getting shot at."

"You won't be unless you touch me, in which case I'll shoot you myself."

"Fair enough." He pocketed his hands and stepped back.

The distance helped. So did the fact he didn't call her bluff. Luciana's limbs shook too much to pick up any weapon. At one time, she'd been furious with him for abandoning her when she'd needed him most. Although he'd bowed to her parents' pressure and hadn't fought to save their future together, her emotions had faded to regret and resignation.

"So, you decided to drop in after fifteen years without a word, and you don't have a clue why?" Okay, maybe her anger hadn't faded.

"I didn't come to see you."

"Ouch. Thanks for being straight with me, rather than sparing my ego. I think."

He winced. "I didn't mean an insult. I'm supposed to be in Des Moines to consider a potential property for my company to add to their hotel portfolio. But the limo took me here instead and then left me."

Limo. Hotel portfolio. If he hadn't been out of her league before, he'd traveled far beyond her social realm. "So, are you one of those 'if I build it, they will come' visionaries?"

"No, I'm a market-feasibility, make-sure-every-aspect-is-viable-before-I-sink-a-penny-into-it type of executive. I don't have a reason that makes any sense for why I showed up here, and my cell phone isn't getting reception. If I could borrow your landline to make some calls, I'll get out of your hair as soon as possible."

He hadn't come to see her. He'd arrived by mistake and wanted to get far away without further ado. Once upon a time, they'd shared a rare, special love. She remembered it and regretted losing it, even if he didn't.

"Of course you can use the phone." She threw her weight into closing the barn door against the wind, secured the latch then strode toward the house, not glancing back to see if he followed. Without seeing or hearing him, she could sense his presence.

"Do you live here alone?" he asked, falling into step next to her.

"No. Mama's in Des Moines for a couple of days, and Alejandro still uses his room when he's on leave." Although this time, he got to sleep in an uncomfortable hospital chair next to their mother, and if he valued his life, he'd stay gone for a long time after his "trade the mortgage money for a one-night stand" stunt.

"Leave from the Army?" Blake guessed.

"Marines."

A pickup with a bad muffler rumbled along the gravel road as she led the way through the front door. She flinched, praying the vehicle would continue down the road without stopping. Overwhelmed on every front, she didn't need to deal with an angry neighbor, too. Besides, her cows couldn't have strayed far. She'd just finished the milking.

Except the first cows through the chute had been done two hours ago, plenty of time for them to wander to the end of the pasture and succumb to the temptation of the ripening corn on the other side of the rotting fence she never had enough time to replace.

Inside the house, she turned to face Blake. After spending years dreaming he would return for her, she'd never expected their reunion to be reduced to banal conversation over borrowing a phone. She gestured to the relic on the wall. "It's still in the same spot."

"Gotta love the rotary dial," he murmured.

She tried not to think about all the times she'd wrapped herself in the cord as she'd whispered to him through the receiver. "Not much changes around here."

Outside, the rumbling muffler grew louder then cut off. "Luciana!"

Her heart sank. Whatever stereotypes had evolved concerning neighborly visits in the country, Trevor seemed determined to bust the myth.

"Make yourself at home," she told Blake. "If my cows got loose again, I'll be gone for a few hours. I'll understand if you've already left by the time I get back."

She paused in front of him, studying his gorgeous face and wind-tousled, light-brown hair. Chances were she wouldn't see him again for another fifteen years, if ever. Reaching up, she ran her palm down his cheek, scratchy with five o'clock shadow. Luciana lingered against his skin, her fingers tingling. Unable to resist, she stood on tiptoes and brushed her lips across his jaw.

"Your lousy cows are trampling my corn again," Trevor shouted through the screen door. "I'm suing you for damages if you don't get the hell out here now and fix your pathetic excuse for a fence."

Blake stood frozen as Luciana ran out the door, calling breathless apologies to her not-so-understanding neighbor. Despite his shock over seeing her again, time and distance had allowed him to treat her as a casual acquaintance.

Until she'd touched him.

He trembled as if he were a single hand pump away from coming in his pants. Only she had that effect on him. For years, he'd chalked it up to youth and out-of-control hormones. Despite not being young anymore, hormones he hadn't lost control of in years surged from the slight contact.

Outside, Luciana spoke in low, soothing tones to her neighbor, while pressing her palms against her heart. The guy spat on the ground and stomped away. He gunned his truck and drove off.

After he disappeared, her shoulders slumped. Blake stepped toward the door, ready to wrap her in his arms. But she didn't glance his way, as she headed to the barn. A couple of minutes later, she emerged, wearing work gloves and maneuvering a wheelbarrow with a roll of barbed wire, metal stakes, and who knew what else inside.

Toying with following her into the field behind the barn, he discarded the idea. He'd been a town boy, never a farmer—another thing for her family to hold against him, although being a non-Hispanic, non-Catholic had been more than enough reason for them to hate him on principle.

Turning his attention to the interior of the house, he studied the familiar kitchen wallpaper peeling apart at the seams. An overturned wooden chair lay in the corner next to a bottle of glue, a clamp holding the leg support in place.

As he picked up the phone receiver, the stretched-out cord fell to a pile on the floor. He should call for a taxi, a helicopter, a damn rescue mission to take him straight to San Diego—screw the Des Moines location. And he would have, if Luciana hadn't touched him with the same sweetness and reverence as when they were kids.

He spun Marcia's number in the dial. "It's Blake. Do you want a raise?"

"Of course. Who doesn't? But where are you? We've gone through everything with the site development team, and I'm running out of stalling ideas while we wait for you."

"I'm not coming. Wrap up and take the company plane home. The expansion debrief file I started is saved on the server. Finish it and deliver the presentation to Mr. Sunburst at ten o'clock tonight."

"You want me to give the presentation? What do you want me to say about this site?"

"Whatever you think. Might as well earn your raise." At the moment, he couldn't care less about the hotel expansion plans, not when he had a chance to rediscover the woman who owned his past, whose single touch illuminated everything lacking in his successful, workaholic life.

"Yes, sir," Marcia said. "But what are you working on? Is everything okay?"

"Interesting questions. Maybe I'll have answers to them by morning." He hung up the phone, his shoulders light. He'd bought a solid twelve hours with no interruptions and no responsibilities. Whether he could make the most of the time remained to be seen.

Dang, he wished he'd been prepared with a pair of jeans, T-shirt, and sneakers. He'd networked with enough people to understand when an expensive tailored suit worked to his advantage. It wouldn't with Luciana.

He'd have to leverage what he did have going for him. She hadn't forgotten him, and he'd wager she wouldn't have caressed his face if she'd been involved with anyone else.

Her father had given him no choice but to walk away from her. He'd intended to return once everyone had settled down. Then she'd lost the baby and hadn't returned his calls—calls her overprotective parents had likely never told her about. Meanwhile, his brother offered him a one-way trip to California, and he'd jumped at the opportunity.

He'd moved on with his life—far beyond whatever they would have created together. He loved his job, even with his cranky boss. But the night stretched before him, beckoning him to forget about his responsibilities and consider what life would have been like if he'd never walked away from his first—and only—love.

Chapter Three

*W*ith a lot of cajoling and strong nudges, Luciana convinced the cows to return to the pasture, but not before one of the gentle animals nudged back, sending her flat on her ass in a cow pie. She pounded in the new post and strung more barbed wire.

Satisfied the animals would stay on her property, she returned the supplies to the barn then limped back to the house. Her bruised hip put up a good argument for cutting her losses and selling the cows as soon as possible, but she'd have no farm left without the steady but slim milk income.

Ahead, Blake stood in the doorway, raising his right hand in greeting. Her heart lurched, wanting the sight to welcome her every time she returned home.

He sauntered down the front walk. "Are you hurt?"

"Nah. A cow and I just had a minor disagreement over space."

"Some disagreements aren't worth it, even when you're right," he said, a twinkle in his eye. Although he teased about the livestock, perhaps he'd also believed their love hadn't been worth the trouble of fighting her parents.

"Did you find a ride out of here? Alejandro has my pickup, and I value my life too much to drive the tractor in the city."

"I don't need a ride. I'm right where I want to be."

A pang of longing shot through her. Years ago, when he'd gazed at her with those bright blue eyes, she'd believed without question they lived in their own special world where they would be together forever. But not only was she not part of his world, she didn't even understand the type of life he led. "I'm supposed to believe you want to build your fancy hotel right here?"

"No. You're supposed to believe I want to spend the evening with you."

"Oh." Luciana hadn't considered the possibility, didn't know why he'd want to. Maybe if she had a few hours or weeks, she could get used to the idea.

"I'd hoped for a bit more enthusiasm." He reached toward her waist.

She jumped back. "No, you can't touch me."

He lifted both arms as if to prove he had no intention of forcing himself on her.

Despite wanting to believe she had more will to resist him than when she'd been a teen, she wouldn't bet on it, assuming her brother had left her any money to bet with. "I fell in cow manure in the field. You don't want to get it on your nice suit or get close enough to smell me."

She squeezed her eyes shut. Did she have to spell out the details of how far beneath his station her life had become? "I'm going to stick my babbling mouth in a soapy shower."

His eyes gleamed. "Anything I can help with?"

"I think I can handle my own bath." Her cheeks heated as soon as the words left her mouth. When they'd been kids sneaking around, the clandestine meetings in the cab of a pickup or in an open meadow hadn't allowed them an opportunity to explore each other's naked body. She doubted she'd be able to refuse the chance if he offered.

"I meant in general." His eyes sparkled, as if he were imagining her naked under the spray. "Anything I can do to make myself useful while you're getting all fresh and sweet-smelling?"

She didn't need much encouragement to get fresh with him, a prospect that both terrified and aroused her. "If you want to stay, you can help by opening a can of whatever's in the pantry for dinner. If nothing appeals to you, the freezer might have more interesting options. No promises though."

"I can cook dinner," he assured her.

For a moment, she imagined what her mother would think of her asking a man to cook for her in her own kitchen. Best not to think about her parents in conjunction with Blake Wellington. She couldn't cope with her own explosive emotions, let alone her family's reaction.

She shed her boots outside then watched him from the corner of her eye as she made her way to the bathroom, afraid to hope he might be in her house when she emerged. But he hadn't left while she'd worked on the fence. The further hope invaded, the more fear paralyzed her.

Why had he come back into her life, and what did she plan to do with him while he graced her with his presence?

Nothing, that's what. She didn't have anything to offer. Even when he'd loved her, he wouldn't have considered marrying her if she hadn't been pregnant.

After the shower, Luciana dressed in her bedroom then leaned against the window. Craning her neck, she could see the top of the dead tree swinging violently in the wind. As soon as she finished the milking tomorrow morning, she'd cut it down before it fell on the one part of the farm she'd poured her heart into—the only memorial she had to what could have been, to the life that had never had a chance.

She shoved away from the window and left the bedroom, pausing at her desk in the living room. Despite the empty mortgage folder, she still had a little money in the emergency envelope, enough to make a good-faith payment to the hospital for her mother. Caring for Mama came first. Then she'd worry about saving the farm.

Luciana had survived the loss of her baby before she'd had a chance to hold him or her in her arms, before the child had been real to anyone but her. She could survive the money troubles on the farm, Mama's recent setback, and whatever maelstrom Blake created with her emotions.

Grounded, she headed for the kitchen where he sprinkled an assortment of chopped ingredients over the eggs sizzling in a fry pan. "You're making an omelet."

He glanced at her. "Don't sound so surprised. I'm not a gourmet chef by any means, but give me a skillet and I can fend for myself."

The food didn't surprise her as much as the threat of domestic chores hadn't sent him running. Stepping around the suit coat and tie he'd draped over a chair, she peered into the pan. "Peppers, tomatoes, mushrooms, sausage, and a hint of hot sauce. Very nice."

He grinned, looking way too comfortable with his white dress shirt rolled up to the elbows, displaying the enticing light brown hairs on his forearms. "The first one's ready if you can bring me two plates."

She did, and he flipped it onto the plate then repeated the process of making the next one.

"Anything I forgot?" he asked.

Too overwhelmed to speak, she shook her head. She'd assumed he'd forgotten *her*. Instead, he stood in front of her stove, cooking for her.

He took the plates and set them on the table then held out her chair.

"You don't have to do this." She didn't expect to be pampered and catered to. As a matter of fact, she no longer remembered how to graciously accept special treatment.

His lips curved in a sensuous promise. "I want to."

She sank into the chair, frightened by how much she wanted him to shower her with affection and attention. When had she become so starved for it? Or did she crave affection only from him? "We can't pick up where we left off. Too many things have happened. Too many years have gone by. We're different people now."

"I'm all for getting reacquainted." He sifted his fingers through the ends of her hair then walked around the table to take his seat.

Suppressing a shiver, she refused to reveal her vulnerability to his touch. "As you can see, my life hasn't changed."

"Then why do you say you're a different person?" he challenged.

Because life had worn her down so much she didn't recognize herself anymore. Her dreams had morphed into a desperate grasp for survival—medical care for her mother and a roof over her head. "I'd rather hear about your glamorous life," she said. "I assume you went to college like you planned."

She remembered the fear in his voice when he'd confessed he wanted to continue his schooling despite her pregnancy and their plans to marry. He'd worried about juggling a full class load while supporting a family. She'd sworn he wouldn't have to give up his dreams because of her. At the time, she'd believed their love would carry them through any adversity, not that she'd get left behind while he pursued his ambitions.

"I went to college, not quite the way I envisioned, definitely not glamorous, but it worked out well in the end. Remember, my brother had moved to California to work in the movie industry? He offered to let me crash on his couch."

Prior to her accidental pregnancy, she'd spent six months terrified he would choose to go to college on the West Coast rather than at one of the nearby Iowa schools. The few times his brother had talked to her when he'd returned for holidays, he'd warned she would hold Blake back from his full potential if they stayed together. Of course, he had been right.

"I got a job working nights at the Sunburst Hotel front desk and went to school during the day," he continued. "I interned at the hotel in the summers, and they offered me a full-time job on graduation. I took the job, but I also kept going to school—this time at night for my MBA. Pretty soon, I'd worked my way up to vice-president of Marketing, then of Operations. Then CEO."

Luciana chewed on her omelet, savoring the spicy burst of flavor he'd created. A CEO had cooked her dinner. She wished she had a close friend to share a giggle over the gossipy tidbit, but the farm chores took up too much time to have any left over for friendship, let alone giggles.

"Congratulations, Mr. CEO." She toasted him with her glass of water. "I'm impressed but not surprised, considering you managed your parents' hardware store while you were still in high school." A natural leader, he'd had her as his number one follower.

"That store took a lot of effort for little return," he mused. "But at least Mom and Dad are enjoying their hard-earned retirement. They have a lot of fun visiting the locations where Rob films his movies."

"His marriage made the entertainment news." She might not have paid attention if he'd married an actress, but he'd fallen for a curvy, Hispanic teacher with a sweet smile. "No word about you, though." Her cheeks flushed. Not the smoothest way to dig for information.

"I'm not entertainment-news worthy, thank goodness." Blake smirked. "Engaged, twice. Never married."

Food forgotten, she stared at him. "Twice?"

"You were number one."

"We didn't even have a ring, and it was a shotgun situation."

He lowered his fork. "Please don't use the word shotgun. I'm still trying to recover from your father coming after me with one. But I asked and you said yes, so we were engaged, even if it only lasted a week."

She blinked. He sounded like he'd wanted to marry her instead of being backed into it.

"I managed to make my second engagement last for a year, right up until the week before the wedding."

"Did you love her?" she asked, not sure how she wanted him to answer. The thought of him loving anyone else filled her with a terrible jealousy, but the man she'd known never would have married if he hadn't been in love, even if the woman had been pregnant. She didn't want to learn he'd turned cold in the intervening years.

He scratched his cheek. "Good question. We had some affection. Caroline is the daughter of the man who owns the Sunburst Hotels. Her father pushed for the relationship, and she seemed interested. Then, a week before the wedding, she called it off. She hooked up with some guy from her past. I had no idea he existed, let alone she was so hung up on him she wanted to marry him instead of me."

"I'm sorry," Luciana offered, sorry he'd gotten hurt, not upset he hadn't married someone who hadn't deserved him. Had he ever mentioned her name to his fiancée or told her about their baby? Or was she his dark, ugly secret he didn't want anyone to find out about?

Chapter Four

"So, you still live here with your parents and brother? I expected you would have...." Blake hesitated, not wanting to insult Luciana. She'd acquired strength of spirit over the intervening years but also an aura of sadness. She used to smile and laugh. The few times her lips curved, the joy didn't reach her shadowed brown eyes.

"Grown up? Moved out? Gotten a life of my own?" she supplied. "I had my own apartment when I was in my early twenties. I took some college classes and had a job in Des Moines. Mama worried about me living on my own but not married. Then Papa had a bad farming accident." Her eyes clouded, and she paused.

"How bad?" Wanting to offer comfort and support even though he was years too late, he reached for her hand.

Her fingers trembled beneath his. "The tractor rolled and pinned him under it. The doctors kept him in a coma for four months hoping he'd make a recovery, but he was gone."

"God, I'm so sorry. I had no idea."

"Why would you? It's not something that makes the national news." She flashed a watery smile. "Anyway, with Alejandro in the Marines, Mama asked me to come home to help her with the farm."

"That doesn't seem fair."

She pulled free from his touch. "Whoever said life was fair?"

He couldn't argue. If life were fair, they never would have split up.

"I don't know if you remember," Luciana continued, "but Mama's lived with diabetes for a long time. Over the past couple of years, she's dealt with quite a few complications, including surgeries on both her eyes. Yesterday, her doctor admitted her to the hospital so he could monitor her kidneys."

"I'm sorry." The words rang hollow and inadequate in his ears, and he wished he could offer something more substantial. "Sounds like a rough time."

She laughed without a shred of humor. "Rough is a good word."

"So, you're here while she's in the hospital?" As much as he wanted to spend the evening alone with her, he wouldn't keep her from visiting her mom.

"Somebody has to milk the cows morning and night. I'll see her the day after tomorrow and can be at her side within an hour in an emergency. Trust me, this is becoming routine for us. We got lucky this time with Alejandro home on leave to stay with her and fill me in on medical updates."

Blake glanced around the outdated kitchen, beginning to understand Luciana's life. Instead of a kid still living with her parents, as he'd first assumed, she'd taken over both sets of responsibilities and balanced an oppressive weight on her slim shoulders. "How often does your brother come home?"

"When he can. Sometimes it's better if he stays away." Her mouth tightened. "Don't feel sorry for me. I'm content to be the good daughter and take care of my mother and carry on my father's legacy. It may not be a spectacular life like yours, but I can hold my head up with honor."

"I don't feel sorry for you. I want to rescue you," he admitted, longing for the adoration that used to shine from her eyes.

Instead, she glared at him. "So I can feel indebted to you for the rest of my life? No thanks. The only time I waited for you to rescue me, you never came." She stabbed at her last bite of food, as if the omelet had personally wronged her.

"Your parents forbade me to come." And he'd decided she hadn't wanted him around either.

"But I needed you. I lost *our* baby, not theirs."

His throat swelled. They should have had a baby together. They should have been a family. Less than a week after they'd learned of the pregnancy, she'd miscarried. He hadn't had time to think of the person they'd created as a child before it was gone, too small to have left any physical reminder. He abandoned his silverware and reached across the table for her. "Luciana, I am so—"

She held up her hand. "You've had plenty of time to track me down if you wanted to apologize or talk about it. Don't force words you don't mean because I cornered you. My fault for bringing it up." She rose to her feet. "Do you want an apple empanada from the freezer? They're not quite as crisp as when they're fresh from the oven, but close."

"No." He wanted to steer the conversation back to the baby and the fact that he'd never seen her after the miscarriage. Her parents had kept her locked in the house, refusing him entrance. With graduation behind them, he couldn't even run into her at school. Without the responsibility of impending fatherhood, he'd cut his losses and left town, deciding she would be better off without him. After all, she had her parents to take care of her.

She reached for his empty plate, but he covered her fingers on the dish. "I'll take it to the sink. You don't have to wait on me."

Once again, she pulled away from his touch. "You cooked, so I'll clean up."

He stood and faced her. "How about we do the dishes together? I'll wash and you can dry and put them away."

Her lips curved, and her shoulders relaxed. "You were always good at compromises."

"Not good enough if I couldn't come up with one to make your parents happy and keep us together." He slid his palms up her arms, cupping her shoulders, regret coursing through him again.

"Oh, Blake." She leaned into his chest. "We all share the responsibility for what happened."

He wrapped his arms around her and held her close, absorbing her warmth and sweetness and, for the moment, her trust. With his lips pressed to the top of her head, he inhaled her strawberry-scented shampoo.

Tipping her face up, she studied him with sober eyes. At last he understood why his engagement to Caroline hadn't worked, why no one he'd dated had been "the one." Because Luciana had already claimed the honor. His heart had always been reserved for her alone.

"Are you thinking what I'm thinking?" she whispered.

That they needed to kiss, letting it segue into making love in the kitchen then in the hall against the wall then in her bed? Yes. Absolutely.

"That we shouldn't kiss," she continued, "because if we do, we won't want to stop."

"We need work on getting in sync with each other because your reason is an excellent argument for why we should start kissing." Dipping his head, he brushed his lips over her eyelids and down the crest of her nose.

"I missed you," she admitted.

His chest ached. He'd missed her, too. So damn much. Until he'd held her again, he'd had no notion of the lack in his life.

Rising on her tiptoes, she touched her lips to his. He braced his hands on her waist, but she didn't need his support. She'd acquired both physical and mental strength while they'd been apart.

He sank into the fullness of her warm, sweet mouth, hanging onto her as if she were a mirage from his dreams he needed to savor before it vanished. Instead, with each passing second, she became more real, more alive.

He pressed his tongue against the seam of her lips, and she yielded, meeting him. His head spun with desire and memories. Gripping her tighter, he backed her against the counter. Wanting to take in everything at once, he smoothed his palms over her cheeks, down her shoulders, and along her T-shirt and then up to tangle his fingers in her thick black hair.

As a teen, she would spread her hair along his skin as she pressed her ear to his chest, creating an ultimate peaceful moment. No one else had ever taken an interest in the beating of his heart. But every detail had mattered to her, and he longed for evidence something still mattered.

Coasting his palms over her rounded breasts, he reveled in her gasp. Sheer pleasure of her sweet, unguarded response coursing through him, he kissed his way down her chin and along her neck.

Lifting her head, she allowed him access to her bare skin, fueling his desire. Despite him abandoning her in her most vulnerable moments, she opened to him again. He would honor the opportunity, so it ended with good memories instead of regrets.

He didn't belong on an Iowa farm, and she had too many responsibilities to leave. But the more he touched and kissed her, the more he couldn't deny a part of him would always belong to Luciana.

Luciana moaned, arching against Blake as he skated his hands under her shirt and cupped her breasts through her plain white bra. He took her from innocent to full-throttle in a heartbeat until she longed to rip away their clothing and let him draw her nipple into his mouth. After he sucked until she cried out, she would open his pants, drop to her knees, and give his cock the same attention.

Instead, she clasped his chin and lifted his head until he focused on her. "We're going too fast. We don't know each other anymore."

His blue eyes blazed into hers, hot and fierce. "Not touching each other in fifteen years is fast?"

"You know what I mean."

"We need to make up for lost time and rediscover each other."

If only recapturing their lost years together could be so simple. She wrapped her arms around his neck, tangling her tongue with his. His hardness wedged against her pelvis, the heat from his body transporting her to a realm of heady pleasure.

But those fifteen years were gone. They couldn't make up for them. They couldn't wish the time away with enough kisses or pretend they hadn't changed from the kids they'd been.

Older and wiser, she had the necessary tools to protect against accidental pregnancy, but she still didn't have a clue how to apply the same protection to her heart.

She savored the sweetness of his kiss for another long minute then pushed him away with firm gentleness. "We have to stop."

"Says who?" He nipped at her lip.

"Me."

"Why?" Nibbling some more, he coaxed her to continue kissing him.

She steeled against the urge to give in. "You can't swing into my life, have a quickie with me, and then sail out for another decade or two."

"I have no intention of making this a quickie. We have all night."

And then what? She'd reopen her heart to him so he could break it all over again when he left? She didn't have anything to offer a CEO on a long-term basis. Heck, she couldn't even give as much as she had as a teenager when she'd come to him with nothing. Her responsibilities to her mother and the farm came before she could consider sharing a part of her life with anyone else.

"We're not going to make love. We're going to do the dishes," she said, summoning all the authority in her voice to drown out her desire. "Afterward, I'll show you to Alejandro's room where you can spend the night. If you don't like that plan, you're welcome to call for a taxi."

"Works for me," he agreed. Instead of retreating, he placed his hands on her hips and sidestepped, gliding her along the edge of the counter with him until they stood at the sink, her back to it as she faced him. He reached around her and turned on the faucet.

"You can't do dishes with me standing in your way." Her intention had been to put distance between them, not play sexy games.

"Watch me."

If she ducked under his arm, she could end the sensual tease before it started, but he left her too mesmerized to move.

Leaning his upper body against hers, he reached for the dish soap, dumping a generous amount into the basin. "Now, I'm going to scrub in a circular motion."

Exaggerating his movements, he washed the plate behind her back, rubbing his chest against her breasts and his hips against her pelvis.

"You have way too much rhythm and coordination for your own good," she whispered, her nerves on sensory overload, her nipples pebbled and aching.

"It's for your good, too." He leaned in and kissed the side of her neck.

A breath away from melting in his arms, she turned her back on him and stared into the sudsy basin. By concentrating on the dishes, she could prove disinterest in his seduction even as her body betrayed her.

His sharp intake of breath along her neck destroyed her plan. His erection pressed against her ass through their clothing, driving heat to pool between her thighs.

He lifted his hands from the soapy water, gliding them over her chest and dampening her T-shirt.

"Blake," she begged, both for more and for him to be the sensible party.

"Don't worry. I can get these wet clothes off you."

In spite of her intention to resist, she smiled. "Do women fall for that line?"

"You tell me. I'm using it for the first time." He peeled her shirt up, planting a line of kisses along her back above her bra strap.

Oh, yeah, she fell for everything he cast her way—dove for it.

Shifting her hair to the side, he kissed her neck. Her eyes stung from the reverence in his caress.

She pulled her shirt over her head and tossed it aside, then turned to face him again. "I want to see you while you kiss me."

"Luci." He whispered his old nickname for her with a groan. Gathering water droplets from the faucet, he tipped his palm against her chest. The stream trickled into her cleavage, and his eyes dilated.

She'd never experienced anything so sexy. Despite her earlier intentions, she became desperate for more of his sensual teasing.

"Do it again." She unhooked her bra then peeled it off and tossed it aside. Her breasts ached for his touch. "Please."

Gaze serious, he dribbled another cool stream of water down her cleavage. Then he caught the flow in his palm as it reached her navel and slid a damp trail over her nipple.

She arched into his touch. The heat of his skin and cool wetness traveled straight to her core, igniting her.

With his index finger, he placed a single droplet of water on her other nipple then bent his head and touched the tip of his tongue to it. After a lingering moment of anticipation, he circled his tongue around the bud then drew it into his mouth.

She gripped the edge of the counter behind her, reveling in the sensual contact. If she touched him in return, she'd rip his expensive clothes trying to get her hands on his skin. But oh, how she'd missed not just the caresses and heady desire coursing through her but the adoration and physical interaction with a man she loved.

Tears filled her eyes, and she couldn't stop them from overflowing.

He lifted his head and stroked his thumb over her damp cheekbone. "Luci, baby, what's wrong? Did I hurt you?"

She shook her head but couldn't speak.

"You said no. I'm sorry. I got carried away." Expression stricken, he stepped back, reaching for her clothes strewn across the table.

"No, it's not you." She wrapped her arms around him. He hadn't done anything wrong. She welcomed everything he'd given her. But she also wanted so many things he would never give her, things she could never accept if he did offer.

Her mother needed her. The farm needed her. Blake didn't. She would never have a happily ever after with him.

Chapter Five

*B*lake finished the dishes with grim efficiency while Luciana put her shirt on and hurried out of the room. Outside, the wind blew strongly enough to make the old farm buildings groan and creak, leaving him grateful not to be on the corporate jet enduring turbulence at thirty thousand feet.

"I put fresh sheets on Alejandro's bed and set out clean towels in the bathroom for you," she announced, returning to the kitchen, her T-shirt still damp with his handprints.

She'd explained she didn't want to sleep with him and didn't want to kiss. But just like when they were kids, when he pressed, she denied him nothing.

He would not take advantage of her. He'd honor her wishes and would not let her regret his detour into her life. "Thank you. I'm sorry for causing you so much trouble."

"No trouble." She squeezed her knuckles against her fist. "I'm the one sending mixed signals by saying one thing then doing another. I didn't expect you, and I haven't done a good job of pulling myself together."

He frowned. He hadn't meant to traumatize her. "What do you mean?"

"I never really got over you," she admitted, the simple words shattering his heart. "With mourning our baby, it took me a while to realize you were gone and even longer to understand you were never coming back. By the time I'd managed some space from my parents to contact you, your parents had sold their store and left town. I didn't have any way to reach you—no phone number, no address."

"I abandoned you when you needed me most, and you think I'll do it again." Worse, he would. He couldn't ask his assistant to cover his deadlines and work obligations indefinitely.

She shook her head, sadness and determination in her gaze. "No. You won't do it again because I won't let myself need you that much ever."

Unable to refute her, he picked up a sponge and began wiping the counter. A massive crack split the air outside. He looked out the window as a large dead tree fell alongside the barn.

"What was that?" Luciana joined him at the window, her torso pressing against his side as she strained to see.

"A big tree. You're lucky it didn't fall on a building." With his hands on her waist, he scooted her closer so she had the right angle to view the fallen debris. "The wind gusts tonight are incredible."

Her body turned rigid. "No."

He released her. "Sorry, I—"

"No!" Instead of shouting at him, she stared in horror out the window. Without glancing in his direction, she dashed out of the house.

Assured she hadn't run from his touch, he followed to help her fix whatever mayhem the tree had caused. Maybe she had to mend another fence.

By the time he caught up, she was straining to lift the trunk off the ground, but the two of them together wouldn't be strong enough to raise it an inch. Luckily, it hadn't fallen on a building, an animal, or the fence. "You can't lift it," he said.

"I have to. Help me, please." Tears streaked her cheeks.

"Why? What's underneath?"

"Sam. Our baby."

"What?" His heart stuttered. His legs turned to rubber, putting him on the verge of collapse. Their baby hadn't even warranted a birth certificate.

"It's not a grave, just a fifteen dollar plaster of Paris kit I used to mark the baby's life, but it's all I have." She scrubbed her short nails under the dirt and leaves on one side of the thick tree trunk, revealing a faint slab of white.

"Sam," he repeated, half-numb, halfway to tears.

She knelt at the spot, expanding the cleaned area, until he could see an S that appeared to have been etched with a stick. "I never knew if we had a boy or a girl, so I picked Sam to stand for Samantha or Samuel. I come out here every day to be with our child, to know I'm not alone, and to remember the love from his or her creation. It's all I have," she repeated.

"Luci." Blake sank next to her, gathering her in his arms. "Oh, God, Luci."

She clung to him for a moment but pulled back long before he was ready to release her. "I'm going to get the tractor and pull the tree out of the way. Stay with Sam for me."

He nodded, unable to speak. His heart fell in love and shattered all at once. He'd lived with the facts that she'd been pregnant with his child and the baby had died before it ever had a chance to live, but he'd never felt like a father. He hadn't experienced the pain of losing a child—his child.

His frustration and heartbreak had centered on losing Luciana. He'd anguished over the helplessness of not being able to do anything for her as she lost blood and cried in panic while her parents whisked her to the emergency room and he followed behind, only to be left sitting on the hard waiting room chair.

All his worry, fear, grief, and regret had centered on her well-being. Underneath the despair of her physical pain had been twin hints of relief and guilt. At eighteen, he hadn't been ready for the responsibility of a wife and baby.

The rumble of an engine interrupted his memories. A dull green tractor chugged into view. Luciana jumped down from the cab. She tugged an assortment of thick metal chains behind her, wrapping them around the tree trunk and securing them to the back of the metal frame with an efficiency that underscored her experience with the task.

"Stand back," she shouted.

He obeyed while she settled inside the open cab. Intense concentration filled her gaze as she watched over her shoulder and pressed the accelerator. The chain tightened and strained. Black smoked poured from the exhaust pipe, and the chain creaked.

Concerned the metal links would crack under the stress and having no desire to be flayed by them, he took another step back. The oversized wheels inched forward, tugging the huge tree along.

After little more than twelve inches of progress, the engine belched another cloud of black smoke and, with an ominous clunk, turned silent. On the ground, with indents on the dirt on either side from the fallen tree trunk, he could see a plaster slab with the letters S-A-M etched across it and two large crisscrossed fissures along the surface.

"It's far enough," he called.

Luciana bounded to the ground and jumped over the fallen tree, dropping to her knees in front of the stone. "Sam." She traced her fingers over the cracks.

"Sam!" Her anguished cry echoed off the side of the barn as she dropped her face to the stone.

To him, the baby had been a mere condition and complication until it simply disappeared from existence. But her grief made the loss real. Their son or daughter had never had the chance to grow up, to walk, to talk, to hug, to smile. He had lost. Luciana had lost. And they could never win it back.

He knelt next to her, tucking his arm around her and shielding her body from the wind with his own. Used to assessing problems and tackling them head-on, he wanted to point out that the tree hadn't touched their child. He could replace the plaster with something bigger and better. But she didn't need cold logic. So, instead, he settled for the most inadequate, clichéd words on the planet. "I'm sorry."

For a long time, she didn't reply. Then she turned and kissed him with an urgency that knocked him flat on his ass. She pulled his shirt open and kissed her way down his chest.

"Luci."

"I don't want to talk." Her eyes burned bright and fierce, while the gusts whipped her hair around her face.

His conscience revolted. He couldn't take advantage of her distress and make love to her while she grieved. But he needed the connection. Even more, she needed it. He could deny himself but not her. Their coupling wouldn't make up for what they'd lost, but maybe it could help them both move on.

She rose over him and tugged off her jeans and panties. He swallowed, unable to move as he stared up at her, naked from the waist down, her T-shirt rippling against her chest with the breeze. Luciana, grown into a confident, aggressive woman, enthralled him a hundred times more than the timid girl who'd let him initiate every encounter. The girl had rocked his world. He feared the woman could destroy it.

He pulled a condom from his wallet. He wouldn't take a chance on recreating the hurt and drama from the past.

Luciana nudged his chest until he lay on the grass as leaves fluttered and blew around them. She unfastened the button of his pants, her eyes crazed, expression desperate, and fingers shaking. A broken stick poked his thigh, and he tossed the twig aside, unsettled by his own powerlessness. But he wouldn't change the dynamic. They could only go through with the encounter if she wanted it and needed it without him seducing her.

"Luci, you don't want to make love to me." He tried to inject some sanity into their turbulent emotions. "You laid out your intentions inside the house. I promised to honor them, but good God, I'm not a saint."

She grasped his cock, freeing him from his briefs. "I changed my mind since then. I want to have sex with you."

Have sex, not make love. Despite the swelling of his dick, the difference churned his stomach. He could only love her, never use her for sex.

She stroked her thumb over the head of his erection, the heat of her hand a striking contrast to the cool air, and he gasped, trying not to come in her hand. "I'm not asking for forever," she said. "But I want to remember how our bodies connect, how alive I am with you, how right the world becomes when we're together."

Then they would make love, because they'd never just had sex.

"Are you sure?" He clenched his fists at his sides to keep from grasping her hips and seeking relief for his raging hard-on.

"I am." She rolled the condom over his length and then sank onto him, taking him all the way in with a single thrust.

He groaned. He'd come home. No other words could explain the all-encompassing bliss. Luciana, his first love, the girl who'd believed him when he'd sworn he would love her forever, welcomed him back with open arms.

Skimming her hands over his chest, she pumped her hips, her breath coming harder and faster, matching their rhythm. They needed each other too much to bother with finesse or lingering. He reached between her legs, gliding his index finger against her clit as she thrust down.

She gasped and clutched his shoulders, riding him harder. Fingers slick, he massaged her, drinking in the sound of her moans. Her muscles shuddered around him, and she cried his name then whispered it, collapsing against his chest. Her spasms sent him out of control. He thrust his hips upward, his release exploded from him, and he shouted, "Luci!"

Her name echoed off the wall of the barn. Then another wind gust carried it away as he wrapped his arm around her, holding her while she shivered.

At last, her body stilled, and she lifted her head, tears glistening in her eyes. "I think I just used you, Blake."

Chapter Six

"You didn't hear me complain, did you?" He strived for a light tone. She hadn't used him. "Using" implied they'd only had sex, but their encounter had been much more.

She sighed and pulled farther away.

He hugged her tighter, needing to connect with her while they were still intimately joined. "I'm sorry you didn't have me by your side after you lost Sam. Your parents didn't want me to see you, and I thought I could make life easier for both of us if I disappeared for a while. I didn't mean to stay gone, but once I left, I got absorbed in my own life and tried to avoid digging up the past."

She gave him a tremulous smile and eased off him, leaving him with a chill that had little to do with the windy evening and everything to do with the loss of skin-on-skin contact. "I'm as much to blame for not standing up for us. Without Sam, I guess we didn't have enough of a relationship left to save."

Blake sat up, the chill turning his skin to ice. "You really believe that?"

Not meeting his gaze, she picked up her jeans and stepped into them. "Of course. You just admitted how easy it was to walk away from me."

"No. Leaving you was the hardest thing I've ever done. Jesus, it ripped my heart out."

Her fingers trembled as she tugged on her jeans zipper. "Regardless, our relationship is over and has been for a long time. I'm going to get a shovel and attempt to unwedge these pieces from the ground without breaking them more."

"Aren't you going to put your shoes on first?"

She glanced down at her bare feet. "I left my boots at the house."

The entire time they'd been outside in the dirt and rocks and sharp sticks, she hadn't had shoes on? He stood and secured his pants, then looked down at the dirty, scratched tops of her feet. He could only imagine how battered the soles were. How could he not have noticed sooner? "You ran out here, drove a tractor, and moved a tree with no shoes?"

She winced. "Yeah, not the smartest thing I've ever done, but when the tree fell, I panicked."

"I noticed," he whispered. "But your safety should come first. How badly did you hurt yourself?"

"I'm not hurt, but if you make a big deal out of it, I'm going to limp and groan for sympathy."

If she expected him to play down her injuries so she'd suck it up, she'd picked the wrong strategy. Closing the space between them, he turned her palms up. They were red and scratched from trying to lift the tree. He glanced from the rusted chain still wrapped around the trunk back to her scrapes. "Tetanus shot?"

"Current."

"Good. Then you don't need medical attention, just pampering." He wrapped his arms around her hips then hoisted her over his shoulder.

She squealed. "What are you doing?"

"Taking you inside the house." And taking the opportunity to hold her any way he could.

"I can walk. Put me down before you hurt yourself."

"The only thing in danger of injury is my ego from your comments. I'm enjoying the excuse to put my hands on your ass."

She relaxed against him, no longer fighting him. "You'll spoil me."

"I don't think I can do enough spoiling in one night to affect your expectations." But even as he teased, he proved the statement wrong. With the sun descending below the horizon, his expectations already exceeded his original plans. He wanted so much more than the single evening he'd allotted them to catch up.

∞

Blake didn't release her until they were inside the house. Then, with a gentleness that stole her breath, he lowered her to her feet. Despite the quicker, more efficient shower inches away, he turned on the water in the oversized clawfoot bathtub.

The water flowed over his wrist as he tested the temperature. After dumping in a generous scoop of bubble bath, he glanced over his shoulder and met her gaze. "Need some help getting out of those clothes?"

Luciana swallowed. Considering she'd had her shirt off earlier and then her jeans off a few minutes ago when she'd jumped him, she shouldn't be nervous. He'd already seen all of her, including her tears over Sam's memorial. She didn't have any more secrets.

"Your pants are ripped," she noted. "You don't belong on a farm."

"Says the woman who drove a tractor with no shoes," he teased. "I don't care about the clothes. You can rip them to shreds if it means I get another chance to connect with you."

He lifted the edge of her shirt and pulled it over her head then reached behind her and unhooked her bra. His tender gaze locked with hers as he drew it off. "We're going to take our time making love. I want a chance to love all of you."

She needed to push him away. If she let him cherish her, she'd set the stage for a massive heartache after he left. But her heart had ached for so long, she wanted to soak up his affection to treasure later while she dealt with overdue bills, her mother's medical needs, and obnoxious neighbors.

Taking her in his arms, he clamped his mouth over hers. He kissed her as if she was his whole world and he never intended to let her go again. She allowed the fantasy to sweep her away, for the one man she'd ever loved to be hers.

With his lips, he caressed her chin and down her neck. Then he shifted his hands to her waist and bent his head, his beard stubble grazing her breasts as he unbuttoned her jeans.

Her nipples pebbled, and she gasped, shocked by her sensitivity to every brush of skin, no matter how incidental.

Raising his head, he smiled then dipped down, repeating the contact.

"Tease." She grasped his shoulders for balance.

"Only because you like it." He eased her jeans down her legs. "Into the tub. I promised you pampering."

"I don't need pampering, just you."

"Consider this your lucky night. You get both." Not flinching at the grime on her extremities, he guided each foot over the edge of the tub.

She sank into the hot water, her sore, tired body disappearing under the bubbles. Enveloped in the warm, soft cocoon, she groaned and closed her eyes to savor the moment. She never indulged in baths. Practical showers suited her lifestyle and time constraints much better. Any quiet moment she could spare, she elected to spend outside by Sam's memorial.

The water sloshed against her chin, and she opened her eyes. At the other end of the tub, Blake submerged to the middle of his torso. For the first time, she appreciated the huge basin. Even with their legs tangled together, she didn't feel crowded.

He lifted one of her feet and caressed his fingertips over her scrapes and bruises. Running outside barefoot had been stupid beyond belief, but she'd never been rational when it came to Sam. The loss of the baby had also meant the loss of Blake's love.

He circled her ankle and began massaging her calf. She closed her eyes and savored his touch. "You always know how to make me feel special."

"Because you are special." The water sloshed again, and his lips touched hers.

She didn't argue, not with his warm mouth covering hers and his hands kneading her overworked muscles. Deep down, common sense overrode his declaration. Women didn't come more ordinary and mundane than her. Perhaps, that explained why she'd never tried to track him down over the years. He could do better and go further without her.

But fate had presented her with one night to make memories to last for the rest of her life, to create fantasies, to enjoy special status. Determined to make the most of it, she opened her eyes and sat straighter, placing her palms on his chest. Her parents and her church had forbidden her to touch his naked flesh. She no longer worried about their judgment, but his body still intimidated her.

He'd grown up and moved on from their awkward, clandestine liaisons, leaving her with no idea of what he liked or how to please him. More than anything, she couldn't bear to disappoint him.

He trailed his fingertips along her cheeks then cupped her neck. "What's wrong?"

"I don't know what you want anymore."

"I want you."

"I know." Even if she had trouble believing it. "But what do you like? How can I please you?"

"Whatever you do will make me cross-eyed with pleasure, just like it did when we were eighteen."

"That easy?"

"Trust me, when it comes to you, I'm so easy, it's all I can do not to embarrass myself."

A nervous giggle escaped from her lips. Under the water, she caressed his leg above the knee. He groaned and shifted his hips. Assured the same man she'd loved all those years ago still lived inside him, she relaxed and stroked his inner thigh.

He picked up a bar of soap and rubbed it across her breasts then down her stomach. The soap slipped from his grasp, but he continued to massage her chest.

Fighting the temptation to succumb to his touch, Luciana grabbed the block as it floated by and skimmed it over his thigh and balls. His cock hardened, and she rewarded him by gliding the slippery bar along his length.

"I can't decide whether I like getting clean or dirty with you better," he murmured.

"You don't have to choose. You get both. It's your lucky night." Abandoning the soap, she continued to stroke him.

"If you don't want me to come in your palm, you have to stop." He panted against her neck.

"Where do you want to come?" she challenged.

He lifted his head and stared into her eyes. "In you."

She shivered, wanting him to fill her, to jerk and shudder on top of her as his pleasure spilled from him. "Then we need to get out of here."

"We'll never get rinsed off with all the soap and bubbles in this water."

"I guess we'll have to make use of the shower, too."

With the water sluicing over them and Blake's body inches from hers, she reveled in the unobstructed view of his flesh while his fingers and mouth traveled over her skin. Touching him in turn, she filled her head with his short gasps of pleasure and moans of her name.

The more he caressed her, the weaker she became, until she had to admit, "I can't keep standing."

"Good, because I want to take you lying on your bed." He flicked off the water and snagged a pair of towels, wrapping her first.

A moment later, she lay on her bed with her wet hair spilled across the pillow, her skin still damp but not chilled. No chance she could become cold as long as she kept her gaze on him. He dropped his towel and leaned over her, kissing first her lips then her neck, showering attention on her breasts then down her navel to between her legs.

"What are you—" She stopped as his plan to love her with his mouth became obvious. She'd always wanted to experience the intimacy and beauty and had all but given up hope of getting the chance.

Lifting his head, he gazed up her body at her. "I've dreamed of loving you like this. Please let me."

His poignant words unraveled her. "Yes." With her fingers tangled in his hair, she guided him down to touch her with the intimacy they both wanted. She bent her knees and arched her hips, giving him access. Everything belonged to him. Not only did she trust him with her flesh, her heart lay open for his taking, too.

Kissing first, he brought truckloads of pleasure and an insatiable need for more. With each lick and suck, he delivered her to a delirium she'd never known. "Please." She lifted her thighs higher.

He thrust with his tongue, and the orgasm rolled through her. She cried his name, but the wave of pleasure left her greedy to have more of him. Reaching into the nightstand drawer, she grabbed a condom. "I want all of you in me. I want you to come, too."

As soon as he suited up, she grasped his waist, pulling him down to her. But unlike the fast and hard connection she'd initiated outside, he slid in gradually, drawing out the pleasure until she strained toward him, begging him to give her everything. And he did, filling her with a satisfaction that transcended any physical need.

Balancing his upper weight on his elbows, he cupped her cheeks in his palms. "Luci, you make me whole."

He lowered his head and kissed her with a sweetness and reverence both rare and beautiful. With her arms wrapped around him, she held him in a tight embrace, riding an earth-shattering orgasm while they came together.

For one night, he offered her everything.

But only for a night.

Chapter Seven

*B*right light shone around the edges of the heavy curtain, proof Blake had slept late in the morning, not surprising since he and Luciana had stayed awake most of the night, unable to get enough of each other.

Luci. He rolled over but encountered an empty bed. Maybe, while he cooked breakfast, they could talk about what last night meant. He needed to see her again. Of course, she couldn't walk away from her responsibilities, but they had to find a compromise. Despite craving more than a long-distance relationship, he'd start there if she couldn't handle more yet.

Sitting up, he scanned the room. His clothes lay folded at the end of the bed. He frowned, pretty sure he'd left them scattered in the bathroom. Stretching across the mattress, he snagged the pants between two fingers and drew them to him. After turning the fabric several times, he located the rip, sewn so well the thread blended with the fabric, no pleats or pucker to give it away.

Luci had been working while he'd slept. He would have preferred to keep the tear as a reminder of their unbridled passion. He dressed and emerged from the bedroom to an empty house.

A glance at the clock assured him even with the time difference, the workday would be in full swing in San Diego, so he picked up the house phone and called Marcia. "It's Blake. How did the presentation go?"

"Not great, but okay. Mr. Sunburst had a lot of questions I didn't have the answers to. I promised we'd get him all the information as early as possible today. I forwarded the questions in an email."

He checked his phone, but of course he didn't have service. "Let me see if I can get an Internet connection with my air card and log in on my computer. Can you work on booking me a flight out of Des Moines and a ride to the airport?"

"Of course. I can't wait for you to get back. We're lacking direction without you in the office."

"Thanks." He didn't smile as he hung up. Unable to entertain the option of working from a remote location, he needed to be present for his job.

Trying not to disturb the manila envelopes and papers scattered across the desk by the living room window, he set his laptop on the surface. While he waited for the machine to power up, he wandered out of the house, needing at least a good-morning kiss.

A chainsaw lay next to the fallen tree beside the barn, the smaller limbs already cut away and piled in preparation for a bonfire. He must have slept like the dead to not have heard the saw running. He stepped around the tree trunk. A hole in the ground replaced Sam's memorial. Four dirt-stained, fist-sized chunks of plaster lay in a pile next to it.

He picked up the top one and traced his finger over the bottom half of the letter M.

"If you want to keep a piece, you can," Luciana said from behind him.

He spun to face her. "Are you sure?"

She nodded, her gaze sober. "I've decided to take the pieces inside and put them away in a box. I'm never going to forget the past, but I need to move on, too."

His heart quickened, as he hoped for her to consider her statement beyond the figurative context. "Do you ever think about moving on from the farm? My condo has plenty of space, and you'd never have to milk cows or worry about fixing fences or getting rid of fallen trees."

She shook her head before he finished speaking. "You know I can't."

He did. Asking had been selfish of him. "I have to leave soon, but I don't want to go without firming up when I'll see you again. What if I buy you a plane ticket to visit me later this month?"

Her gaze shifted to a point beyond his shoulder. "Don't make this hard, Blake."

Fear bubbled through him, morphing into anger. "Is that what I'm doing? Because it would be a lot easier to walk away knowing I'm going to see you again."

"I'm not in a position to make any promises."

"Because I'm not Hispanic?" he demanded. "Am I still only good enough to sneak around with?"

Her eyes flared with anger. "I never snuck around. God, I thought I was the luckiest girl alive to have you. If you were my boyfriend again, I'd believe the same thing. It's not about my family's approval. It's the fact that they need me." She met his gaze, her expression so sad he had to fight the urge to weep. "And you don't."

"Don't I?" he challenged. "Of course, I can live and work without you, but inside"—he thumped his chest—"I've been dead for the past fifteen years. That's the real reason my ex-fiancée dumped me. I don't want to go back to soul-sucking survival mode."

He took another step toward her. "We're amazing in bed together, Luci. I've never stopped caring for you. I want to raise a family with you. You're my heart and my soul."

She stared at him for so long, he feared the heart in his throat would choke him. Then she whispered, "I'm sorry. But I don't need you. You can have all the pieces of Sam's memorial. That's all I have to give."

She turned and jogged around the tree where she picked up the chainsaw and yanked the starter rope. The engine whirred, and she attacked the trunk with a vengeance.

Hoping she'd reconsider, he stood immobile. As she continued to work without glancing at him, tension radiating from every movement, he picked up the broken plaster pieces and trudged to the house. He might still be in love with her, but she had other things in her life that mattered more, leaving him so far down her priority list he might as well mean nothing to her.

He needed a miracle to get to the top of her list, if, in fact, he rated a place on it at all.

CஐB

Luciana's arms and back ached by the time she finished cutting the tree and moving it into piles for firewood and a brush pile to burn as soon as the wind died down. Plodding inside the house for a glass of water and a sandwich, she froze at the sight of the long black limousine coasting down the gravel road away from the house.

"Blake." Her heart pounded. She'd been abrupt with him earlier, trying to sort out a way for him to be part of her life and hitting a dead end with every option. Letting him go had been the right choice, her only option. But she hadn't expected him to leave without saying good-bye.

She also hadn't expected him to proclaim her as his "heart and soul." How ridiculous to think she meant something to him. One night of sex did not allow enough time to fall in love.

Unless he'd never stopped loving her, just like she'd never stopped loving him.

Refusing to cry, she blinked away the blur of tears. After choosing her family and the farm years ago, she should be thankful for the opportunity, rejoicing over the second chance to have him in her life for a brief evening.

Inside the too quiet, too empty house, she moved to each room, but he'd left no sign he'd ever set foot in her life. She ate a sandwich containing all the flavor of dust, doubting she'd ever rejoice again.

The phone rang as she took her plate to the sink, and she lunged for it. Hearing Alejandro's greeting, she swallowed her disappointment and asked, "How's Mama?"

"Sleeping. The doctors still want to watch her for another day, but her function is improving. How's the farm?"

"I'm holding it together, like always." She tried to sound cheerful, but her throat hurt. She was holding the farm together. How much longer she could hold herself together remained to be seen. Despite surviving Blake leaving her once, she didn't find the second time easier.

"What happened?" Alejandro knew her too well.

"The cows broke through the fence again." True enough, and it allowed her to answer his question without lying. "Trevor, of course, wanted to start a pissing match. Nothing to worry about. Don't let Mama get worked up over it."

"Speaking of Mama, she got a new roommate last night, a total hottie."

"Don't tell me you're scoping out women in the hospital."

"I'm not scoping, but I'm not dead either. Anyway, the hottie in the next bed is an agriculture professor at the university. She wants to start an organic dairy farm for research and stuff. Mama told her we might be interested in selling."

Luciana bobbled the receiver. "Selling? We can't sell Papa's dream."

"Why not? He's not here to live it. I'm not going to live it. You're killing yourself trying to keep up with all the work. And it makes sense for Mama to live closer to medical facilities."

"Don't make any promises right away." The glittering possibility faded as quickly as she entertained it. They owed more on the mortgage than the farm would sell for. Even if she could unload it, she'd have no money left after the sale to buy or rent a home for her mother or pay the medical bills. Based on her education and past work history, Luciana had no illusions she could offer a better life than their current one.

"Pick me up after the morning milking tomorrow," she told her brother. "I have an appointment with the hospital billing office, and if Mama continues to improve, we should be able to bring her home."

She hung up the phone then trudged out to tackle the chores that had taken a backseat to the fallen tree. Instead of freeing her, her conversation with Alejandro weighed on her. She'd given up the possibility of claiming her only true love to tend to the responsibilities around her.

For what?

Yes, Mama needed her, but Luciana already did a lousy job meeting those needs.

Chapter Eight

"*H*ow was your one-night stand?"

Luciana blinked at her brother as he jumped from the cab of her truck. How the hell had he guessed about Blake? Did she have "I had great sex the other night" tattooed across her forehead? "What are you talking about?"

"The one-night stand. I forgot to ask you when I called yesterday. Did the guy shower you with diamonds we can pawn to pay the bank?"

Oh, right. Alejandro's stupid scheme. "Of course not. I didn't leave the farm for any hookup. You need to get a refund."

His eyes widened. "The guy didn't come? I mean, to the farm. I don't need to know if some random guy *came* for you." He cringed.

"He didn't." Blake did not count as a random guy, and he'd shown up to scout a hotel location, not because he'd signed up for a one-night stand with her. She frowned. Arriving at the farm for a one-night hookup with an old girlfriend made more sense than the hotel mumbo-jumbo.

She grasped her brother's arm. "Call that Madame Eve service and ask who they sent to meet me." As much as she hated to admit it, if they'd sent Blake, she wouldn't demand a refund or give Alejandro grief for taking the money. Being with Blake again, even for a single night, had been worth it. "Does your ag professor have her own livestock, or does she want to buy the cows with the farm? If she's willing to purchase the animals first and let them continue living here until the rest of the sale goes through, we'll have enough money to pay the mortgage plus all the back amounts we owe."

"She's not *my* professor."

"You said she looked hot in a hospital gown. Nobody can pull off looking hot in one of those. I say you've fallen in love," she teased. Somebody needed to get a happily ever after. If it couldn't be her, she wanted one for her brother.

"I'll love anyone who saves the bank from foreclosing on us." He sighed. "I'm sorry I screwed up again. I thought this time I would really help."

She touched his cheek. "You did. You helped me to see what's important, and saving the farm isn't."

An hour later, she and Alejandro went their separate ways with him heading for Mama's hospital room and her entering the billing department, clutching the manila envelope with her emergency cash. After a few minutes, a supervisor ushered her to a private office and closed the door.

With trembling fingers, Luciana laid out the money on the laminate desk. "I know the bill is enormous and our income is limited, but we'll make good faith installments every month for as long as it takes."

Instead of sneering at the paltry sum in front of her, the woman smiled. "We don't need to make a payment plan. In fact"—she nudged the bills toward Luciana—"you can take all this back."

"Excuse me?"

"Your mother's bill has been paid in full."

She blinked. "How? I haven't given you anything. We've talked multiple times about how I contribute so little compared to how much I owe that I'll never pay off our past invoices let alone this new one."

"Everything on your mother's account has been taken care of," the supervisor assured her. "Your father's old bill, too. A gentleman came in yesterday afternoon and settled up everything on the spot with a wire transfer. He didn't so much as blink at the total, which gave me a great view of his amazing blue eyes."

Luciana gasped. She had to know more than one person with blue eyes, but only one man came to mind.

"I admit my reasons were less than professional when I asked him out to dinner, but unfortunately, he turned me down flat." She sighed. "If you're dating that guy, you'd be a fool to let him get away."

The supervisor continued chatting as she led her out of the office, but Luciana didn't hear another word. Blake had been there? He'd spent his money to cover her obligations? Why would he do such a thing? Her family had done nothing for him but exclude and threaten him. Worse, she could never return the mega-favor.

She entered the hospital room behind a volunteer. "Flowers for Mrs. Cortez."

Mama beamed and held out her arms at the cheerful bouquet of black-eyed Susans and yellow and orange tulips. "From you, Alejandro?"

"Not me. What do you need flowers for when you have me in the flesh?" He winked as he shifted the bouquet on her tray.

She batted his arm with affection then reached for the accompanying card and read silently. Bypassing him, she held the paper toward Luciana, her gaze inscrutable.

Almost terrified to read the words, she took it in trembling fingers.

Mrs. Cortez, call me if you need anything. I'll do whatever I can to provide it. Blake.

Pressing the card to her chest, Luciana sank to the floor. "He didn't just send you flowers. He paid your hospital bills, all of them, and the ones left over from Papa, too. It's all covered."

Mama gasped. Eyes overflowing with tears, she crossed herself and held her rosary above her head. "I've been praying for a miracle. Thank you, Blessed Mother." Lowering her arms, she reached over the side of the bed toward her daughter. "Why would he do this? We haven't heard from that boy in years."

She squeezed her mother's puffy fingers. "He got in touch with me two days ago."

On the other side of the bed, Alejandro inhaled sharply.

"But don't worry," Luciana continued. "I'm not leaving you."

Mama shook her head. "I'm not worried about that, not with a man who takes care of my hospital bills and sends me flowers. Your papa and I were hard on him all those years ago. We had a vision of you settling down with a Hispanic Catholic boy, but I haven't seen you truly happy since you two were together. It breaks my heart to think I had something to do with keeping you apart."

Hugging her knees to her chest, Luciana said nothing. She'd chosen to part ways this time, and Blake had disappeared without a good-bye.

"Good news, Mrs. Cortez," a nurse said, entering the room. "The doctor's very happy with your kidney function, and he says you are good to go home. He's already signed your discharge papers, so we'll spring you from here and let you sleep in your own bed tonight."

While the nurse recorded Mama's vital signs, Alejandro pulled Luciana to her feet and guided her to the side of the room. "Are you telling me Madame Eve hooked you up with Blake?"

"I'm not telling you anything." She tugged her arm free and began gathering Mama's belongings without looking at him. "Bring the pickup around to the front entrance."

He didn't move, but she sensed his gaze on her. "We just got a windfall—a second chance. Why aren't you jumping for joy?"

"Get the Silverado. Please." She dug her nails into her palm, refusing to cry. She'd had a second chance with Blake, and she'd turned her back on it.

∽

Thoughts of Blake—what they might have been years ago and what they still could have been if she hadn't blown him off when he'd offered options to make their relationship viable—kept Luciana tossing and turning all night. The next morning, she stumbled inside the bank, unable to remember a word of the plan she'd detailed to both pay off her debt and sell the farm to the eager professor.

"What are you doing here?" the bank president demanded, crossing the lobby toward her. "Considering the circumstances, I canceled your appointment."

"You're refusing to see me?" Oh, the irony. She'd come to offer something concrete so he wouldn't have to swallow a loss on her loan, and he'd written her off as a lost cause.

"I have nothing to talk to you about. Your loan is paid off. You'll receive the title in the mail."

"What?" She stared at him. "How can the loan be paid off?" The moment she asked, the answer became obvious. "Blake."

"He stormed in here and rubbed in my face how successful he and his brother are now. I guess he's trying to get back at me for not inviting him to the cool parties in high school, his own fault for hanging out with you instead of me and the other popular kids."

Blake wouldn't have paid off the loan because he gave a rat's ass about the banker. If he'd done it, it had been for her benefit alone.

"He didn't say a word about his success or mention his brother when I did the wire transfer," the teller said from behind the counter. "He only had two non-business comments. First, he asked me to give this to you." She set a parcel a little bigger than a shoebox on the counter.

Bewildered, Luciana accepted it, surprised by its weight. Resting it on the ledge, she lifted the lid. A whimper escaped her lips.

Nestled in tissue paper rested the mold of Sam's name, the cracks sealed together. She ran her finger over the glossy sheen covering the original plaster. A small card poked up from one corner of the box, and she tugged it free.

I'm sorry I couldn't give you what you needed before, but I'm here for you now. Tell me what else you need, and it's yours.

Luciana lifted her head. "What was the second thing he said to you?"

The teller gave her a knowing smile. "The condo next door to his is for sale and—direct quote—would make a great mother-in-law apartment."

Her heart stuttered. After she'd pushed him away and chosen everything else over him, she could only hope he'd forgive her for not giving them a chance to work out their love together. "I've made a terrible mistake. I-I have to go."

CR

Blake clicked through the screens on his presentation, the board eating up every word as he detailed the expansion plans to usher in a new era for Sunburst Hotels.

The conference room door flew open, and a dark-haired woman stumbled in, stopping his rehearsed speech and his heart.

"Wait, he's in a meeting. You can't go in there." Marcia and two security guards followed in her wake.

Luciana, her eyes defiant, stopped at the far end of the table and pointed at him. "You."

"What?" Ignoring Mr. Sunburst with his jaw unhinged to his chest, Blake rounded the table, dismissing the security detail with a flick of his wrist.

"You asked me to tell you what else I needed," Luciana said, her voice clear and calm, her fingertips skimming the lapels of his suit coat. "I need you in my life. I love you."

"Oh, Luci." He wrapped his arms around her, his heart full to bursting. "I love you, too. I never stopped." He covered her mouth with his, soaking in her presence. She'd come to him. He'd been too afraid to hope, even as he'd thrown his risk analysis aside and everything else toward winning her.

"I've got this presentation, boss," Marcia said with a smirk. "You get yourself a room…or a preacher."

He studied the love of his life. "What do you say?"

Her brown eyes shone with love and happiness. "Yes to both. I want more than one night with my groom."

At last, they were in complete agreement, together the way they'd been meant for each other from the start. "Good because every night from here to forever is yours."

ONE NIGHT WITH THE BEST MAN
A 1Night Stand Story

By
Sara Daniel

~Dedication~

In memory of John and Naomi-proud farmers, loving grandparents, extraordinary role models.

Chapter One

*H*ell yeah, Alex Cortez wanted to be the best man at his sister's destination wedding. A party in Jamaica or maybe Bora Bora. Bring it on, baby.

Then Luciana had hit him with the real destination: the dilapidated farm in Iowa where they'd grown up.

Hell. No.

Except he couldn't decline, not after she'd waited a full year while he completed his last tour with the Marines so he could attend.

Maneuvering his sports car onto the rutted gravel road, he pulled to the side before the farm came into view over the hill. When the sale had gone through the previous year, he'd considered it the best day of his life, despite a round of enemy fire and a dinner of MREs.

Why Luciana wanted to have her big day at the place that had stolen their father's life and mother's health then tried to kill her soul, he had no freaking idea. The filtered, air-conditioned air did nothing to disguise the scent of manure, livestock, and fresh-cut hay from outside. He sneezed twice and cursed several more times.

One more mile. He'd survived the deserts of the Middle East and warring factions in Africa. He could suck up his abhorrence of the farm for two days.

Keeping his gaze glued to the road, Alex gritted his teeth as gravel dust and rocks slapped the paint job of the car that, up until a few months ago, he'd only been able to fantasize about buying. But the investment in his buddy Luke's identity theft app had paid off so big, paying cash for his sweet ride hadn't dented his bank account.

But, all the money in the world couldn't help him avoid the upcoming weekend. He steered into the driveway, lifting his gaze just enough to take in the parking situation, but not enough to check out the sad state of the house or the barn. Adding his car to the row designated for the rehearsal guests, he inhaled and exhaled several times before exiting.

An excellent landscaping service, giant white tent, and flowered archway had transformed the normally overgrown grass lot into a manicured lawn ready to host a classy, outdoor wedding. By focusing on the nuptials, he'd ignore the real setting and maybe come through the weekend unscathed.

"Alejandro, you arrived." Luciana waved and beamed at him, her smile too relieved for him not to feel guilty for giving her reason to worry he might not show.

He joined his sister in the open-sided tent, hugging her. Family members and friends milled around, doing a fabulous job of pretending they preferred the manure-scented air over the ocean breeze of a tropical island.

"You look gorgeous." Not carrying the weight of a two-hundred-acre dairy farm on her shoulders had done wonders for her. Beyond radiating happiness, she managed to project an image of utter relaxation, on the eve of the biggest day of her life, no less.

"I can't tell you how excited I am to have my two favorite men in the same room together." Her smile carried an extra-special sparkle as she faced her fiancé, Blake Remington.

Alex offered his hand to the other man. "I'm in your debt." Literally.

Blake had solved the family's insurmountable money troubles when Alex hadn't had a cent to contribute and then Blake had refused his every effort to repay him from his newly-flush bank account.

"There is no debt," Blake assured him, his handshake solid and sincere. "If anything, I'm in yours."

Because he'd set his sister up on a one-night stand that had led the two of them to reunite after fifteen years apart—an act of selfish desperation so Alex wouldn't be forced to return to farm work.

"If you wanted to repay me, you could have found a nicer location for this event."

"Dr. Gundersen was very generous in allowing us to take over the yard," Luciana said.

"She probably needed the money. Or maybe she hoped we'd all take over the milking for a couple days." Alex would pity the woman, except the gorgeous agricultural professor had bought the place despite a host of more palatable options.

"I'd hoped no responsibility and a boatload of money would make you less cynical," Luciana chided.

He wasn't a cynic—except when it came to the farm.

"How long do you intend to ignore your mother, Alejandro?" a woman in a folding chair nearby demanded in rapid-fire Spanish.

He embraced her. "Sorry. I didn't see you. I would never ignore you, *Mamá.*"

"Did you bring a girl with you?"

To the farm? Not a chance. "I haven't been out of the Marines long enough to find a place to call home, let alone meet someone."

"No, no. You meet someone first. Then you make your home together," Mamá said. "Another wedding in a couple of months would be perfect."

He didn't want to be tied to anything he couldn't fit in his car, let alone a woman who would expect something from him. For the first time in his life, he was free, and he intended to savor it—for years, possibly decades. He needed to find someone to hang out with who wouldn't aid his mother's quest to marry him off.

Dr. Susan Gundersen approached the tent. *Well, well.* Talk about perfect timing. Not even his mother would consider tying him to the person who'd taken over their old home. And dang, the woman was even more gorgeous than he remembered. Maybe the weekend wouldn't be so awful, after all.

"Excuse me, Mamá. Our hostess needs some assistance." He patted her hand and escaped.

Being a red-blooded male, he checked the professor out as he sauntered toward her. She had the bluest eyes he'd ever seen, dark-red hair, and the svelte, poised figure of a model. Alex had always had an irrational weakness for blue eyes.

Luckily, hair color and body type didn't hold any special power over him, but he still recognized a hot woman when he saw one. If all college professors looked like her, he ought to continue his schooling. "You might not remember me, but I'm—"

"Alejandro," she finished. "I remember."

"Alex," he corrected. Sure, he could speak Spanish and loved his mother's to-die-for enchiladas, but he also lived and breathed baseball and had given Uncle Sam over a decade of his life. His mother and sister hung on to their Hispanic heritage, but he was 100 percent American.

"How's your gallbladder, Professor?"

The one time they'd come face-to-face, she'd been sharing a sterile room with his mother and had the misfortune of wearing a tacky hospital gown. That chance encounter, combined with her career in agricultural studies specializing in organic dairy farming, had convinced his mother to sell her the farm.

"No idea. I haven't had any contact with it in a year." Her lips quirked.

"It never calls? You two used to be so close."

As her smile widened, his own faded. He needed to shut up. Despite the thrill of flirting with a woman who had more letters behind her name than he'd ever had in his, her excitement about fields of cow pies and dilapidated buildings meant she could only be a distraction from his mother's matchmaking, not a woman he could consider hooking up with.

He didn't want to witness the farm stripping her of her sparkle. He'd put his life on the line—and watched his fellow Marines die—to ensure people in this country had better options than just trying to survive. But she'd used her freedom to choose the hard, soul-sucking life.

"So, are you joining the rehearsal as an honorary member of our family?" he asked.

Her smile disappeared, the corners of her sexy mouth tightening. "I'm not trying to crash your party. I came out here because, in addition to all the stuff you never cleaned out of your room, I found some of your family's things in my attic. I hoped you or someone else would have a few minutes to sort through the items and tell me what you want saved and what I can toss."

He didn't have to worry about creeping into flirtation mode anymore. "You'll have to ask Luciana. If you leave it up to me, I'll pitch everything without glancing at it."

"You have a lot of childhood memories left that you'll regret throwing out."

As if she had any idea what kind of regrets he carried. "I keep my memories in here." He tapped his forehead.

She opened her mouth, no doubt to convince him he needed all that stuff he'd tried so hard to leave behind. So he said the first thing he could think of to shut her up.

"Want to guess my favorite memory of you, Professor? The open-air view of your ass as you toddled around in a hospital gown."

Chapter Two

*S*usan sighed. How pathetic the one time someone found her ass memorable was when it had been hanging out of a hospital gown. Unfortunately, Mr. Tall-Dark-and-Oh-So-Dangerous didn't intend to improve the sad state of her sex life. He just wanted to humiliate her.

She'd long ago accepted her PhD and passion for organic dairy research would never make her a hot-guy magnet. Her one gift with men was boring them into a coma. Stepping around Alex without stooping to demand why he'd resorted to checking out backsides, hers in particular, she strode across the tent to Luciana, with whom she had a good rapport, and once again explained about their possessions still in her house.

"I am so sorry. It completely slipped my mind." Alex's sister gripped her forearm, the gesture full of sincerity. "I'll do it right now." She shifted her attention to her fiancé. "I promised I'd finish cleaning all our stuff out of the house by this weekend. If we can move the rehearsal back an hour, I should be able to finish it today."

"You'll lose the time you were hoping to visit with your aunts, uncles, and cousins. You've been looking forward to seeing them for months," Blake said. "As soon as Marcia returns from fixing the flower snafu, I can have her box everything and mail it to us."

"She won't have time. She's already running behind schedule."

Susan winced. She hated putting Luciana in the uncomfortable

149

position, but with the contractor scheduled to arrive on Monday to remodel Alex's old room into an office, Susan didn't have much choice. She'd been more than generous in letting them store items in her house for the past year.

"Alejandro will do it," Mrs. Cortez decreed, looking like a queen on her folding-chair throne, her gaze sharp and assessing. But the woman had been too far away to overhear Susan's conversation with him earlier.

Susan stepped toward the family matriarch. "Perhaps I could bring boxes out here for you to look through."

"No," she replied. "Today is about family and watching my daughter reach the next milestone in her life. Alejandro can box everything to deliver to my condo."

The back of Susan's neck prickled, and she glanced over her shoulder. Alex stood a couple of paces behind her. He dropped his gaze to her butt. She couldn't stop him from being a jerk—or her body from tingling—but she refused to let him see he'd rattled her.

She focused on his mother again. "You're right. Today should be about your family's celebration. I'll box everything and ship it to you."

"You don't want to box everything. The shipping will cost an arm and a leg. Besides, if we've lived without whatever's still in the house for a year, we're not going to suddenly miss it," Alex said. "Everything needs to be tossed."

"You two go through it right now," Mrs. Cortez said. "If you do it together, Alejandro will be done in the time for the rehearsal and, Susan, you can stop him from throwing out his adorable baby pictures, which I would most definitely miss."

Bracing herself for an insult or an expression meant to offend her, she peeked at him again, but the hard, sexy man who had once been an adorable baby looked surprisingly vulnerable. Uncomfortable warmth stirred in her chest.

"Let's get it over with." He strode away, leaving her to jog to catch up.

At least she'd gotten the result she wanted, even if it lacked graciousness. She fell into step with him. "I've changed a lot of things inside. If you were attached to anything in particular, you might be disappointed."

"I'm the guy who wanted to toss everything, remember? I don't do attachments. Makes it too hard to pick up and leave whenever I want."

"If that's your motto, please don't have kids. You might be able to leave them behind, but I guarantee they won't appreciate it."

He lifted an eyebrow. "You have kids?"

"No, but I'll be sure I'm ready for the commitment when I do." If she had kids, she could guarantee them the same home and her steady presence. Stability. Deep roots. Everything she'd never had.

"Be careful of what you get into. This place will bury you, and bringing kids into the picture will weigh you down more."

Considering the state of her sex life, any discussion about kids was a ridiculous hypothetical. Having said discussion with a man who'd never shown any interest beyond ogling her ass was downright bizarre. She brushed her fingers over his elbow. Electricity sizzled up her arm, proving her starvation for any kind of contact.

"What happened to you as a kid? Were you neglected or something?"

Instead of spilling a dark confession, he laughed and shook his head. "Nope. I was a poster child for the American dream. Baseball star. Homecoming king. Two parents who loved me and worked like hell to give me everything I needed."

How could he not appreciate the rarity and wonder of the strong roots he'd grown up with? Well, she'd appreciate it for both of them. Susan tugged him toward the house, but the closer they got, the more his arm tensed beneath her hand.

"I don't have a lot of sympathy for people who are bitter about having a perfect life," she said.

He pulled free. "I never said anything about perfection. My parents worked so hard, but the farm owned them, not the other way around. If it hasn't happened to you yet, give it another year or two and it will."

All right. She'd offer him the benefit of the doubt since he'd never struck her as the spoiled type before. But regardless of his assertions, she remained convinced his family was perfect. Pulling the back door open, she led the way through the mudroom and into the kitchen.

Alex's mouth opened, but for a moment he didn't speak. Then, "Holy crap. You gutted it."

"I tried to warn you." Her shoulders sagged. Of course, he hated it. She'd taken his cozy memories of meals around a simple wooden table and made the place unrecognizable. She would hate anyone who tampered with her family roots…if she'd had any.

Stepping past her, he ran his hand over the marble cooking island in the center of the room. "I feel like I'm in a stranger's house—one with an incredible kitchen."

"I did splurge in here because I like to cook, but don't worry, your bedroom's the same. Everything from your family is stored in there."

"I like the improvements," he stressed. "But I thought when you bought the place, you were only interested in the farm, not the house."

"That's what I thought, too, which is why I told your mom and sister they could leave their stuff here until they were settled in their new homes. But after dividing all my time between here and the university, I gave up my city apartment and decided to turn this house into a home." She caught herself before babbling on. As if he cared about the details of how she'd ended up remodeling the kitchen. "Are you ready to go to the bedroom?"

"I thought you'd never ask." He winked.

Heat flooded her cheeks. "You know what I mean. Don't try to create a sexual context where there isn't any."

"Professor, from the moment I saw your assets through that hospital gown, all I've thought of is sexual contexts with you."

"Grow up, Alex. And my name is Susan." She gestured for him to leave the kitchen ahead of her.

"Lead the way, *Susie*." He gestured right back. "If I have to go to the bedroom for any other reason, I'm going to revel in being immature and hormonal, and check you out while we walk."

Marching through the living room and down the short hallway, she tried to ignore where his gaze rested, but her stomach flip-flopped and every nerve ending sparked with awareness. "If you're so into backsides, you should have become a doctor, so you could see a new one every day."

"I don't want to see everybody's," he said from behind her, so close his breath brushed her neck. "I have standards, and let me tell you, in those tight jeans, you've met and exceeded every one of them."

Despite the promise of heaven in his voice, the last thing she needed was a guy with a sworn avoidance of all attachments. She did not need a fling with a man who wouldn't stick around. She had a plan for permanence and stability and to build an organic dairy legacy. People would come and go from her life, but she could count on the farm and her university research to always be there for her.

Alex had handled hanging out in the kitchen that bore no resemblance to the one he'd eaten meals in every day for the first eighteen years of his life. He'd enjoyed ogling Susie's butt in her fitted jeans and loved how her skin flushed and her nipples tightened in response.

But one glance inside his old bedroom destroyed the sexy tension. He couldn't distract her with a quickie when his bed was covered with baseball trophies and dried dance corsages.

"All this shit can be thrown away. I'll pay for the Dumpster to come. Done." He dusted his hands together and back-stepped out of the doorway to escape.

"What about this?" She scooted around him, engulfing him in the subtle scent of lilies, and picked a framed photo from a box.

The light reflected the layer of dust over the glass, along with a chipped corner. The metal frame was dull and speckled, the edges uneven. "Dumpst—"

She tipped the frame. The reflection disappeared, allowing him to view the picture. A grinning, dark-haired, four-year-old boy gripped the steering wheel of a tractor, his feet dangling off the lap of a similarly dark-haired man who held him around the waist and beamed with pride.

Entranced, Alex stumbled toward the vision of warm, happy memories. Then reality crashed in. Fifteen years after the idyllic scene had been captured, the same tractor would roll over, pinning Dad underneath it and killing him.

Alex took the frame, intending to hurtle it against the wall, but couldn't let go of the evidence of the bond he'd had with his father. He wanted to sink to the floor and cry like a baby. Hell, he even wanted to make his father proud. Which was total shit. The only thing that would have inspired pride and approval from his father would have been to follow in his footsteps and become a farmer, allowing the work to kill first his spirit then his body.

"Do you want me to give you a minute?" Susie's compassionate voice next to his ear startled him.

Too discombobulated to attempt a callous or flirtatious reply, he allowed the truth to slip free. "Yes."

After patting his shoulder, she strolled toward the doorway. The memories and boxes in the room closed around him as if he'd stepped in suffocating quicksand. He might summon the strength to tackle the task with her at his side, but he didn't stand a chance alone.

"No! Don't go. Please."

Pausing, she raised her eyebrows, but otherwise didn't move closer or farther from him.

A raw sense of desperation, not unlike when an enemy cut off his reinforcements, enveloped him. "I've harassed you and acted like a jerk, and I'm sorry. I promise not to feel you up or jump you. I just really suck at trips down memory lane and could use a little moral support, if you don't mind staying with me."

Her gaze softened, and she slipped her arm around his waist, her warm curves burning through his clothes and into his flesh. "Of course I'll stay. How about if I bring things to you and you can tell me about each item? Judging from your reaction to this picture, I think you'll immediately know which things have meaning that you want to save and which don't."

He scrubbed his knuckles through his hair. It was longer than it had been in years without his regular military trims. "Sure, I can do that much." He took a deep breath, filling his nose with her lily scent again. "I think."

She brushed her lips over his cheek. "Sit down."

Knocked over by her unexpected gesture, he sank to the floor.

"We can get through this whole room as long as I have enough kisses for reinforcement. How about the next one on the lips?"

"How about you tell me about this girl?" She shoved another picture in front of him, steel replacing softness in her tone.

Another junkyard frame, this one encasing a picture of him with the high school's head cheerleader moments after they'd been crowned prom royalty. He glanced at Susie's pursed lips and bit back a grin. If she wanted to disapprove, he'd make it worth her while.

"Her school spirit was the stuff of legends. First time she gave me head, I went out and hit a grand slam. Damn, she was a good time. Jealous?"

"That you took advantage of some girl? Hardly."

His naiveté had been the only thing taken advantage of. "I'll admit to being jealous when I discovered the third baseman and the shortstop also shared her school spirit." Relieved the memories no longer carried the charged, confused emotions of his youth, he set the picture in the discard pile. "Next."

"Newspaper clippings of the baseball state championships."

They'd been his moments of glory until he'd gone off to war. Carrying a wounded comrade to safety and the medical care that would save his life had been Alex's real moment of glory. But no newspaper stories or pictures had documented it. The quiet, heartfelt thanks of Luke's wife had been more than enough reward.

"Better save the papers for Mamá. She was so proud to see me in black and white. It's a shame I didn't die in combat for the Marines. My heroic sacrifice would have made the paper for her."

Susie's grip tightened on the stack of papers. "If you're trying to joke, you're not funny."

"Dying for your country never is." But he'd been prepared to make the sacrifice. His father had given the same life commitment to the farm. Having nothing left he was willing to give his life for left Alex with a strange emptiness.

"If you come across any newspaper articles about Dad's accident, set them aside for my mother. She'll want them, but I'll never be able to look at them. Are there any more pictures of hot, promiscuous girls who corrupted my innocence?"

Susie's gaze rested on him for far too long. Finally, she broke the contact and set the newspapers under the tractor photo. "You're not as shallow as you want me to think."

He resisted the urge to squirm. "Of course I'm shallow. Just because I promised not to try to get into your pants doesn't mean I'm not thinking about it."

"You need to improve your bullshit because you're not fooling either of us."

As if the junk in the room hadn't sent his emotions into enough of a tailspin, his heart clenched and then sped up when she called him out. Unable to prevent a smile, he turned the expression into a smart-ass smirk. "Did you use your teacher voice on me, Professor?"

"It's the only voice I'm using on you from now on. No girls, promiscuous or otherwise, in this picture." She handed him a photo of himself as a skinny, miserable thirteen-year-old wearing overalls and a T-shirt, scooping cow manure from the barn alongside his dad.

"That summer sucked. Dad decided I was old enough to pull a grown man's workload, and I decided to get as far away from the farm as I could as soon as I turned eighteen." Alex had left home, but he hadn't been able to outrun the guilt. If he hadn't left, he'd have been around to prevent the accident that had claimed his father's life.

"The Marines took you pretty far away, I'll bet, but I can't imagine they worked you any less hard."

"I didn't resent it like I did the chores here. Believing in a noble cause made the bad days bearable. Anyway, at the time of this picture, I wasn't dreaming about joining the Marines. I banked on enjoying a big league baseball career."

"What happened with that? You were obviously good." She waved a toy tractor set between the keep and discard piles.

"Keep for Luciana. I fully expect to be an uncle within the next year."

She set it aside with a smile. "So, back to America's favorite pastime."

He shrugged. "Sure, I was good, but you have to be a lot better than good to land a career in the majors. I have no regrets about baseball. I dreamed of being a superstar, like every other boy who's ever played the game. Like all those other boys, reality eventually kicked in, and I needed a backup plan. Which sure as hell wasn't going to be the farm."

Susie held up an ugly orange T-shirt.

He pointed to the throw-out pile. "Now, confession time for you. Why did you leave your pristine classroom to shovel cow pies out of a barn?"

"First of all, I haven't left the classroom." She tossed two more shirts to him, and he dropped them both on the Dumpster pile. "I still carry a full teaching load. Second, I rarely shovel manure or anything else. Have you been to the barn yet?"

"No, and as long as the wedding's not taking place inside it, I don't plan to." He stood and plowed through the box of shirts, pulling one with a hardware store logo from near the bottom. "Keep this one for Luciana. Blake's parents used to run the store. Everything else is trash."

She set the shirt aside while he swiped the corsages and trophies from the bed into the box and pushed it to the junk pile. Family pictures went to the keep side, earning only a cursory glance to weed out old girlfriends, but not enough for him to dwell on the memories within the photos.

Soon, he'd divided the room into two halves. He'd done it. He'd gone through everything and survived with his soul intact.

Susie clasped his palm. "Nice job on conquering your demons. Even better, we have time for a tour of the barn before you have to report to the tent for the rehearsal."

"I already told you I'm not setting foot in there. If we have time to kill, this bed is now conveniently bare and available."

She didn't take the bait. "You can stand in the barn doorway if you're too chickenshit to go inside."

Alex tugged her hand, pulling her flush with his chest. He could seriously get into her body rubbing against his. "You don't call a Marine chickenshit."

She smirked. "Prove it, and I'll take it back."

Chapter Three

$\mathcal{H}$ell if he didn't swallow her bait whole. "You play dirty. I like that in a woman."

"I've seen the kind of women you like. If you're attracted to me, I won't take it as a compliment."

Alex laughed. If she wasn't tied to the one piece of property he refused to have anything to do with, she would be damn near perfect. In addition to being witty and intelligent, she had a compassionate side that threatened to drown him in sweetness. Maybe if he concentrated on the sweetness of her ass again, he'd forget about their destination as she dragged him across the back lot.

Unfortunately, the barn still drew his attention. He'd known it as a white building with peeling paint and a sagging roof, but the structure in front of him was bright red with white trim and not a bit of sag.

The door sported a prominent *University Employees Only* sign. Susie bypassed it in favor of a new section of the building with an entrance labeled *Visitors* and ushered him into a Plexiglas-enclosed observation area.

"Visitors? Do you think you're going to become a tourist destination or something?" Despite the laughable idea, he'd have been the first to encourage his family to take a gamble on it if they could have made any money to ease their financial burden.

"Considering we're running an educational endeavor, we're open to field trips and independent study groups. Mostly, we use this room for academic observation and research." Touching a computer monitor, Susie filled the screen with columns of numbers. "Students and instructors can come here and access the data we've recorded."

"What is there to record besides how much milk you get every day?"

"We keep records about the food the cows are eating. In addition to the quantity of milk, we test the nutritional content at every milking, correlating it with the different feeds the cows are ingesting, while staying away from hormones and antibiotic supplements."

Beyond their glassed-in room, the employee door opened. Three men and two women, some not much younger than him, some barely out of their teens, filed in. Each nodded or waved to Susie, and a couple shot him speculative glances. They strode through the barn, some switching on the milking stations, others opening the large animal doors for the cows to enter single file.

"Those are a few of my grad students. They'll milk each cow, test the milk, and record their findings. Another group will do the same thing in the morning. I have seven students in each group, so no one is stuck trying to run everything and they also get a few days off a week."

Relief raced through him that she didn't have the constant twice-a-day pressure his father and then his sister had dealt with. But raising any kind of livestock required a lot more work than the never-ending milking.

"What about the rest of the farm chores? Do your students do those, too, or are you stuck with the remaining work?"

"A part-time handyman and some undergrads take care of repairing things and other labor-intensive tasks. I oversee the operation, but I'm well aware of who does the heavy lifting, and it's not me."

The buildings and the land might be where his family had toiled, but the similarities ended there. Susie wasn't working herself into the ground, the way his father and sister had. Keeping her teaching job also meant she didn't depend on the operation to pay the bills and put food on the table either. He didn't have to worry about the farm destroying her.

"Come with me. I want to look at the data from the kelp-meal supplement research." Opening a see-through plastic door, she led him out of the observation area, along a walkway with painted lines on the floor.

Stepping across a line, she joined a young woman who measured a small test tube of milk and clamped it into a machine. A series of numbers spilled across a computer monitor, and both women leaned in, studying the screen with the intensity of a Marine on alert for land mines.

Dairy farming had been part of his life since birth, but Alex knew nothing about the operation Susie ran. Sure, he understood every movement of the students attending to the actual milking, but the computers and numbers flipped the focus from back-breaking labor into an intellectual endeavor.

The sexy professor had turned everything he'd thought he'd known about farm work on its head. What other surprises would she reveal if he took the time to uncover them?

Alex stepped into Susan's personal space, his chest brushing her back as he peered over her shoulder at the kelp supplement chart. She took a deep breath and tried to focus on her student's thesis update.

"After I enter all the data on Monday, I'll have six months of findings to draw conclusions on the benefits of kelp," Layla said.

The intensity of Alex's presence traveled down her spine and settled in Susan's core until her thighs quivered.

"I'm looking forward to your analysis and preliminary observations." Thankfully, she managed to find her professor voice and hang onto an appropriate image for her student, no small feat when every fiber inside her burned to twist toward to the sexy hunk at her back and beg him to slide his hand inside her panties.

Layla's gaze swept over him with undisguised appreciation. "Your new research project looks like it will provide very entertaining results."

"Oh, no. We're not—" Susan protested. "Alex's family used to own this farm, so I'm giving him a tour of what we do."

He laughed, undermining her attempt at professionalism. "I'm all about letting Susie use my body in the name of research."

Oh God. She stepped away from his magnetic force field and cleared her throat, trying to pretend her legs weren't trembling. "Sorry for distracting you, Layla. We'll let you return to your work."

She laughed. "No need to rush off on my account."

"I'm pretty sure it's on my account. I have that effect on women." He winked.

"The only research on your body is going to be how fast I can shovel a grave to bury you in. Outside, Alex, now." Susan led him to the employee door, and thankfully he followed her out. She strode around the side of barn, not stopping until she'd gone far enough to be certain her students couldn't see or hear them. Then she spun to face him. "You weren't doing my professional image any favors in there."

His lips curved in an unrepentant smirk. "Professor, you might be a bit out of touch if you think college students have never heard a sexual innuendo before."

He made her sound ridiculous and uptight, but she had a community and a position with the university to protect. "In addition to what you said, you were rubbing against my back in front of her."

"Two fully clothed bodies touching. Oh, the scandal," he teased.

"Don't do it again." She tried for a severe tone, which wasn't easy when she wanted to beg him to touch her.

"Are you suggesting we take our clothes off next time?" He stepped closer, backing her into the barn wall, but not touching her anywhere. "That can be arranged."

"Then arrange for it," she snapped, giving in to her need, since pretending didn't fool either of them. "Preferably while you're kissing me."

"Whatever you want, Professor." He stepped even closer, filling her personal space and heating every single pore.

She'd fantasized about his sensuous attention ever since he'd sat with his mother on the other side of her hospital room and Susie'd had nothing better to do but stare at him for hours on end. She still couldn't think of anything better.

His lips brushed hers.

Oh yes, she could think of something. She needed to feast more than her eyes on him. Parting her lips, she kissed him back, tugging his hard, muscled torso closer to her.

He traced her lips with his tongue then thrust inside. Her knees weakened, and she relied on the barn wall for support. Good Lord, the man could kiss. She threaded her fingers through his thick, dark hair and held him to her.

Despite proving she managed a well-oiled machine with minimal effort, she'd spent the past year working long hours to get all the pieces to flow together, as well as get the research arm up and running. Factoring in the farmhouse remodeling project and moving out of her apartment, she hadn't given a thought to her personal needs since well before her emergency gallbladder surgery the year before.

Those needs commanded attention. And hallelujah, Alex took them in his capable hands. Under her shirt, he caressed her bare midsection, the gentleness of his fingers liquefying every remaining cell. Susan leaned into his touch, craving more, desperate for him to cup her breasts and tease her clit.

Around the corner, the barn door opened, rattling the wall behind her. She tore her mouth from his and froze. Footsteps clomped outside, her students chattering about which cows were obstinate and which were so gentle they'd keep them as pets.

The door smacked closed, and the chatter faded. Alex slid his palm up to her breast, teasing the hard bud of her nipple through the lace bra.

She didn't want the bra or any other barrier, and she didn't want to hide behind the barn, either. They were both adults. They didn't need to sneak around to cop a feel. They could hook up in the privacy of her home, fifty feet away.

A bullhorn blared. "Wedding rehearsal in five minutes," someone called out.

Dropping his arm, Alex pressed his lips to her neck. "I imagined more than the five-minute slam-bam special."

"You're not getting a five-minute special." Susan tried not to sound like she was melting as she straightened her spine. "Come to the house after the rehearsal, and you can have the five-hour deluxe treatment."

His brown eyes lit up, and he grazed his fingertips down her shirt, caressing her breasts. "I look forward to it." Bending, he captured her mouth one more time. "I want you to touch yourself every half hour and think of me until I return."

Moaning, she reconsidered a five-minute special to tide her over for the next few hours. But he'd already spun away, leaving her aching and missing him before he'd left her sight.

Alex Cortez didn't just stimulate her oversexed body. He threatened to burn up her peace of mind. His roots belonged to him. She couldn't share in them, and he couldn't transfer them to her because she lived in his old house, no matter how much she would have given for a piece of them. He'd be gone by the end of the weekend, and imagining they could have a future would leave her brokenhearted.

Ω

Why every person at the rehearsal dinner needed to indulge in misty, idyllic recollections of the good old days on the farm, Alex had no idea. Selling the place had caused everyone to black out the real memories and replace them with sugarcoated dreams, as if every day working themselves to death had been some stupid blessing.

The only thing he thanked the farm for was the opportunity to fall into Susie's arms after dinner. Unfortunately, he couldn't do so yet. The bride and groom rose to their feet, and Blake called for attention. Then Luciana clasped his hand, and they shared a moment of blissful eye contact. Alex looked away. Eye contact shouldn't be too intimate to be shared in public, but with the love between them so evident, their contact was.

"I think everyone knows Blake and I were high school sweethearts reunited after fifteen years apart. What you might not know is the reason we reconnected is because my brother arranged a one-night stand date for me," Luciana said.

Alex shifted in his seat. The plan had made sense at the time—one of those crazy risks that most people wouldn't take, but he'd jumped at without blinking. The expressions of the other people around the table, however, suggested his actions had been sleazy and irresponsible.

"His only stipulation was I give him a one-night stand gift when I asked him to be our best man," Luciana continued.

The anticipation he'd once felt didn't course through him like it had when Susie offered him five hours of heaven in her bed.

"So, Alejandro." His sister shifted around the table and held out a paper to him. "Here is a certificate to the 1Night Stand dating service. Madame Eve will set you up with someone special who will change your life."

He couldn't *not* take the paper, but he had no interest in finding someone special who would tie him down. "Well, I don't need anything that dramatic, but I'd be happy to discover a naked woman in my hotel room for the night."

The others chuckled, as he'd meant for them to. He preferred his encounters with no strings, like he and Susie would have that night.

Except, damn, of course they'd have to deal with strings and complications when she lived in the house where the mementos of his past were piled in his old bedroom.

Worse, his sister being the exception, of course, he recognized one-night stand type of girls, which Susie definitely wasn't. If he slept with her, she'd think they were starting a relationship, no matter how frankly he spelled out the parameters.

He sighed and refocused on the activity around the table as Blake spoke to the woman sitting to Alex's left. "Marcia, you're my saving grace in the office, which is why you're our assistant of honor. Luciana and I want you to find happiness too."

Her face blanched. "I don't need a one-night stand to be happy."

Blake didn't hesitate as he passed her a certificate. "Use it as a kick start to help you get to happiness."

Other bridal party members received gifts of the more traditional variety, leaving Alex and Marcia as the only ones to receive one-night stands. He faced her, but no connection or interest sparked inside him. "Do you think Blake and Luciana are trying to set us up?"

"I hope not," she said. "No offense."

"I have to take offense when you say it like that."

"You're not offended. You're relieved."

He shrugged, unable to deny it. A one-night stand with a random person could expel his pent-up lust and purge the memories of Susie's lips and the heat of her satin skin. But with her connection to Blake and Luciana, Marcia wouldn't be random, and he'd probably cross paths with her again in the future.

"Explain to me why you're the assistant of honor instead of the maid of honor. I know you're Blake's assistant, but I didn't get stuck with the corny label of best brother."

"Because I'm married," Marcia said. "So I'd technically be the matron of honor."

He glanced around. "Did I miss meeting someone?" The guy couldn't be very happy that his wife had received a certificate for a one-night stand.

"No. We haven't been together in…a while."

"Going through a divorce?"

Behind the head table, a light flipped on inside the house, and someone moved behind the curtains. *Susie.* Was she thinking of him? Touching herself? He groaned and picked up his wineglass.

"No. I guess you'd call it a marriage in name only," Marcia said.

"I'd call it complicated." Alex did not need the complications that came with any kind of relationship—long or short-term. Freedom stretched before him—from the farm, from the Marines, from worry about his family.

He'd been thinking with his cock behind the barn. But he wasn't so stupid he'd throw away his liberty because Susie gave him a hard-on. Sleeping with her in the place where his roots still festered would ensnare him in the past he'd tried so hard to get away from.

As soon as he fulfilled his commitment to the bridal couple, he'd drive away without so much as a glance in his rearview mirror. He would not allow anything to trap him and kill his spirit. It had taken his father, but the farm would never own him.

He'd confided his intimate family memories in a woman who cared far too much about the place where those memories had been formed. If he slept with Susie, the farm would own a piece of his soul.

He couldn't come to her like he'd promised. As much as he wanted to feel her skin against his, to save his sanity and his plan for his life, she had to be off-limits.

But the idea of sleeping with anyone else left him cold. He folded the certificate and placed it in his wallet. Some day when he'd forgotten all about Susie, he'd cash it in.

The party started breaking up, and he concentrated on Marcia to avoid looking at the house where the warm, welcoming lights beckoned to him.

"What do you say we go find something stronger to drink than this overrated wine, and pretend like we didn't get a free pass for a one-night stand? At the end of the night, I'll drop you off at your hotel room, and I promise not to try to convince you to sleep with me."

Marcia smiled sadly at him. "With talk like that, you just might steal my heart."

He grinned in return because they both knew he wouldn't, and she wouldn't steal his. His old buddies would laugh if they could see what a play-it-safe guy the biggest risk-taker in the regiment had become.

Chapter Four

Concealed behind the curtain, Susan accepted the pang in her chest as she watched laughter, familiarity, and joy emanate from the private, catered party in her front yard. Luciana had invited her to attend, but she'd made the right decision in declining.

Joining the party wouldn't include her in their group, and she'd had too much experience with others resenting her intrusion on their lives to consider doing so. She could absorb the connection and the closeness from afar. The farm gave her stability, but it didn't fulfill all her hopes for building a community.

Her bond with her students and the other university employees who worked under her didn't extend beyond the classroom and the farm. Her attempts to join their larger social circle changed the group dynamic, leaving everyone a bit uncomfortable and on edge. In addition, the other professors either thought her crazy for starting the organic dairy operation or resented her for diverting department resources from their pet projects to maintain it.

She liked her life—a life she'd built from scratch because no one had given her anything. And she would enjoy its possibilities a lot more as soon as Alex entered the house and stripped her out of her clothes.

Across the lawn, he pushed out his chair and stood, stretching his lean, muscled body, the action accenting his broad shoulders. She squeezed her thighs together. Thinking about him, she became so wet and shaky, she didn't need to touch herself to get ready.

He offered his arm to the woman on his left. Whatever he said made her laugh, and she linked her arm with his, nudging him with her shoulder. Their temporary closeness didn't bother Susan. Within minutes, he would be hers.

When she peeled off his clothes and explored his naked physique, the emptiness in the life she'd worked so hard to create would disappear.

Alex walked the other woman to her car then stood next to her open window, his hands in his pockets until she drove away.

Turn to me. I'm ready for you. Come here.

Instead, he strode toward a little blue sports car farther down the yard. She grasped the windowsill, balling the fabric of the curtains in her fist. He wasn't coming?

For the first time in over a year, she'd offered herself to someone. She'd thought he wanted her, that rejection wouldn't be an issue. Yet, he hadn't given her an explanation for why he'd changed his mind. Just like her father who'd walked out when she was seven, her mother who'd left two years later, and her grandfather who'd died several months after, Alex hadn't given her any notice before abandoning her.

Damn it, she deserved at least an explanation. Running from the house to the driveway, she waved frantically. His taillights reflected off the mailbox at the end of the drive. Then he turned onto the gravel road. A moment later, his car disappeared over a small hill.

Susie dropped her arm. He might have been into her while they'd been kissing behind the barn. But, like the parade of foster families and potential adoptive parents she'd bounced between, he'd blown her off because he'd either changed his mind or gotten a better offer.

She hugged her arms around her chest. She'd had no idea putting down roots would leave her so cold and bereft.

"Dr. Gundersen." Luciana crossed the front yard, the radiant smile on her lips giving credence to every cliché about bridal perfection and blissful happiness.

Somehow, Susan had lost sight of the fact Alex had come to the farm for his sister's wedding, not to satisfy the new homeowner's desperate need for an orgasm.

"Please, call me Susan." She dredged up a smile.

"Even though you refused our offer to pay you for taking over your yard, Blake and I still wanted to offer a token of our appreciation." She held out a sheet of paper.

Susan took it, but standing in the shadows, she couldn't decipher the writing. "What is it?"

"A certificate for Madame Evangeline's 1Night Stand service. Her matchmaking is the reason I'm getting married tomorrow. Trust me, if anything is lacking in your love life, Madame Eve will fix it."

Susan's chest ached. Damn Alex for walking away without any explanation.

She'd learn from the pain and move on. He'd reminded her why she didn't want a guy who could touch her heart and hurt her. She'd given too many people in her past that power.

"I'm okay with the state of my love life, but my sex life could use some action."

Luciana grinned. "Madame Eve will fix that, too. When you fill out the online application, you'll be able to describe what—and who—is your one-night stand holy grail."

A one-night stand would be a sex-only proposition. If she cashed in the certificate—and stocked up on the highest quality condoms—she could get her much-needed orgasm without involving her emotions and mistaking a few kisses for something meaningful the way she had with Alex.

Behind Luciana, Blake approached them, a bottle of wine in his hand and a satisfied swing in his step. He offered Susan the wine. "This is also part of your gift. I recommend drinking it while you fill out Madame Eve's application."

"Uh, thanks." She took the bottle, trying not to sigh as Blake wrapped his arms around Luciana's shoulders and hugged her from behind. They were so sweet, so obviously in love and delighting in every touch.

"Do you two need any last-minute help getting ready for tomorrow?" She'd rather pull an all-nighter tying up little bags of dinner mints or fashioning bows to hang on the chairs in the aisle than think about how desperate she'd have to be to let a service match her up with a stranger for sex. She *was* desperate for already considering it.

"Nope, everything is all set." Luciana leaned into Blake's embrace. "You'll be there, right? I'll stop the ceremony to drag you out of the house if you're not."

The possibility both amused and horrified Susan. No way did she plan to put the bride's threat to the test. "I wouldn't miss it."

"Good." Luciana draped her arm around Blake's waist and together they strolled away, exchanging a long, sensuous kiss.

Susan hugged her chest tighter, but a paper certificate and a wine bottle weren't the warm, cuddly partners she craved. She returned to the house, locking the door behind her. Without table favors to keep her busy, she could power up her laptop and study the statistics on which types of pasture grass allowed for the most nutritious milk. A Friday night of analyzing data beat obsessing about Alex driving away in his fancy sports car, probably laughing at how he'd led her on and left her hanging.

She sized up the wine bottle. Might as well indulge and drown her disappointment. Watching a wedding in her front yard would be the closest she'd come to experiencing a real, forever love. With the laptop booting up on the center island in the kitchen, she uncorked the wine then settled on a barstool. Instead of opening the spreadsheet of data, she clicked on the Internet icon and typed the link from the paper certificate that directed her to an online application. Taking a long swallow of wine, she read the first question.

Why do you want a one-night stand?

The same reason any woman would. She wanted to have an orgasm. She typed then revised the words to *multiple orgasms*. If she chose to actually use the certificate, she'd darn well make the encounter worthwhile. The next several questions consisted of basic personal information.

Then, *describe the person you want to have a one-night stand with.*

Black hair, brown eyes, hard, lean, muscled physique.

Pausing, Susan gulped her wine. Hell. Her subconscious hadn't given up on the Alex fantasy. Attaching his picture would be easier than trying to use words to capture the nuances of his stubborn jaw, how the amusement ebbed and flowed from his expression, and the way he tried to pretend he didn't feel his emotions simmering beneath the surface.

She didn't want a one-night stand with him. Forcing someone to match them together when he'd rebuffed her would be awkward at best, stalker-esque at worst. Typing on the questionnaire, she clarified her interest in wanting someone with similar physical characteristics, since her body obviously responded to his type.

All similarities ended on a superficial level, though. She preferred a man with an interest in agriculture and organic health, someone loyal and trustworthy from a large, welcoming family. After refilling her wine glass, she typed more specifics, not pausing until she reached the Send box at the end of the application.

Clicking the button would formalize her request for a single night of sex. She could accomplish the same thing by picking up a random person in a bar. Letting someone else choose her companion came with more risks, and Susan was not a risk-taker. Even the purchase of the farm had been a carefully weighed consideration.

Sipping her wine, she reread her responses on the application. If the service could match her with a man somewhat close to the type she'd asked for, he'd be worth checking out.

Using the laptop touch screen, she tapped her index finger on *Send.*

Chapter Five

*A*lex's attention should have been on his sister pledging the rest of her life to the man she loved. He kept his eyes on the couple, refusing to squirm as Susie's gaze bored into him from the rear of the audience. If looks could kill, a recovery team would be removing chunks of his mangled flesh from every square inch of the yard.

He'd made the right decision by not going to her the night before, but blowing her off had been beyond rude. He should have explained his reasons for changing his mind. She might have even appreciated hearing she deserved better than a guy who'd sleep with her and then walk away.

Even if she'd professed to being okay with him moving on after they spent the night together, he feared he wouldn't be able to. The farm played no role in his future, and she and the farm were a package deal.

The wedding ceremony concluded, and he took his place in the receiving line, shaking hands and then posing for seventy million photos. After the toasts at the reception, he and Marcia fulfilled their obligatory waltz. Then he danced with his sister, his mother, and a multitude of cousins and distant relatives.

Finally, he gave up his place on the dance floor for a much-needed drink and ended up facing Susie. He didn't know who she'd been dancing with, but judging by the surprised expression on her face, she hadn't sought him out.

"Hey," he said. The song switched to something slow and weepy that called for him to hold her.

She jerked away from his touch. "Why did you stand me up last night?" Of course, she had every right to be furious with him.

"Because I'm a total ass, and I decided to do you a favor by not using you."

"At least, you're telling the truth." Her lips quirked in a wry smile as she crossed her arms and rubbed her biceps.

The self-protective gesture made him want to hold her more, but he didn't try again.

"I doubt you were having noble thoughts about doing me a favor when you left last night," she said. "In fact, I'm curious how the asshole internal monologue went. Something to the effect of 'thank God I got a better offer than wasting my time with her,' maybe?"

If she'd watched him leave the farm, she probably assumed he'd spent the night with Marcia. He'd rather she stewed over that conclusion than discover he'd come to think of Marcia as a sister. If Susie screamed at him and hated on him, she'd keep her distance and he wouldn't have to worry about his feelings for her careening out of control.

"I'm sorry. I can't handle your connection to the farm." Instead of purposely pissing her off, he spoke from the heart, surprising himself. "I have too much baggage over this place. I need a clean break from it, and if I sleep with you, I'm not sure I'll ever be able to get one."

Her frozen demeanor melted, and she reached out as if she wanted to heal him. He wasn't broken, though, not as long as he stayed away from the place where the thankless, unending labor crushed his spirit, the place that left his father disappointed in Alex for his choice to leave, and the place that ultimately stole the life of the greatest man he'd ever known.

"How about we have one dance and then I'll make it easy on you and walk away?" she suggested, her gaze sad but understanding.

One dance. Yes, he wanted to cradle her in his arms and hold her to his chest one more time. Surrounded by relatives and neighbors on the packed dance floor, they were guaranteed not to go too far and lose control.

As Alex enveloped her in his embrace, Susan rested her head on the lapel of his tuxedo jacket. Instead of a lightning bolt of lust she could extinguish with a single romp in the bedroom, he incited a long, slow burn that promised to grow stronger with each encounter. Good thing she didn't have to worry about future encounters endangering her heart.

Of course, she had no intention of letting him off the hook by agreeing he'd done her a favor by blowing her off. "I touched myself last night," she whispered in his ear.

Along her midsection, his semi-hard shaft thickened and twitched. His breath caught and then quickened at her neck.

She slanted her hips closer. "After you drove away, I kept touching myself. When I came, I screamed your name."

His erection throbbed full and hard, teasing her softness through their clothes. Her core ached for a more intimate caress. As soon as she returned to the house, she'd touch herself to achieve the release she'd never get directly from him.

"I can feel how sorry you are that you missed it, but I had a damn good time without you."

Sure, sex with him would have been better, but the fantasy of him still packed a hell of an orgasm.

He growled in her ear. "Since you can feel exactly what you're doing to me, you would be wise to stop now."

Biting her inner cheek, she withheld a smile. "Good thing you don't need me either."

Tipping her chin up with a single finger, he met her gaze then skimmed her lips with his, sending sweet desire thrumming through her veins and tingling her limbs. He dipped his tongue into her mouth, drenching her in heat and need.

She kissed him in response, her body—and her heart—ignoring her head's plea to stop and move away from him. Although she was willing to make changes to accommodate a man in her life, she refused to compromise over the farm. She needed its roots and the connection she'd been searching for her entire life. Anyone who rejected it, rejected her.

She didn't have to explain her stance to Alex. He understood. Unfortunately, the farm was also his deal breaker.

Susie broke off the kiss and ducked out of Alex's arms as the final notes of the song drifted through the speakers and his heart thundered in his chest. "I'll pack up your keeper pile of mementos and ship it to your mother."

"Good." He needed to say a million things, none of them about the stuff sitting inside her house, but his voice wouldn't operate beyond the single word. Knowing he would never hold her in his arms again, never see her again, was anything but good.

"Good-bye, Alex." She stood in front of him, maintaining eye contact.

What the hell could he say? He couldn't tell her how badly he ached to bury his cock inside her after he'd explained her connection to the farm stopped him from all further contact. Anything he said would lead her on and hurt her more.

So, he drank in her beautiful blue eyes, dark-red hair, and clear, smooth skin until she hugged her arms around her chest once again and swiveled away from him. Even then, he continued to stare, mesmerized by the sway of her hips and the proud, straight set of her shoulders until she disappeared into the house. A moment later, a light switched on inside, creating a warm glow through the curtains.

Tearing his gaze from the building, he weaved between the joyful, gyrating bodies on the dance floor to the head table. At his seat, he sat and drained his water glass then poured a refill from a nearby carafe.

Although the open bar tempted him, drinking anything stronger than water wouldn't erase his need for her. He'd tried that path last night, to no avail. He could, however, with a willing partner, release the sexual energy Susie'd inspired in him. Unfortunately, everyone on the dance floor was either related to him or married.

He lifted his gaze to the partygoers congregated around the tables. His former science teacher, Mrs. Santiago, who'd been ancient back in the day, lifted her head from the quilted bag attached to her walker and winked at him. He waved a weak greeting and chugged more water. He would not be hooking up with anyone in attendance.

He'd hit rock-bottom, in desperate need of a last resort. From his wallet, he unfolded the certificate Luciana had bought for him. With a new cell tower on the corner of the land, he had a signal on his cell phone. Quickly, he typed a text to Madame Eve, hitting send before he could second-guess his actions. An immediate reply directed him to an online application.

As he finished filling in his personal information, two of his cousins approached the head table, their obvious goal to drag him onto the dance floor. Application complete, he pocketed the phone and resolved to put his needs aside for the duration of the party.

Two hours later, Luciana and Blake left for their honeymoon suite while the DJ finished packing away the sound equipment. Alex hesitated halfway to his car. Maybe he should apologize to Susie one more time.

The house loomed dark and silent behind him. If he woke her to ask forgiveness, he'd have to apologize for waking her too. Anyway, he deluded himself. If he knocked on the door, he wouldn't stop with an apology and a stilted good-night. She was better off without him messing with her head and toying with her emotions.

But he would suffer the loss of never holding her in his arms again.

༄

Returning to his hotel, he debated then discarded the idea of hanging out in the bar, and headed to his room instead. As he stepped inside, his phone vibrated with an incoming text. Madame Eve had come through for him.

Go to the hotel across the street to claim your one-night stand.

He stripped off his tux, redressing in jeans and a T-shirt. Then he filled his pockets with condoms and followed the instructions. At the front desk of the new hotel, he picked up a key card for his assigned room and stepped into the elevator.

The silence enveloped him, but he refused to listen to the inner voice insisting he no longer wanted a random encounter. He needed to go through with it to forget about Susie. Walking away had been the right decision. Though prepared to rethink his views on freedom and being tied down, he'd never settle on the farm.

Exiting the elevator, he strode down the hall. After unlocking the door, he stepped inside. Six feet away, a gorgeous redhead wearing nothing but a blue low-cut bra, matching thong, and four-inch stilettoes peered over her shoulder, inspecting her smooth, curvy ass in the mirror.

She whipped toward him. Her blue eyes widened, first with surprise, then horror. Lunging for a shirt lying over the arm of a chair, she tripped on her fuck-me shoes.

Alex shot forward, catching her in his arms and breaking her fall. Her breasts and hips imprinted on his body, destroying the control and barriers he'd worked so hard to erect. No matter how many battles he won, he'd already lost the war.

"Let me go. Please, let me go." Susan struggled in Alex's arms, her throat clogging with the tears she tried desperately to hold back. "What are you doing here? Please tell me you're not my 1Night Stand date."

"Apparently, I am." He caressed her bare back, his hand gentle and oddly comforting. "If it's any consolation, you were the last person I expected to find when I opened the door."

"It's no consolation. Please leave," she whispered. She had to get him out before he noticed her nipples shrinking to hard points as her breasts wedged against his shirt. Frantic longing tempted her to undulate against him, swelling her humiliation to epic proportions.

His arms relaxed around her. He didn't release her, but held her lightly enough she could have stepped out of his grasp if she had any willpower. "What did you tell Madame Eve you wished for?"

You.

But Susan had enough pride not to admit it. "Orgasms." She met his gaze defiantly. "A lot of them. Now go away."

His brown eyes smoldered. "I can't."

"Why not?"

"Because I want you too much."

"You don't want me at all." Because she came as a package deal with the one thing he hated more than anything.

He laughed, his voice lower and rougher than normal. "Rub the front of my pants and feel how badly I want you."

She refused to glance down. She'd felt his desire earlier in the evening. Any woman could fill the need, which he'd no doubt been banking on when he opened the door. She'd seen the surprise in his eyes—he hadn't expected to find her.

"Your lust isn't for me personally. You'd have the same reaction to any woman standing in her underwear."

He palmed her bare ass cheek. "You underestimate yourself. Let me give you what you want—orgasm after orgasm, pleasure only for you, nothing for me."

"Why?" Already so weak with need, she wanted to unzip his jeans and drag him inside her. He didn't have to strike a bargain that would deny him pleasure.

"I want you to get what you came for, and I can't stand the thought of any other guy caressing you."

Susan could have reassured him she didn't want anyone else touching her either. She'd yearned for only him since she'd seen him standing in the tent before the rehearsal the previous day. No, from the moment she'd laid eyes on him in her hospital room a year ago. "You can touch me, but you'd better make it good."

A wicked smile spread across his strong, chiseled face. "You have my word. Tell me what position you want to come in the first time. Then, after we do it your way, for the rest of the night I'll decide how you'll come."

He intended to pleasure her more than once. Sure, she'd fantasized about it, but reality suggested the unlikelihood of the possibility. Regardless, he offered her an orgasm. She'd take it—and revel in it.

"I really like your hand on my butt," she started, not sure what she had in mind. Her fantasies had been more about him than positions. "Maybe if I lie on my stomach but keep my underwear on." The thong didn't offer much coverage, but she'd take the tiny bit of modesty it offered. Facing away from him, she could accept the pleasure without focusing on or connecting with him.

Smacking her bottom lightly, he released her. "Lie on the bed."

Flooded with unexpected hunger and aching to please him, she jumped and took a step toward the bed then glanced at Alex, hoping he'd embrace her. Surrounding her and rubbing his naked skin against hers was what she truly wanted.

But not what she'd asked for. Teetering on her too-high heels, she turned down the covers, revealing a plain white sheet. She lay face down, the linen cool in contrast to her hot flesh. Pinching her eyes shut, she prayed she hadn't made a huge, foolish mistake.

Muffled footsteps crossed the carpet. Alex brushed her back then leaned over her. "Put this under your stomach."

She opened her eyes as he plucked a pillow from the head of the bed. As he brought it closer, she lifted her midsection. He tucked the cushion under her pelvis, so her butt stuck up in the air. Good God, what had possessed her to suggest such a vulnerable position?

"Excellent." His voice trembled a bit. "Now reach for the headboard."

She did, but, too defenseless and exposed, she shoved onto her elbows to maintain control. "Let's start with something else. How about missionary sex instead?"

He cupped her shoulders then slid his hands down her arms, gently straightening them again. "Trust me, Susie. I'll make this good for you." He glided his lips across her temple.

Her fears ran in the opposite direction. What if he rocked her world and the rest of her life felt empty and unfulfilled because she'd had a taste of him?

Alex had promised her two things—he'd give her pleasure, and he'd never return to the farm.

Chapter Six

*H*e caressed her arm from her shoulder to her fingertips then over her wrist, elbow, and collarbone before tracing a path down her spine and over the bump of her bra strap. At the base of her back, he massaged under the elastic band of her underwear, tugging the thong string taut but not moving lower to touch her the way she craved. She raised her hips to signal for his attention.

Instead, he stroked up her sides then down her back. Again and again, with gentle caresses meant to relax her. But she was too knotted with need and anticipation to unwind.

"You're not doing what I requested."

"You don't want this?" He paused along the side swell of her breasts, at the edge of her bra cup.

She wanted everything. "I want you to grab my ass while you slide your fingers inside me."

"Plural?" he verified.

Oh God. Her insides turned molten with desire. "Yes."

"Your wish is my command." He shifted on the bed, spreading her legs, his jeans brushing her inner thighs as he knelt between them. Settling his palms on her ass, he rubbed in a circular motion.

Oh yeah. She moaned into the sheet and tried to lift to give him a better angle, but, with him kneeling between her spread legs, she'd lost her leverage and was at his mercy. She gripped the headboard and squirmed.

He slapped one cheek lightly. Gasping, she wiggled again, unable to control her eagerness. With another smack, he dipped inside her.

"Alex." Her head spun with wonder and exhilaration while her body trembled.

"You're so wet for me," he whispered. "I could glide another finger in you already."

"Yes, yes." With tears and screams threatening, she begged for him, every emotion building like a volcano on the verge of eruption.

Giving her what she wanted, he stretched and filled her. "God, you're so tight." His voice deepened and strained as he brushed his lips across her back.

"Yes. Omigod." She couldn't control her shaking. If only she could see him. Yet, not being able to move or face him strengthened her desire.

He twisted his wrist, and, without warning, she detonated. Great spasms shook from her very core. When he squeezed her ass, pure ecstasy raced through her veins. He caressed the sweet spot inside her.

"Alex." Nothing had prepared her for such an incredible orgasm. More than a release, it tilted her entire world on its axis.

He withdrew and shifted from between her legs. As she shivered with aftershocks, he rolled her onto her back, sweeping his lips over hers, his gaze so tender she wanted to drown in it.

"You are so responsive. Feeling you come the moment I slide into you makes me tremble and feel like a superhero at the same time."

The world tilted again, and she stared at him, unable to reply. Responsive? Her? The few encounters in her past had left her with the uncomfortable suspicion she skewed toward the frigid side.

He smiled and stroked her jaw. "This time I plan to watch your face while you come."

"You want to do it again?" Susan had assumed they'd move on to her reciprocating with a release for him. After all, he had to be dying with lust, and her explosive orgasm should have satisfied her for years, not mere minutes.

His smile widened, revealing an adorable set of dimples. "You did specify multiple orgasms, 'a lot of them,' to be exact. I have no intention of letting you down."

He caressed the swell of her breasts spilling over the top of the demi bra then nudged the cup down to expose her nipple. Bending, he took the bud in his mouth, swirling his tongue around it before sucking gently. Desire slammed through her, and she bucked her hips.

He draped a palm over her navel then covered her mound through her thin panties, trapping the heat inside her, building it until she thought she'd explode. The underwear that had seemed so sexy when she'd bought them became a source of frustration. She didn't want anything between him and her skin.

Before she could rip the panties off, Alex corralled her hands, removing them from the intended target and interrupting his own caresses, too. She whimpered, a sound she wasn't proud of, but she'd become too desperate to care about anything but him touching her again.

He released her to unclasp her bra. "I'm doing the pleasuring and choosing how to deliver it this time, remember?" Pulling the garment off, he tossed it to the floor.

"Just get back to sucking and kissing me, please. I miss your mouth on my skin."

"Already?" He rubbed a palm over her nipple.

Nodding, she arched for him. "As soon as you move away, I miss it. I can't get enough of you."

With a groan, he nudged her panties down. Leaning over her, he teased her breasts with his tongue while inching his thumb through her wetness, massaging her clit then dipping into her.

She writhed on the mattress. and he sank deeper, giving her what she wanted before she could think to ask for it. Still pleasuring her pussy, he tasted and kissed his way down her chest and over her navel. He flicked his tongue along her clit, inciting intense pleasure and the vortex of a mind-shattering orgasm.

Alex loved watching Susie come. His only regret was not being able to watch her face and her pussy at the same time so he wouldn't miss a moment of her pleasure.

Keeping his thumb nestled inside her, he waited while she opened her eyes and refocused on him, her lips curving in a satisfied smile. He drew back then plunged in to fill her again.

She gasped and raised her hips.

His chest clenched at her instinctive plea for more. "You want to come again?"

"I don't think it's possible."

"Sure, it is." Torrid dampness encased his fingers as she sprang to life around him. "But not on the bed. Stand up, and we'll try something different."

She started to obey then looked pointedly at where he remained lodged inside her. "How about moving your arm so I can get up?"

"I'll move it, but not remove it from you, if that's what you mean." He grinned at her dismay and rotated his wrist, loving the way her gaze softened and her mouth slackened. Each moan and gasp rocketed straight to his agonizingly hard groin.

She clung to his shoulder, steadying herself as she shifted into a sitting position, driving him deeper. Then she stood. He circled his thumb around her clit then rubbed across the length of her slit.

"Okay, I take it back. More orgasms are possible." She gasped, gripping him tighter. "Anything's possible with you."

Kneeling on the floor while she stood over him in nothing but her stilettos, he repeated the journey with his index finger.

"Alex. Oh, the things you do to me. I never dreamed—"

He surged inside her, and she cut off with a gasp. Her body hugged him, shuddering around him.

"My shoes…still on…forgot." She panted.

"We didn't forget. I want you to leave them on." Nudging her legs wider, he settled his shoulders between them while she trembled. He had no idea how he'd gotten lucky enough to be allowed to explore and worship every inch of her incredible skin, but he intended to make the most of the opportunity.

"Grab onto me for support if you need it, and tell me how much you like this." He swirled his tongue around her clit.

"Yes." She latched onto his hair. "Yes, I like it."

He wanted more than a tepid *like*, even if she spoke the word with heartfelt enthusiasm. He shimmied a second digit into her pussy.

"Omigod! Alex. Oh, Alex."

He clutched her ass, and she came hard against his hand and face. He continued sucking and plunging. She shuddered and came again, harder than before. Her knees buckled, and she collapsed onto him, her body soft and pliant and utterly his.

Lifting her, he laid her on the bed and peeled off her shoes. Then he hunkered over her, swiping her hair off her face. She smiled at him, face glowing, eyes dewy with tenderness and other emotions that should have terrified him, but he had no fear. With her, he was invincible.

"Taste yourself, Susie. You have so much passion bottled up inside." He kissed her, and she stabbed her tongue into his mouth, groaning with eagerness. *Damn.* Despite making her come four times already, he still wanted to give her more.

"You've got to be dying right now," she whispered. "Take off your clothes and come inside me." She spread her legs wider, so his hips rested between her thighs, then hooked her calves around his waist.

She offered him heaven, but as long as he didn't take it, he wouldn't feel any guilt about leaving her at the end of the night. "Tonight's not about what I can get. It's about what I can give you."

"But—"

He wiggled lower on the mattress and cupped her core, morphing her protest into a moan. Then he stroked her inner thighs, drinking in her incoherent pleasure. When her desire turned to desperation, he pressed both thumbs into her at once and sent her flying over the edge.

Afterward, she lifted her head, awash in contentment and sweet smiles. *Something* shimmered in her eyes, an emotion he didn't dare analyze. He tucked the sheet around her and kissed her on the lips before she could speak the words that had no place coming between them. Her body needed a chance to recover, and their emotions needed a break in order for both of them to gain some perspective.

"I'm going to get a bath ready for you," he said and strode to the bathroom. Like in the bedroom, playtime in the water would be a one-way street. But, eventually, he'd get his release. For years to come, he'd jack off while remembering the heat of her sex, the shuddering of her muscles, and the ecstasy on her face. And her name would forever be on his lips and in his heart.

He would leave in the morning knowing he hadn't hurt her. When he'd offered to satisfy her fantasies, he'd thought Susie wouldn't touch him, but her passion was too great not to rock him to his very core.

He couldn't protect himself, but he'd do whatever he could to protect her from him.

C8

Susan finally convinced Alex to shed his clothes down to his boxer briefs. Really, the huge Jacuzzi convinced him, since he couldn't stay dry while touching her, and wet denim didn't do anyone any favors. She toweled off while he dried his legs, the soaked boxer briefs undermining his efforts.

"Take them off, Alex. You've seen every bit of me. I can handle seeing what you have hiding in there." It didn't hide well. She roamed her gaze over the impressive bulge. When she lifted her eyes to meet his, he wore a tortured expression.

"I promised you all the satisfaction and nothing for me," he said, his tone defeated. "I can't keep that promise if we're both naked."

His defeat equaled a win for both of them. "I release you from your promise, and I'll give you a new one. I'm going to make love to you until you scream my name and demand why we didn't do this hours ago."

She peeled his underwear down and then knelt before him, sipping a water droplet from his thigh. He hissed then whispered an oath, his cock bobbing for attention. While licking it dry, she rubbed the water from his tight buttocks with her hands.

"I'm not taking pleasure from you this way. Not the first time." He lifted her to her feet and they stumbled into the bedroom.

Needing to take charge, she grabbed a condom from the desk and faced him so he stood with his back to the wall. She ripped the package open with her teeth and rolled the protection over his length.

He gripped her hips and set her on the edge of the desk. Tilting back, she surrounded him with her legs, drawing him closer. With a single thrust, he drove into her, filling her in a way that transcended the physical, turning every cliché she'd ever heard about one person completing the other into a reality.

He encircled her body, hugging her to his torso. Carrying her, he staggered to the bed and sat with her on his lap, clutching her ass and driving deeper into her. She wouldn't have thought it possible to top the pleasure he'd already bestowed on her, but Alex managed the impossible.

She couldn't only take pleasure from him. She wanted to return it. Shifting her legs on either side of him, she prodded his chest until he lay flat. Then she rose above him until the tip of his cock titillated her pussy.

"Susie." Her name spilled from his lips in a plea, or maybe a prayer.

"What?" she teased, wanting him to voice his desperation, to admit he craved her the way no one ever had.

"I have to be inside you. I need you."

On the verge of detonating from his simple proclamation, she sank onto him.

"Yes, Susie. Oh. Yes." Ecstasy and agony intertwined on his face.

She rocked frantically, intent on making his release as amazing and memorable as the ones he'd given her. Pumping her hips, she drew him out then slammed down to claim every last inch of him until she couldn't hold out any longer.

The second she began splintering apart, he came with her, clinging to her, shouting her name, even as she cried out for him. He caught her, pulling her to him. She rested her head on his sternum, draping her arms over the crown of his head, absorbing the rise and fall of his chest against her cheek.

She'd found heaven.

Continuing to lie with her head tucked under his chin, she didn't dare risk meeting his gaze for fear he'd see the truth she'd never admit to him but could no longer deny to herself.

She'd fallen in love with him.

Despite their short time together, living amongst his roots and his memories, she knew him and understood him. So, she also understood too well why she couldn't share her feelings.

Because of the farm, he would never love her in return.

Chapter Seven

*T*rying not to disturb him, Susan finally eased off him and then the bed.

"Where are you going?" Alex murmured, his eyelids heavy, his face relaxed and content.

Unable to completely sever contact, she brushed her mouth across his. "Washing up and getting rid of the condom."

He fondled her hip. "I don't want you to go that far away, even for a minute."

To stop herself from agreeing, she kissed him again. "Just go to sleep." Once slumber had overtaken him, she would dress and head for the one place he wouldn't follow her—her home.

When she emerged from the bathroom, he remained sprawled across the king-size bed. She couldn't help but stare at the lean lines and muscles of his gorgeous male form.

A red puckered scar ran the length of his thigh. Another smaller, faded one marked his shoulder. His years in the Marines had been far more than an escape from farm work. He'd given up relative safety to put his life on the line for his country and not without a couple close calls.

His cock twitched. "Are you coming back to bed, or are you going to stare at me all night?"

Neither. She planned to walk away while she still could. Except she couldn't make her feet move in the direction of her clothes or the door.

Reaching out, he grasped her fingertips. "Spoon with me, and I'll show you what a good cuddler I am."

She eyed his swelling cock, heat unfurling in her belly. "If you plan to spoon with that, uh, fork, we'll end up with a spork."

He laughed, deep and sexy. "Guilty as charged."

Giving up the pretense of attempting to leave, she crawled over his naked body and lay next to him, wiggling her backside into his heat. If she only had one night, she'd wouldn't leave before it ended.

He rolled toward her, his cock, full and proud, nudging her ass. She delighted in his desire and squirmed closer. He draped his arm around her and sank into her, their bodies so close she couldn't determine where one stopped and the other began. Closing her eyes, she lost herself in the connection.

ᙉ

They made love again and again throughout the night, sometimes with insatiable energy, sometimes with quiet tenderness that pierced her heart. As the sun began to rise, Susan shifted out of Alex's arms while he slept. In silence, she put on her clothes and located a complimentary hotel notepad and pen. Pausing, she considered how to achieve a clean break without taking away from the perfect memories they'd created.

I have farm chores to attend to. Don't worry. I know how you feel about those. Thanks for the fun night.

After scrawling her name at the bottom, she tiptoed from the room barefoot, carrying her stilettos in her hand. She wouldn't cry. She'd agreed to have a one-night stand. The night was over, so their relationship also came to an end.

If her real life looked a little duller in the first blush of morning light, giving her students a hand with the milking would help her remember her blessings and put her life in perspective.

Good sex was a fun pastime, but she could live without it. As for the other emotion that had taken root during the night, well, she'd figure out how to live without that, too.

ᘓ

Alex blinked and rose onto his elbows. Although alone in a hotel room, he definitely hadn't dreamed he'd spent the night with Susie— her unique scent and the faint hint of lilies permeated everything.

"Susie?"

No answer.

He dragged himself into a full sitting position, trying to ignore his morning wood. Damn, as often as they'd come together in the past twelve hours, he should have been out of commission for a month. But she'd tapped an insatiable reservoir inside him.

Maybe they could call for room service and spend the morning repeating last night. She hadn't been able to get enough of him either. Every time he'd touched her, she'd been ready to come for him. He couldn't wait to watch the pleasure spill across her face once again…as soon as he figured out where she'd gone.

Stumbling into the bathroom, he flipped on the light then splashed water on his face. Bent over the basin and reaching for a towel, his face inches from the counter, he couldn't miss the note addressed to him. Water dripped from his chin onto the notepad, smearing the ink, but unfortunately not enough to turn the words illegible.

Thanks for the fun night.

Was a fun night all he'd been to her? An epic sex-fest?

Alex had wanted those things when he'd come to the room to claim his one-night stand, but from the moment he'd seen her checking out her ass in the mirror, everything had changed. Susie hadn't just touched his body. She'd imprinted herself on his soul.

Fuck that. He wadded the note in his fist. If all he'd done was get her off, then she could say it to his face.

ᘓ

An hour later, Alex steered onto the gravel road to the farm, gunning the engine and spraying rocks from under his tires. A crew from a rental company had taken over the front yard to disassemble the wedding tent. He drove straight up the driveway and skidded to a halt in front of the house.

Jumping from the car, he dashed to the front door and depressed the bell, holding it down to annoy her into answering. No one did, however, and no lights were on inside. Undaunted, he strode around the house and toward the barn, entering through the visitors' observation room.

Two men doing their damnedest to grow beards on their baby faces looked up from a laptop screen full of numbers.

"Is Susie here?" he asked.

They glanced at each other. "Who?"

"Your professor. Dr. Gundersen." Funny how he'd almost forgotten about her important title. She never held her years of education and mega-brain over his head, unlike other intellectuals he'd encountered who considered a high school diploma and military enlistment signs of idiocy.

"She's testing the day's milk. Do you want me to get her for you?" one of the boys offered.

"No, I know the way." Alex yanked open the plastic door and strode through the barn, around the milking stations to tables of assorted science experiments. Standing with her back to him, she measured white liquid into a test tube.

He waited until she placed it in a machine, then demanded, "*Thanks for the fun night.* Is that all you think we shared?"

She jumped then swiveled in his direction, her eyes guarded beneath her safety goggles, her expression wary. "Wasn't it?"

All he had to do was agree with her and walk away. He would be free, exactly as he'd wanted to be. No responsibilities, no ties, no roots. Except being apart from Susie was the last thing he wanted.

"Not for me. I mean, yeah, I had a lot of fun. But it went beyond fun. It meant something. Here." He smacked his fist on his chest.

She tugged off her latex gloves and shoved her goggles to the top of her head. If he hadn't already lost his heart, her red-rimmed eyes would have clinched it. The cost of leaving him was still evident on her face, proving she hadn't been unaffected by the night they'd shared.

Other than her shaking hands, though, she didn't appear ruffled as she stepped toward him. "Alex, I like you a lot, but if you're going to march in here and make a big, sweeping profession, you need to understand the consequences."

"I can handle consequences." His heart thundered. He had to do more than simply chase after her. He had to prove he had something to offer.

"Can you? If you're asking for more than one night with me, then you're asking to be a part of this." She spread her arms.

He followed her gesture, studying the high ceiling of the renovated barn, the cows standing patiently in their respective stalls, and the students who'd given up any pretense of carrying on with their business to gawk at them.

The knee-jerk hatred that had festered in his preteen years and swelled throughout adolescence, then exploded with his father's death, didn't rear up and overwhelm him. He had no interest in diving into eighteen-hour days of farm work, but if she asked him to lend a hand occasionally, he'd step in without hesitation.

He returned his gaze to her. "I respect the work you're doing here and the operation you're running. I'm not going to interfere with it or ask you to give it up. You're carrying on my father's dream and my family's legacy in a more fulfilling way than Luciana or I ever could have. Because of you, Dad can rest in peace."

An inner calm settled over him. He'd come back to profess his love to Susie and ended up finding closure for his grief and guilt over his father.

She blinked at him, surprise and pleasure stamped across her features. "Thank you. I'm honored you think so, and I'm even more glad you're not tortured by those demons anymore."

"Enough about my family and the farm. I came for you because I'm crazy about you. I spent the past year telling myself I couldn't stop thinking about you because I was so relieved you'd taken this burden away from my mother and sister. But I deluded myself. I couldn't stop thinking about you because you're you."

"I thought about you this year too," she whispered, infusing him with precious hope.

He took a deep breath, preparing for the biggest risk of his life. "Last night was more than sex. Every time I touched you, I did it because of how I feel in here." He thumped his chest again. "I know it's too soon and you're going to think I'm crazy, but I love you, Susie, and I want to spend the rest of my life with you."

"I do think you're crazy," she said.

The hope mushrooming inside him deflated.

"But I'm just as crazy because I feel the same way." She sashayed over to him.

The hope ballooned again. He closed the remaining distance between them and wrapped his arms around her, lifting her off her feet. "Say the words."

"I love you, Alex. I don't need you to be a farmer or to change anything about your life for me. I just need you to accept me and my work for what it is."

He molded his lips to hers. Cheers and moos rang out from around them, but he didn't care about their audience, only her sweet mouth and generous heart. "How long do I have to wait for you to finish your work so I can take you to the house and make love to you?"

"Given the circumstances, I think I could call in a favor for someone finish up for me." She tipped her head at her students. "Extra credit for whoever finishes my recordings and cleans up my station."

Every single kid jumped to do her bidding, extending congratulations and best wishes to both Susie and him.

He nodded his thanks to the group, but had eyes only for the woman who had captured his heart. Together, they sauntered across the yard. She tucked her hand in his back pocket, and he threaded his arm around her waist, his heart so swollen with love and happiness he feared it might explode.

But he was more than willing to accept the risk. With her at his side, the odds would always be stacked in his favor.

ONE NIGHT WITH HER HUSBAND

A 1Night Stand Story

By
Sara Daniel

~Dedication~

For anyone who fell in love and married while in college.

Chapter One

A quarter million stolen credit card numbers was the best news Adrian Torres had heard in seven years.

"*You* want to lead the team to San Diego to repair Sunburst's image?"

"Yes, sir." Adrian didn't flinch under his boss's skeptical stare. "If you've read my proposal, you know I have a solid plan to reinstate their reputation as one of the most venerable, trusted names in the upscale hotel industry."

He'd spent hours perfecting the plan, so he could be Marcia's knight in shining armor. Business success mattered more to her than anything he could do on a personal level to convince her their marriage deserved another shot.

Mr. Gladstone rubbed his hand through his thick gray hair. "Sunburst is an important account, one I courted personally. You haven't proven yourself with a campaign for a client half this size yet, let alone one in this much turmoil. Why should I trust you to lead the charge?"

Adrian leaned forward. Regardless of the sweat dripping down his back, he'd be damned if he'd show his uncertainty to the older man. If he couldn't convince someone he'd worked side by side with for the past six months to have faith in him, he wouldn't have a chance with the woman he hadn't seen in seven years.

"Excuse my bluntness, sir, but my career didn't start the day you hired me. I turned down a partner position with my former employer, where I successfully revamped the reputations of accounts larger than Sunburst Hotels. I can remove the tarnish from their image, and, if you look at my plan, you'll agree."

"You're a cocky bastard, aren't you?"

"Sure of myself, sir." With the business portion. He only hoped his confidence would translate to his personal life, where he needed it most. "I won't let you down."

Gladstone nodded once. "You're leading the team to San Diego, using your PR plan as a guide. If you succeed in saving Sunburst's reputation, the account is yours. If you fail, you're fired."

Failure was not an option, and it had nothing to do with Adrian's career.

؃

With her boss taking leave to be at his wife's side for the birth of their first child, Marcia's sole responsibility was to keep the company humming along on autopilot. But at the precise moment Luciana went into labor, hackers had broken through Sunburst Hotels's firewalls and stolen sensitive account information, including credit card numbers and addresses of past and present hotel guests.

By the time Blake texted, *it's a boy!* Marcia had hired the best Internet security firm in the country to patch the breach. Over the past three days, she'd hovered over the tech team, ensuring their system would never be compromised again.

Crisis over.

If only.

Instead, the real crisis had just begun. The media hit them harder than the plethora of retailers who'd been in and out of the news with the same compromised security. No one wanted to share their credit card information with a company whose trustworthy reputation had been reduced to a joke and a disgusted shake of the head. Their corporate promise of a worry-free night's sleep had become the opposite, the hotel lobbies across the country resembled ghost towns, and the marketing VP and publicity director had both quit.

"The Gladstone PR people are getting settled in the conference room," her secretary informed her.

"Thanks, Cindy." Marcia headed toward her last hope to save Sunburst Hotels. The promotion to Vice President of Operations she'd been working toward for over a year had disintegrated, as had her marriage seven years earlier when she'd made a career her first priority.

Leading her team into the conference room, she marched with her head held high, refusing to let her uncertainty show. Three people sat on one side of the table, all of them appearing to fall into the same category as the team following her—far too young and inexperienced to trust with her company's future. She needed their boss, the much older Mr. Gladstone with his familiar, thick gray hair to infuse her with the confidence she could no longer continue to fake.

But the man was nowhere to be found. The only other person in the room had dark-brown hair that curled around his ears, a trait she'd always found adorable but that did nothing to calm her growing panic. Accented by a dark suit coat, his shoulders appeared broader.

Dear God, with all the stress, she'd lost her mind. She couldn't have found a worse time to start hallucinating about her past-relationship mistakes.

Her laptop slipped from her hands and clattered onto the table.

Her husband lifted his head from his iPad, and his fathomless brown eyes met hers. "Might want to be more careful with that."

Okay, so she hadn't lost her mind. Yet. Not the least bit comforted, Marcia stared at him, the faint Hispanic lilt in his tone coiling tendrils of heat through her middle. What was he doing here? Why now?

If only she'd been more careful with her marriage. But she hadn't, and she couldn't deal with the past and couldn't change the reality. The reality of him in her conference room amidst her colleagues, though, made no sense. The only thing she knew for sure was the most handsome man she'd ever met had become more gorgeous than ever.

Meanwhile, she— *Oh shit.*

Her appearance had definitely changed, too, and not for the better.

Chapter Two

𝒫ushing back his chair, the man who haunted her dreams rose to his feet and smoothed his tie over his flat stomach. "I'm Adrian Torres, a relatively new member of Gladstone PR. However, I've been in public relations for my entire career. I have a lot of good ideas to turn your image around."

Okay, so he hadn't appeared out of nowhere to suddenly reclaim their relationship. His appearance made more sense, but damn if she didn't feel let down. Of course, Marcia had no right to be disappointed when he'd chosen the same work-over-relationship priority she had.

"You'd better," she choked out, fumbling with her laptop. Either they'd become such complete strangers Adrian thought he needed to reintroduce himself or he didn't want the others in the room to catch on that she knew him. Hell, she more than knew him. She could have written a report on the amazing experience of his cock thrusting inside her.

Not that anyone would believe he'd once found her attractive enough to cuddle with. Working late and shoveling down meals at her desk had caught up with her until her curvy figure had become undeniably fat. She'd left him to build her career, but she'd stayed away until she could return to the same physical shape as when she'd left. Unfortunately, she continued to move further from that goal, rather than closer.

Karma, the bitch, hadn't given Adrian a gut and a double chin. Nope, he'd become more fit, along with giving every appearance of being on the road to a successful career.

Instead of attempting to shake her hand, he glanced at her junior-level marketing team seating themselves around the oval. "I assume we're still waiting for a few more people before we get started?"

Since she alone represented upper management, somehow she had to push all her personal turbulence aside and match his fixation on business. "Everyone is here, except Mr. Sunburst, who is under strict instructions from his doctor not to overexert himself. He will, however, be in later today to hear our report." And Marcia needed to deliver good news if she had a hope of saving her career.

"Let's start with introductions." Adrian nodded to his team to go first while she settled into the empty seat across from him. She'd assumed, if they ever faced each other across a table, divorce lawyers would be present on both sides. So, despite the surreal experience, the situation was far better than the worst-case scenario she'd both imagined and dreaded through the years of minimal phone and mail contact with her husband.

The introductions traveled around the table until, all too soon, the collective gaze turned to her. She cleared her throat. "I'm Marcia Johnson."

Adrian arched an eyebrow.

She'd never officially taken his name after they'd married, and, despite his silent challenge, she had no intention of cluing in the employees who looked to her for guidance that they were witnessing her reunion with her estranged husband. Especially since he'd given no indication he wanted to clue them in. His unwavering composure suggested they weren't in the same room by coincidence. But surely he recognized he'd dropped into her life at the worst possible time for her to deal with a personal crisis.

"I'm the executive assistant to Blake Wellington, Sunburst's CEO," she explained, pushing down her inner turmoil. "I am acting CEO this week while he's out on family leave."

"Hell of a week to be in charge," muttered a woman from the Gladstone team who'd introduced herself as Jasmine.

"Tell me about it." Marcia shared a wry smile with the woman, grateful for the opportunity to tear her gaze from her spouse. Legalities aside, could she still claim him as hers? He could have moved on to someone who would put her relationship before her career. She balled her hands into fists under the table.

While mentally tallying the ways she came up short in comparison to any new woman in his life, she recapped the hacker damage to their computer systems and the mass exodus of the marketing department to bring the Gladstone people up to speed. "The security leak is fixed. We have the very best firewalls, encryption, and consumer protections in place so this will never happen again. We just need to convince our guests and the public they can hand over their credit cards, book a stay with us, and carry on with business as usual."

"I have a plan to make that happen," Adrian said, his voice confident and authoritative.

For the first time since the crisis had begun, someone offered assurance instead of looking to her to provide it. Tears pressed against her eyelids. She didn't have to be strong on her own anymore. Someone had her back.

"We'll start by appealing to your most loyal customers, the ones you never thought would go elsewhere, the ones who never planned to leave you," he continued.

That sounded personal. He'd meant a business context, not their past, right?

"Shouldn't we ensure they have something to return to, first?" she asked.

If he no longer loved her, having him in the same room didn't matter. And how could he love her? She no longer bore much physical resemblance to the woman who'd attracted him in college, when they had been so crazy in love they'd eloped over spring break of their junior year. Eight years later, she lived alone without so much as a pet goldfish to keep her company and only contacted her husband to discuss official things, like their tax-filing status.

"These customers are the heart of your business. If they come back, you can save the company. If they don't...." His sentence hung in the air.

She'd left him and never returned, and he'd never chased after her. After years of minimal, strictly-business contact, they had nothing left to save. Working until at least 10:00 p.m. each night, she had no friends other than her boss's family and turned to food for comfort when the loneliness became unbearable. Instead of taking Adrian's words and his presence personally, she needed to focus on the corporation and career she still had a chance to salvage.

"Are you suggesting we give our loyal customers a free night's stay?" She could do the same thing. Her pathetic, warped brain refused to give up the personal angle. When Blake and Luciana had gotten married, they'd given her a certificate for a free night with a one-night stand matchmaking service as a bridal party gift. She could call the number and ask for a night with her husband. But would he accept a freebie with her? If he did, she had to brace for the possibility her new physical shape would turn him off for good.

"A free night is a tool at our disposal, but we need something bigger for the main thrust of the campaign." He captured her gaze and leaned forward. "You need to win back their trust and prove you deserve their loyalty."

Marcia's stomach twisted until she fought the violent urge to heave. She couldn't prove she deserved him because she didn't. Maybe if she'd returned to his side within the first couple months, they could have worked out their differences, but the years hung between them, a chasm of time...and heartache. After she'd already left him once, she couldn't imagine why he'd ever trust her again. The meeting continued, but with despair overwhelming her, she couldn't process the flurry of words.

"I'm losing you," Adrian said.

Through no fault of his own. Once again, she'd proven herself unworthy.

"Everyone take a ten-minute break," he continued. "Get some water or coffee, whatever helps you focus. I expect 100 percent attention when we reconvene."

A break. She could escape and regroup without every eye in the company watching her reaction and counting on her vote of confidence.

"Marcia," he called.

Pretending not to hear, she bolted from the room. She needed every second of those ten minutes. The elevator doors opened, and she jabbed the button to the sub-level parking garage before anyone could follow her. As soon as the doors opened, she hurried toward her car, tears blurring her vision as she fumbled in her purse for her keys.

Not yet. Hold it together a minute longer.

At last, she yanked open the door and climbed inside, slamming it behind her. Finally, she was alone. All alone. Her life stretched before her as an endless, empty highway.

A sob burst from her throat. When she'd bought the one-way plane ticket to California, she'd expected her husband would follow and they would make up and pick up their relationship where they'd left off.

But he hadn't followed. And they no longer had anything left to pick up.

Chapter Three

$\mathcal{F}$or the first time since he'd found his "in" with Sunburst Hotels, Adrian's confidence wavered.

Other than the initial laptop incident, Marcia hadn't been rattled by his appearance. He'd hoped for an outburst. Anger or outrage would have been welcome, anything to show she still had feelings for him.

Pride had kept him from going after her when she'd left. But it had gradually been replaced by a choking fear she would look at him and feel nothing, that they would be strangers with nothing between them as confirmed by every phone call and mail correspondence to deal with their joint lives.

He watched the numbers at the top of the elevator plunge to the lowest level and then questioned a nearby employee, who explained the building had an underground parking garage. Determined not to repeat the mistakes of the past, he took the next elevator down and walked through two rows of cars before he found Marcia. Through the car window, she slumped over the steering wheel, shuddering with heart-wrenching sobs. Opening the door, he settled his palm on her back.

She lurched, horror mingling with the pain in her eyes—pain he'd caused. "No! Go away."

He flinched, the urge to weep alongside her welling inside him.

But he'd cried for her before, and it hadn't changed shit. For better or worse, he would not live the rest of his life in a suspended, married-but-not-married state.

"I'm sorry I shocked you with my presence." He wasn't sorry for surprising her, but he regretted how unwelcome his surprise had been.

She swiped at her eyes and began rummaging in the glove compartment. "You have my phone number. You could have warned me you were coming."

His chest tightened. "Those stiff, formal calls don't change anything, except suck away my soul. I needed to shake things up."

"So you decided to burst in during the biggest business crisis I've ever faced?" She extracted a pack of tissues from the compartment and mopped her beautiful face. "I hope you have a better strategy to save my company, or we're doomed."

With the pressure to convince her to believe in him more intense than during his meeting with Mr. Gladstone, he crouched next to her seat. "While we work together to fix Sunburst's crisis, we have a chance to bridge the distance between us, too."

Mouth gaping, she met his gaze again. "Your idea of bridging the distance is to ambush me in my own conference room and then introduce yourself like we're freaking strangers?"

Failure tasted metallic and bitter in his mouth. In his plans, he'd skipped straight to wowing her with his marketing prowess. He hadn't considered he'd upset her so much she wouldn't stick around to listen to his spiel. "No, I played my ace card. You put your trust in Gladstone PR. I made myself the face of Gladstone so we'd have enough common business interests that you wouldn't immediately kick me out of your personal life."

Marcia squeezed the steering wheel until her knuckles turned white. "I don't have time to think about anything personal right now, and I certainly can't let my employees see me as an emotional wreck. They're counting on me to lead them with a solid plan."

Business and her career didn't just come first in her heart. They owned her whole heart. Adrian had been a fool to lose sight of that. Burying his own hurt and frustration, he said, "I have a beautiful plan for the company. We'll put it in action together." Afterward, he'd have to decide if he could handle coming in a distant second place with her for the rest of his life. "Trust me."

She stared at the steering wheel for a long time before turning to him. "I have to. You're my only hope."

He'd take her acceptance, however grudging. Despite the awkwardness of her sitting in the car and him kneeling outside, he wrapped his arms around her, pulling her warm body against his chest for the first time in far too many years. Oh, how he'd missed the closeness and sweetness of holding her. "Have dinner with me tonight, so I can tell you all the things I'm still holding out hope for."

With a gentle but firm nudge, she forced him to release her, the calm, professional façade once again encasing the woman he'd vowed to love and cherish forever. "We are having dinner together. In a conference room. With a half-dozen people from both our companies who are looking to us for guidance."

He stood and backed away. At least she'd stopped screaming at him to get out of her sight, as she had when he'd first opened the car door. In fact, they'd scraped the surface of a serious conversation.

"Your ten-minute break is over. I'll meet you upstairs." She emerged from the car. Heels clicking on the concrete floor, she marched toward the building, never glancing back.

Her raw emotions, though, proved she still felt something for him. And he'd circled his arms around her, however briefly. The day had been his biggest breakthrough in seven years. Best of all, it wasn't even half over.

 C&

Marcia repaired her makeup with careful precision, thankful she'd splurged for the very best concealer. She couldn't reverse Adrian seeing her in a moment of weakness, but she could ensure no one else in the meeting room guessed she'd been sobbing her heart out.

Smoothing the flyaways escaping from the sleek bun at her nape, she studied her reflection in the mirror. Assured she'd fixed every imperfection that could be concealed, she took a deep breath and strode from the restroom to the elevator.

Entering alongside a couple of anxious employees from accounting, she plastered on a confident expression. After they exited, she kept the mask in place as she continued to the executive level and headed for the conference room, prepared for another face-to-face encounter with her husband.

As she stepped into the room, Adrian lifted his head and acknowledged her with the kind of nod that symbolized respect rather than threatened to spill the details of her humiliating crying jag.

Needing to establish her leadership position, she made eye contact with each person at the table before sitting down. "Is everyone ready to resume the meeting?"

"I'm eager to pick up where we left off," Adrian said, holding her gaze.

They'd dated for a mere six months before they'd married. Then they'd spent their first year of married life having sex, studying for senior exams, having really hot sex, writing term papers, having more sex, interviewing for jobs, arguing, and no longer having sex. They'd self-destructed, with nothing left to pick up where they'd left off.

"The theme for the rest of today is rediscovering the magic," he continued.

Rediscovering every inch of his magic would be her greatest pleasure. First, she'd straddle him in his chair and bump her hips with his in a lap dance that would drive him wild. Then she'd demand he take her across the table, and he'd drive into her until she screamed…or until the table collapsed under her weight.

Shit. His body might still be magical, but hers sure as hell wasn't.

"Your customers started coming to Sunburst for a variety of reasons," Adrian said, his tone all business but with the ever-present Spanish accent that warmed her insides and dampened her panties. "The ones who returned did so because they fell in love with your hotel."

Right. They were talking about the company crisis, not their marriage and definitely not the magic they used to make between the sheets. Or in the shower. Or on every inch of counter space.

She squirmed in her chair, but nothing eased the need spreading through her core.

"We've damaged the bond and tested their love, so they don't feel comfortable coming back on their own."

He was right. Once she'd left him, she'd been too afraid to return, afraid she wouldn't be welcome, that he wouldn't love her anymore.

"The bond, however, is only damaged, not severed. We need to entice them to rediscover the magic now before an irreparable break occurs."

The sound of his voice could entice her to do anything and follow him anywhere.

"We need to brainstorm some fun ways to hook our customers into returning to us, and we need to craft an apology. I propose we split into two groups. I'd like to see what kind of ideas everyone comes up with without Marcia and me influencing your direction. So, while you all do that, she and I will go to a different room to work on a soul-baring apology for our mistakes. Sound good?"

Her breath caught. Were they going to address the company gaffes or really bare their souls and wade into their personal mistakes? So far, she'd failed at keeping her focus on the former.

"Yes, we need to apologize to our customers and the public before we can move on. We can set up a press conference for later this afternoon." Finally, she sounded like the professional everyone expected her to be.

"Perfect," Adrian said. "Lead the way to where you'd like to work."

The outward focus might be in the right place, but her energy and lusty thoughts were consumed by the man and the things she could do alone with him. Her big wooden desk *would* hold their weight.

Heart pounding, she led him down the hall. As she held open the door, he glanced from the name plate to her. "Your office, huh?"

"Yep. Some things need a little extra privacy."

"Indeed they do." He winked and brushed her chest as he sauntered inside.

The arousal blooming in her shriveled. How could he not notice how big she'd gotten when she interfered with his ability to walk through a doorway?

Chapter Four

$\mathcal{M}$arcia slapped the door shut with more force than necessary. Better to keep everything professional and avoid making a fool of herself. But neither of them would be able to concentrate on business if they didn't clear the air first.

"Let's get the personal apologies out of the way, since we both know I've owed you one for years." When he opened his mouth, she held up her hand, needing to say her piece so she could move on. "After we got married, every time I talked to my mother, she harped about how she didn't want me to waste my college education to follow you to your job and support your career."

"I remember." Cold bitterness infiltrated his tone. "According to your father, all the money he spent on your education should have gotten you a lot better husband than a lousy Hispanic whose family sent money to 'those drug lords across the border' every month."

Hearing Adrian say the words in her father's typical arrogant tone, Marcia cringed. Not only would he have said such a thing to Adrian's face, he'd believed it, too. "I can't even begin to apologize for his bigotry."

"Don't apologize for him. You're not responsible for his actions."

But begging forgiveness for her father's bad behavior was easier than admitting her own. She paced around the desk. "I swore to my mother I'd have a career of my own and wouldn't sacrifice my dreams for yours."

"Congratulations. You kept your promise."

To her mother. But Marcia had made promises to Adrian, too.

"You have a damned good career here," he said, brushing his fingers over her desktop.

"I did until this week," she corrected. "My determination to prove to my parents that marrying you didn't ruin my chances of a good career led me to interview and take a job on the West Coast without consulting you."

"Because even talking about it with me would have ruined your career?" Sarcasm edged into his tone as he stalked behind the desk.

"Because you might have talked me out of it and then they would have been right." She sighed. "At that point in my life, nothing seemed worse than hearing my parents say 'I told you so.'"

What she wouldn't give for a do-over, but she couldn't alter her choices, only the future. And she'd already sacrificed her future with Adrian for her career. Marcia sank onto the desk chair. "Let's work on this company apology and see if we can save my job. Although, for the record, my career wasn't worth it."

He whirled the chair until she faced him. Bracing his palms on the armrests, he loomed over her. "What do you mean?"

Staring into his eyes, she wished she could lose herself in the deep-brown depths the way she often had when their relationship had been a blissful fairy tale. But she had apologies to make, first the personal and then the professional one. She didn't have time to get lost in fairy tales and wishes.

"Throwing away our marriage, turning my back on our relationship, and blowing off our partnership wasn't worth whatever success I've achieved. I'm sorry. I screwed up. I was wrong."

She attempted to spin away, but Adrian held her in place, bending toward her as though he might kiss her. After three long heartbeats, he released her without a word.

She would never be forgiven and didn't deserve to be. Forcing herself to move on to the business at hand, she opened a blank document on her laptop and typed, *I'm sorry. I screwed up.*

"Change 'I' to 'we,'" he said over her shoulder.

Her fingers trembled on the keys. His correction focused on the preferred pronouns for a corporate statement, rather than admit he'd contributed to their relationship missteps. After all, he'd argued they should hash out their post-graduation plans together, and she'd pushed him away.

While he pulled another chair next to hers, she typed a couple lines about the company's security problem and the technical repair.

"But we know we can't just fix the tangible problem. We have to address the ways we've failed and thereby hurt you," Adrian dictated.

As his pathetic excuse for a wife, she'd failed and hurt him. "We broke your trust, and we have to earn it back. We don't expect that to be easy, but we'll—"

Throat too clogged, she couldn't speak the word *try* as she typed it. No bonds remained in their marriage for them to try to repair. The apology could serve both a personal and professional purpose, but the reparations only had a chance on the professional side.

Adrian placed his palm on her cheek, rotating her head toward his. "We *can* try. Look at us. We're in the same room, wanting the same thing."

Chest aching and electricity zipping through her, she couldn't look away. "How could you possibly know what I want when I don't even know?"

Leaning closer, he brushed his lips across hers. "You want this."

Yes. *Dear God, yes.*

He caressed her mouth again, lingering.

She closed her eyes, savoring his warmth and gentle strength.

"You want more. I know because I want it, too." Using both hands to frame her cheeks, he pressed his lips to hers, his tongue probing for entry.

She'd never been able to resist his seduction. Oh, how she'd missed the way passion sizzled through her veins and filled her core. Tears leaked down her cheeks.

Breaking contact with her mouth, he kept his palms on her jaw, smearing her tears across her cheeks with his fingertips. "What did I do to make you cry?"

She shook her head and gulped in deep breaths, refusing to think about enduring the rest of her life without his embrace. "I'm just a giant waterfall today." Wrenching free, she plunked a tissue from a nearby box. So much for her expensive concealer.

"Most gorgeous waterfall I've ever met."

She couldn't accept his compliments and indulge in sexy banter, not without falling for him all over again. "We're supposed to be working. I don't flirt and kiss in my office."

"Do you do those things somewhere else? Say the word, and I'll go there with you."

She didn't make out anywhere with anyone, not because of a personal policy, but because she'd never had eyes for anyone but him. If only she could take him up on his suggestion. They could sink into each other and pretend they were still young and head-over-heels in love.

But unlike when they'd blown off class because they couldn't take their hands off each other long enough to get dressed, the moment he touched her curves, neither of them would be able to pretend nothing had changed between them.

Refocusing on the company apology on her computer screen, she added, "We recognize all the gimmicks in the world won't bring you back unless we can establish a bond of trust, one stronger than the bond we broke."

"For the record, I don't consider kissing to be a gimmick," Adrian said.

Staring at the screen, Marcia willed her eyes not to blur. If she turned to him, she'd mold her mouth to his and let the taste of him send her to blissful oblivion, gimmick or not. "I'm the one who's supposed to apologize, not you."

"You don't think I'm as much to blame?"

She shook her head. The responsibility lay with her. She'd left him, and she didn't deserve forgiveness, let alone a chance to fix what she'd ruined.

"Instead of trying to find a job in the same area as you, I interviewed for jobs on the opposite side of the country," he said. "Call me stubborn, defensive, hurt, just plain stupid, whatever. I was all those things when I decided we could both play the 'I refuse to compromise my career' game."

Instead of angering her, Adrian's admission filled her with relief. The entire blame in their relationship no longer rested on her shoulders.

He tipped her face toward him. "You can't use any of that in your Sunburst statement, so take your hands off the keyboard and look at me. We both made mistakes. We both have to apologize."

And then what? They'd thrown away something so rare and precious because they'd been too shortsighted to see what a gift they had in each other, and they couldn't simply retrieve it. "Can we move on together from this apology, or have we just tied up the loose ends so now we have nothing left between us?"

"That's up to us." His regretful yet sensuous smile caressed her from the inside out. "What do you think?"

Her heart lightened, and she returned his smile. "I want to try your kissing gimmick again."

Unable to get enough of her smooth skin, Adrian stroked his wife's cheeks, her chin, and even her temples. When he embraced her like she'd asked, she melted against him. Oh yes, he could make out with her forever. Being so stubborn and letting her get away had cost them both too much.

He traced his tongue over her lips, rejoicing as she parted for him. She'd never played games or withheld her affection and passion. Circling the back of her neck, he pulled her closer, thrusting his tongue into her mouth and wallowing in her warmth and sweetness.

She squeezed his shoulders, his bulky suit coat and starched shirt preventing her nails from biting into his skin. He longed to shed his clothing and absorb the pain. Then, after she'd scored him, he craved her tender exploration down his chest.

Dragging his fingers through her hair, Adrian popped out the pins holding her fancy 'do in place, allowing the auburn tresses to fall in silky waves over his hands. What he wouldn't give for her hair to sweep across his bare chest while she kissed her way down to his aching groin.

The intercom on the desk buzzed.

She leaped away from him, her expression shocked and horrified.

"Mr. Sunburst is here," a woman's voice announced.

Guilt added to the horror on Marcia's face. Hands shaking, she gathered her hair at her nape, the action pulling her blouse tight against her lush chest.

Damn, if everything didn't tighten inside him, too. He held out a bobby pin to her. "Can I help?"

Snatching the pin, she gestured toward his tented pants. "For God's sake, get rid of that before the company owner walks in here."

Chapter Five

"While I'm watching you all mussed and knowing I'm the cause? Not likely," Adrian said. He'd never tried to hide his desire for her and didn't intend to start.

"What have you done to me? We're supposed to be working." Her cheeks flushed a deep red. "I have never been this unprofessional before."

"Never?" Satisfaction rolled through him. "Let me wipe away your lipstick smudge." She paused, which he took for agreement. Slowly, he slid his thumb over the errant stain. Too bad it hadn't smeared all over her face so he would have had an excuse to keep caressing her. Reluctantly, he pulled his hand back. "Do I have a matching smudge?"

With round blue eyes, she scrutinized his skin and then scraped her nail against the corner of his mouth. Once again, white-hot lust shot through him.

"Should I send Mr. Sunburst in?" the woman on the intercom asked again.

"The evidence is gone," Marcia whispered, her gaze locked on his lips.

"Doesn't mean you have to stop touching me. Rake those nails down my chest and across my back." Adrian couldn't wait another minute to take her. If they both got fired, they could start over together. He'd use the chance to make the right choices in their relationship instead of letting their stubbornness and insecurities guide them.

Although her eyes dilated, she shook her head. "Stop. We're adults with serious responsibilities." She depressed the speaker button. "Send him in, Cindy."

To cool his desire, Adrian mentally recited his public relations plan for the company. By the time Mr. Sunburst entered the room, he managed to stand and shake the man's hand without embarrassing himself.

The three of them prepared the final draft of the company statement, fine-tuning the exact wording of the speech as well as the parts Mr. Sunburst would speak and where Marcia would take over.

"Blake should be taking the heat next to me, instead of you," Mr. Sunburst said to her. "Let's see if he can drop in for a half hour. After he and I issue the apology, you can step forward with the positive promotions your PR people have come up with."

"Not having a stronger tech security system wasn't any more Blake's fault than anyone else's in this company," she said. Not only did she not balk at the idea of standing in front of a half-dozen television cameras and apologizing to the world, she embraced the difficult task, proving to Adrian how strong and capable she'd become in their years apart.

"I've texted Blake," she continued. "He's willing to drop by at some point, but not this afternoon. His wife and son are being discharged from the hospital, and he's focused on settling them in at home."

"We can't put off the press conference any longer. The apology needs to come today," Adrian said. The ease with which she spoke of her boss's plans pointed to a familiarity beyond the office. But the way she spoke of the man's devotion to his wife and baby didn't hint of jealousy, so he couldn't muster any resentment.

"I agree," Marcia said. "Let's give the speech a dry run before the press gets here." She printed copies for everyone and led them from the office.

Following the sway of her seductive hips, Adrian would have

gone wherever she led him. Unfortunately, she adhered to the business plan and stopped in the spacious downstairs meeting room where they'd speak to the media.

For the next hour they practiced everything from posture, to tone inflection, to eye contact. Adrian had no trouble critiquing Mr. Sunburst's delivery, but he lost all objectivity the moment Marcia made eye contact with him. The apology turned personal, and he couldn't separate the present situation from their past.

No matter how many times they confessed their regret over their mistakes, they couldn't change the decisions that had led to their separation. Instead of going after her when she'd taken the job in California, he'd chosen to wait for her to realize she needed him and return to him. But she hadn't needed him.

His strategy to come to her during a company crisis had been based on the belief she would finally need him. But he'd been wrong. Despite his grand publicity plans, he hadn't done anything she wouldn't have been able to do without him.

After the reporters and video crews filled the room, Marcia stepped in front of the microphone and looked into each camera lens. Her poise and professionalism didn't waver as she delivered her rehearsed segment. Once the company got through the crisis, she would have a bright, successful career, with or without his help.

Waiting for the perfect moment to reunite with his wife had backfired. Adrian had nothing more to offer to convince her they should be together. As an innocent college transfer student, she'd relied on him to show her around campus, to help her meet new friends, and to tutor her in lovemaking.

But in the past seven years, she'd found her own way in life. Without him.

Each question from the reporters required Marcia to repeat her contrition and her vow to do whatever necessary to win her customers back. Needing moral support so she didn't reveal her growing frustration with the repetition, she glanced at Adrian.

How soon would she grow frustrated trying to fix their relationship? Even if she did everything right, she had no guarantee she could win him back. And if she did, she owed him years of apologies. After a while, she'd resent begging for forgiveness.

At last, the session concluded and the media packed up and left. After Mr. Sunburst also departed, she and Adrian headed to the elevator to meet up with the brainstorming team in the conference room.

Pushing the button for their floor, she leaned against the wall. "How many more times do I have to say I'm sorry?"

"We'll send emails to the entire Sunburst mailing list and follow those up with snail mail letters, echoing what we said in the press conference. Then the apology portion is over," he said. "From here on out, we'll focus on the future, specifically on what we're doing right and what we're doing to win customers over."

"Is anything going right?"

Adrian's lips curled in a sexy smile. "We're alone in a confined space. I say a lot is going right." He advanced toward her and rested his forearms on the wall on either side of her face. "Let's test all the good things we have in our favor."

As he slanted toward her, she let her eyes drift closed. She needed to lose herself in his kiss, to believe she could count him as a good thing in her life.

The ride stopped, and the doors opened. Someone cleared his throat. "Should I take the stairs?"

"Yes," Adrian said.

"No." Opening her eyes, she nudged him away before he could push the button to close the door in the face of the pizza delivery man. "The elevator's all yours. Thank you for delivering food for my team."

Exiting, she pulled a few bills from her purse and pressed the tip into the man's palm. Up ahead in the conference room, a chaotic scene of ravenous twenty-somethings grabbed pizza slices and cans of soda.

"They won't notice if we duck into your office and finish that kiss," Adrian pointed out.

Yes. Every nerve in her body leaped in agreement. But to truly finish what they'd started, they'd have to explore each other's bodies and make love. Maybe if she'd lost even half the excess weight, she would have had the confidence to let him put his hands on her skin. But no way could she risk the chance of turning him off.

The vibration of her phone provided the perfect distraction in the form of a text. By staying focused on business, she'd be judged on her merits and competence, not on her figure.

"Anything important?" Adrian asked, his lips too close to her ear to be business appropriate.

"Blake gives us a thumbs-up. He watched the press conference on TV and thought we handled ourselves well."

"You did," Adrian affirmed.

"I had a good coach." She tucked the phone away, steeling herself against the lure of his handsome face so close to hers and the heat of his body radiating against her arm.

"Your parents will be so proud when they see you on the news," he said. "Did you let them know?"

She shook her head, all warmth deserting her. "I doubt they'll notice. We're not very close."

His mouth dropped open. "What do you mean? I thought they'd follow every second of your career."

Of course, he expected unconditional support like his parents offered. But her family situation was decidedly more complicated. "We haven't spoken much since I moved to California."

"You left me to get their approval, but then you stopped speaking to them? So, you have no one in your life?" He cupped her shoulder.

"Not no one." She shrugged away and strode into the conference room before he could hug her. She didn't need his sympathy for her less-than-perfect choices. The sooner they were surrounded with witnesses, the more likely they'd keep their hands to themselves and resist temptation...and heartache.

"Blake and Luciana more or less adopted me into their family," she explained, as he followed her to the food table. "Luciana's brother, Alex, treats me like a kid sister, and Blake's sister-in-law, Sabrina, enlists me to take her shopping whenever she needs something red-carpet worthy."

Jasmine, one of the junior Gladstone members, dropped her pizza

227

slice, cheese side down, on the table and swung toward her. "Did you just say red carpet, as in Hollywood red carpet?"

"Yeah." At first Marcia had been a bit star-struck, too, but she'd known Sabrina when the other woman had been a poor inner-city teacher, and money and fame hadn't changed her. "Blake's brother is Rob Wellington, so Rob and Sabrina have to show up for his movie premieres."

"OMG. You're friends with the most famous movie director on the planet?"

"I'm mostly friends with his wife," Marcia murmured, wishing she'd taken more care not to let her private conversation with Adrian be overheard.

"OMG," Jasmine repeated. "I have the most awesome idea. Can you convince Rob Wellington to be caught on camera checking into the hotel and handing over his credit card at the front desk?"

"I don't think so." Rob hated being exploited, and Sabrina hated when someone used Rob for his power and connections. Marcia's stomach churned at the thought of abusing their friendship.

"If they'd do it, the publicity would be great and would go a long way toward reassuring our customers," Adrian agreed, nodding his approval to Jasmine.

"I'll ask Sabrina," Marcia said, longing for his nod of approval to tip in her direction. Despite not relying on anyone else and making her life as independent as possible, she'd needed him to travel across the country to bail her out. She'd messed up every major relationship in her life and couldn't afford to lose Sabrina's friendship, too. "If she declines, then we give the Wellingtons their privacy. We won't ask anything else from them and definitely won't advertise their presence if they prefer privacy when they stay in one of our hotels."

"Of course. This is going to be so amazing." Ignoring her overturned pizza slice, Jasmine ran to her computer and began typing. Others gathered around her, offering suggestions of how to best utilize Rob's star power.

Marcia rubbed her forehead. One more aspect of her life had spiraled out of control. The possibility of losing her best friend made her turn to Adrian, once again seeking help. "I mean it. If Rob and

Sabrina don't want to be dragged into our mess, then that's the end of the discussion. Period."

He wrapped his arm around her shoulders and hugged her to his side. "Don't worry. You and I have the final say, and we're a team. I won't do anything you don't agree with. Where's the spinach, tomato and pineapple pizza you love?"

Focusing on the spread of food in front of them, she took a thin slice of veggie pizza. "I can't find anyone willing to eat it with me."

"Order it, and I will."

Trying to keep her hope in check, she filled the rest of her plate with salad, maneuvering the tongs to evade the jalapeños.

"Still avoiding spicy foods, I see," he teased.

"I'm a certified wimp," she agreed. "Does your mother still cook authentic Mexican dinners whenever you come home?"

"Of course. And I still get the same lectures that I'm not eating right."

She glanced at his fit torso. He certainly looked like he'd been making healthy food selections. If his mother had issues with his choices, she'd be appalled at Marcia's staple of microwave meals and quick takeout scarfed over reports and while catching up on e-mail.

"Mom's given up trying to teach me to cook. Her goal now is to stuff me enough to last a month every time I visit."

"And you still see her once a month?"

"At least." He smiled, and another pang hit her. If they'd stayed together, she would have drifted apart from her parents regardless, but his would have embraced and welcomed her.

Marcia carried her plate to the opposite end of the table from the junior marketing execs making plans to capitalize on her Hollywood connection. Adrian followed her.

"Any new skills you've learned in the past seven years?" she asked, enjoying the easy conversation more than she wanted to admit.

Setting his plate next to hers, he brushed her shoulder as he sat. How she'd missed the casual, familiar contact. "I can knot my own neckties. As a bonus, I can do it with my eyes closed, allowing me a thirty-second nap."

"Nice. I hope you put that on your résumé. More people need that talent so they're refreshed and stay awake during meetings. Unfortunately, my skills haven't progressed. I still can't drive a stick shift."

His brown eyes twinkled. "If it's any consolation, the whiplash I suffered after I tried to teach you has healed."

She laughed.

"But I never got over my need to kiss you," he continued.

Chapter Six

"Shh." Her laughter died, and her cheeks warmed. A glance at their colleagues confirmed they hadn't figured out Marcia's personal connection to Adrian. Although she wanted him, she wasn't ready to share their private moments.

With the others focused on the possibilities of rubbing elbows with a movie star, she had far more interesting topics to explore. "Tell me about your life now, like I'm a stranger. What don't I know about Adrian Torres?"

He twisted open a water bottle. "I've cut soda from my diet, and I steer clear of alcohol. After too many nights drowning my sorrows, I had a lightbulb moment that I needed to find a better habit while I still could."

She'd expected silly little tidbits, not a dark confession, and certainly not the bombshell that she'd nearly turned him into an alcoholic. "Thank goodness you were too strong to be broken by your selfish wife's actions."

"Strength of spirit had nothing to do with it. I knew I'd lose any shot I had at you taking me back if I became a drunk."

Her skin warmed again, and her heart swelled with hope. At one point, he'd wanted her to come back badly enough to turn his life around for her.

"So, after that, I funneled the money I used to spend at the bar into a gym membership."

"I've thought about joining a gym for the past few years." The admission felt more shameful than admitting a drinking problem. "Thinking about it is as far as I've gotten." If only she'd spent three years sweating on the treadmill, she'd have a body she couldn't wait for Adrian to explore with his eyes and hands and mouth.

"I had to make a commitment and a lifestyle change. I get up at five every morning to work out."

"Wow." She tried to wrap her mind around the insanely early routine. "When we were together, I don't think we ever crawled out of bed before eight." Neither of them had had any ambition to move away from the other's naked flesh.

"Nothing to stay under the covers for anymore," he said with a shrug. "I'm open to renegotiating my mornings if you're part of my nights."

She met his gaze and then glanced away. How long could she hold herself in check before she dove at him? Would anyone notice if she crawled under the table, unzipped his pants, and took him in her mouth? Yes. Unfortunately.

"We're not discussing sex lives." Marcia stabbed at the lettuce on her plate.

"Good, because I have nothing to share and don't want to hear about yours."

"Good, because my vibrator collection is none of your business."

He choked on his water.

Shit.

She hadn't really admitted her only action came from toys, had she? Yes, she had. Needing a safe topic, fast, she asked, "I assume you own a gorgeous house?"

"Actually, I rent a bland, modest townhouse."

She blinked. Adrian had planned to buy a house as soon as they landed their first jobs. Home ownership had been one of his top priorities. "I always pictured you in a place of your own. I rent, too, also something bland, a studio apartment with an empty fridge to be exact."

"Hmm, I have milk in my fridge, but I think it expired a couple weeks ago. Try to guess what I drive." His lips curved in a hint of a smile so sexy it should have been illegal.

"A beige sedan with the highest consumer safety rating." *Without a doubt.*

"Please." He shot her a pained look. "How bland do you think I am? I have a motorcycle."

"A motorcycle? You? Mr. Conservative?" She couldn't picture it.

"I also joined a skydiving club a couple years ago, and I've started taking lessons to get my pilot's license." He grinned as if he found his own words funny. "Those two don't go together. I don't plan to jump out of the same plane I'm flying."

Marcia stared at him. The cautious business student who'd longed for a traditional, lazy suburban family life owned the most vulnerable vehicle on the road, jumped out of perfectly good airplanes, and dragged his sculpted ass to the gym every morning. She might be legally married to him, but the man sitting next to her was *not* her husband.

"What do you do for fun?" he asked.

Nothing she could spin as even marginally interesting. "I...uh—I work."

"What do you do when you're not working?"

Collapse on her bed, sometimes before she had a chance to change out of her business suit. Maybe pull out one of those vibrators and see if the batteries still had any juice. "I don't go to the gym. You saw my safe, boring car. I don't have any hobbies. I've been so focused on an upcoming job promotion I haven't thought about anything else."

"You don't have a life outside of this office?"

"No, and I don't plan to get one." Marcia stood and dumped her plate in the trash. Of course, she'd disappointed him. She'd walked out on their marriage. Dreaming they could pick up where they'd left off would only lead to more heartache.

ଙ

"Marcia, I'm so glad to hear from you. How are you holding up?"

Sabrina asked.

"I'm surviving. I'm still at the office right now." While the others polished off the pizza, she paced to the window overlooking the city.

"I expected nothing less," Sabrina teased.

"Yeah, well, this time I'm not working alone. My PR group is bouncing around ideas to improve Sunburst's image, and their favorite plan involves channeling some star power. I know how you feel about people using Rob, so you can say no and it won't change anything between us. But I'd like to run our idea by you."

Her friend agreed to hear it, so she explained. The expectations of the room weighed on her, but, even more, she longed for a deep relationship like Sabrina's where she knew someone so well she could speak on his behalf.

"We're coming into town to see Blake and Luciana's new baby tomorrow, and of course we're planning to stay at Sunburst," the other woman said. "I don't see why we can't do a staged check-in. I'd rather have our entrance officially recorded than snapped by some sleazeball jumping out of a ficus tree."

"No sleazeballs in ficus trees. I can accommodate that request." Marcia gave the marketing group a thumbs up. Adrian's approving nod squeezed her heart.

"The only thing I can't commit on is timing," Sabrina warned. "Rob's trying to wrap up a shoot before we leave, and it's not going as well as he'd hoped."

"We'll work around your schedule. Whatever time you arrive, we'll be ready. Thank you."

"Marcia, are you sure everything's okay? I listened to that apology on TV, and it sounded way too personal for just a business screwup."

She glanced at Adrian again, and the squeeze around her heart turned to pain. "Just business. You know how committed I am to my job."

"I forgot you're not alone. On our next shopping trip, I expect full details."

"Deal." Trying not to think about how those details would be revealed as she cried on her friend's shoulder, Marcia exchanged good-byes and then turned to the PR group. Excitement kicked everyone into overdrive, and they spent the next few hours solidifying plans for Sunburst's revival.

When the meeting finally adjourned, the junior employees discussed heading to a local nightclub for dancing then disappeared into the elevator.

"Did we ever have that much energy?" she asked Adrian.

"For a nightclub? No. In our bedroom?" His gaze smoldered. "We had more."

Her core ached, and she sucked in a breath. She circled the table and brushed her knuckles over the back of his neck. "I miss it."

"So, what are you going to do about it?"

Good question. She didn't have anything to offer him, except the stability of her career, which she could no longer count on. He'd been appalled at her dismal personal life. "What can I do?"

He jumped to his feet, backing her against the wall. "Tell me to take you on the table right now."

She swallowed, the harsh wildness in his gaze exciting and unsettling her. "Not the table." Not with how it wobbled as everyone had leaned on it to get closer to Jasmine's computer. She needed a sturdy surface in an unlit room.

"You're right. We don't need the table." He pressed a knee between her thighs, wedging them apart.

"The custodial team could walk in on us." She grasped his hands before he could discover how much larger and less perky her boobs had become beneath her support bra.

Confusion filled his face, and he pulled his hands free. "Are you making up excuses because you don't want me? Does the idea of me sliding my finger along your slit leave you cold?"

Oh my God. She bit her lip to keep from whimpering, aching for him to follow his words with actions. If he touched her, he'd discover her heat and wetness, but first he'd glide his palm over her soft, protruding stomach. Then he'd have to squeeze between her thighs as they rubbed together. She couldn't bear to watch disgust replace desire in his gaze.

Pacing back, he ran a hand through his hair. "What a mess, huh?

We live on opposite coasts, have different interests, and have grown so far apart I can't even turn you on anymore. I guess we don't have any hope of saving our marriage."

How could he think he didn't turn her on? Marcia teetered on the verge of coming just thinking about him stroking her. "You really don't see any hope?"

"I think we'd be deluding ourselves to imagine any other scenario."

She sagged against the wall. "Then why did you come to me?"

He sighed, defeat etched across his face. "I had delusions that if you needed me, we could have a happily-ever-after reconciliation, but I was living in fantasyland."

Still desperate to remain in the fantasy he was shattering with every word, she forced her legs to hold her upright. "Does this mean you want a divorce?"

Expression unreadable, Adrian stared at her in silence.

Say no, please say no. If her voice would have cooperated, she would have begged him with more than just her eyes. But after throwing the word divorce between them, she couldn't speak anything else.

"We can't keep going like we have been," he said, his voice barely above a whisper. "And if our relationship is over, then, yeah, a divorce is the next logical step." He turned away and picked up his tablet and briefcase.

He wanted a divorce. Because it was a logical move. After not seeing him for seven years, she should have been prepared, but she wasn't.

Her legs unable to support her, she sank to the floor. "You go ahead and file or do whatever needs to be done."

"Yeah, I'll—" His voice cracked, and he walked out of the room, taking all her hopes and dreams with him, just as she'd done to him seven years before.

Chapter Seven

"Ms. Johnson, are you okay? What happened? Are you hurt? Ill?" The night custodian rushed to her side.

Marcia had no idea how long she'd sat on the floor, too shattered to cry. All the hope she'd carried through the limbo of their years apart had disintegrated in a single moment. Adrian wanted a divorce.

"I was just resting, Anna. I'm fine." What a lie. She'd never felt less *fine*.

"You must go home. Sleep," the woman prodded, concern lining her weathered face.

"You're right." Marcia stumbled to her feet, wincing at the stiffness in her legs. How long had she sat in a miserable stupor? "I do need a good night's sleep. I'm sorry about the mess of pizza boxes. I meant to clear them out earlier."

"No worries. I'll take care of everything. Let me call the night guard to escort you home."

"I'm fine. Really. Thanks for checking on me." She gathered her belongings, trying not to give away her shaky, fragile state.

Instead of an escort from the night guard, she wanted Adrian to drive her home. The moment they'd enter her apartment, she'd wrap her arms and legs around him and kiss him until he forgot all about the ugly D word, until he didn't notice the weight she'd gained, until he only cared about thrusting inside her again and again.

But he wasn't waiting next to her car. Instead, she waved to security and left the parking garage alone, driving through the empty streets to her apartment. Not a soul peeked through the curtains in the other units as she shuffled to her door and let herself in.

Leaning against the door to close it, she let her purse and work bag slide from her shoulders. Her husband had traveled across the country to see her. He'd even kissed her like she was special and precious and he'd missed her. And then, he'd ended it.

They hadn't attempted to discover if they still had the magic that had made them inseparable the first time around. She hadn't grabbed hold of the second chance to explore his body or lose herself in his treasured embrace. She would never be loved by him again.

God damn it.

She kicked her shoe loose, hurtling the low-heeled pump across the room. It hit a tray with a precarious stack of papers on the counter. The tray wobbled, and bills and notices slithered in slow motion to the floor. With a yank, she freed her second pump, intent on throwing it, too.

But when she drew back her arm, the anger drained out of her, and she lowered her hand to her side. She hadn't blown her chance in the past few hours. She'd blown it when she'd walked away from Adrian all those years ago.

If only she could have a chance to hold him and make love to him one more time. Instead of all the what-ifs and what-could-have-beens that would haunt her forever, she'd treasure him and store up memories to cling to.

Trudging across the room, Marcia sighed at the mess of papers on the floor. They'd have to wait. She had no energy for anything but regrets tonight.

As she picked up the errant footwear, a paper came with it, the heel stabbed through her certificate for Madame Eve's 1Night Stand service. She ran her fingertip over the gold-embossed lettering. What a ridiculous gift. Why would she ever cash it in when she had no interest in a one-night stand with anyone except her husband?

Her heart stuttered. Could Madame Eve deliver what she desired most?

She had nothing to lose by asking.

ⓒⓈ

Adrian tossed and turned, unable to get comfortable on the hotel bed. But he couldn't blame the bed for his problems. Why the hell had he told Marcia he wanted a divorce?

He'd wanted to make love to her in the conference room against the wall, on the table, at her apartment—pretty much on every available surface. Hell, he wouldn't have let the lack of a surface stop him. He ached for her so damned much, he might never sleep again.

But she no longer wanted him. The way she recoiled from his touch chilled his heart. Even in the days and weeks before she left him, she'd never led him to believe his touch repulsed her.

Giving up on sleep, he headed to the fitness center. Although he pushed his muscles and stamina until he could barely stand, the workout didn't numb the pain slicing through his heart. Somehow, he had to work alongside his wife while the clock ticked on the moments they had left together.

With his career the only thing going for him, he needed to deliver on his promise to Mr. Gladstone. As soon as Adrian returned home, he'd request to be transferred off the Sunburst account. If Gladstone refused, he'd find a new job, maybe open his own PR company. Or, hell, maybe he'd chuck it all and become a skydiving instructor.

After showering and ordering room service, he checked his phone, scrolling through the monotony of messages. His finger paused over one from *1Night Stand service* that must have snuck through his spam filter. If random hookups were the only thing he had to look forward to, his future would be bleaker than he'd ever imagined. No longer having a marriage to hold out hope for, he clicked for a preview of the kind of sleazy offers he could expect.

Dear Adrian,

I have an unusual solicitation I hope you will consider. Your wife, Marcia, has contacted me requesting a one-night stand with you. If you are interested, arrangements will be made to have the encounter take place within the next twenty-four hours. I will send more details later in the day.

Madame Eve

Yes, Marcia had sent an unusual request. No, Adrian didn't have to think twice. He wanted his wife.

Why, though, had she looked up a service to get him to sleep with her? He'd chased after her all day, all but begging for sex. She'd treated him to flashes of desire, but in the end, she'd coldly rejected his advances. To turn to a hookup service after they'd decided to officially go their separate ways didn't make sense. What critical information was he missing?

He couldn't allow his last chance to sleep with her turn into a repeat of their married life—spectacular in the bedroom with no carryover into their real life. He had to convince her he had more to offer, a reason for her to stick with him for good times and bad, in sickness and in health.

Once again, he hit the same brick wall that had kept him apart from her for seven years. She didn't need him to take care of her. He couldn't offer her anything she couldn't do for herself. Many of those nights in the bar, he'd lamented his failure to provide for Marcia had driven her away, and if he'd only waited to marry her until he had a full-time job capable of supporting them both, he wouldn't have lost her.

But an offer of economic stability would mean nothing. What else did he have to convince her to stay with him after the orgasm's afterglow faded? He had to think of something or accept their marriage would be over by the end of the following night.

He could not waste the second chance Madame Eve's 1Night Stand service had provided.

Chapter Eight

"Reservations for two at seven o'clock. Your best table, please. This is a special occasion," Marcia said. She jotted down the confirmation from the maître d' of the city's most exclusive restaurant then moved on to ordering premium robes for the hotel room.

Next came a hair appointment, manicure, pedicure, and bikini wax scheduled over an extended lunch hour. Finally, she contacted the hotel's personal shopper. Despite having done so plenty of times before, she'd always called on behalf of important hotel guests and high-level executives, never for herself. But she needed appropriate attire—not to mention the best shapewear on the planet—both for dinner and for later.

Her night with Adrian had to satisfy her for a lifetime, and she wouldn't skimp on her efforts to create every illusion of perfection.

"You're thinking too hard." Adrian poked his head inside her office, sending her erratic heart into overdrive.

"Professional hazard." She forced a smile as she covered her date night notes and then stood. One more thing—she needed to message Madame Eve to find out what had made him agree to the hookup. Surely, the matchmaker had been cagey when explaining his date's identity. If he'd wanted to have sex with his wife, he would have done so last night, instead of calling for a divorce.

If Marcia canceled their dinner plans, they could meet in the hotel room, narrowing his window of time to change his mind. On the other hand, she could use the dinner date to convince him to give the evening—and her—a chance.

She pushed the dilemma aside to focus on business. "Mr. Sunburst and Blake are coming by first thing this morning so we can update them on our publicity plans. Afterward, we have a studio across town booked to film our new commercials. Rob and Sabrina had hoped for a 5:00 p.m. check-in, but they've already pushed it back to an ETA of six. Everything else looks to be on schedule."

Adrian shoved his hands in his pockets. "You have everything under control without me lifting a finger." The words should have been a compliment, but they sounded more like an accusation.

"Only because you set the wheels in motion," she said. He'd set their breakup in motion, too, and, no matter how desperately she tried, she couldn't find a way to slam on the brakes.

"Everything will go great." He smiled. "I'll make sure Mr. Sunburst and your boss know how much you deserve a big-ass promotion."

Compared to saving her marriage, a measly promotion no longer mattered. "I don't need you to suck up for me."

"Believe me, I know you don't need me." His smile disappeared, and bitterness tinged his tone. "But you're still stuck with me for the rest of the day and all night as well."

Her mouth dropped open. He knew? "Madame Eve told you I was your date?"

"I wouldn't have agreed to anyone else."

Her heart lurched with hope.

"You're wondering if I'll still be as good as you remember, and you want a last chance to indulge in those memories of us," he continued. "I'm curious, too. And I'll deliver exactly what you want."

The hope shriveled along with her heart. He'd signed on for good-bye sex and curiosity sex, with no interest in the last chance to win each other back she'd thrown her final hopes into. They hadn't even undressed yet, and he already had a foot out the door.

"I'm sure you'll be nothing short of amazing. I'll meet you in the conference room in a minute." After she had her emotions far enough under control she wouldn't act like a needy, clingy wife.

Despite wanting to sleep with him, taking charge of the arrangements, and hearing from his own lips that he approved of the plan, Marcia looked like she'd prefer to meet with an execution squad than hook up with him. The ray of hope Madame Eve's text had infused in him dimmed to defeat, and he plodded down the hall.

"Adrian, my man, did you ever impress me yesterday." Mr. Sunburst slapped him on the back outside the entrance to the conference room.

"I'm flattered you think so, sir, but Marcia can make anyone look good."

"Yes, she certainly can. But you hold your own just fine."

He'd been holding his own for far too long. He wanted to be part of a team again—her team.

"You may have noticed our internal marketing and publicity staff is lacking talent and experience," Mr. Sunburst continued. "I'm not the kind of man who steals good employees from jobs where they're happy, but if you're looking for a change...."

"No disrespect, sir, but I'm not sure I'm the right person for the position." He wouldn't even consider the opportunity without Marcia's blessing.

"Don't give me an answer now. Think about it." Mr. Sunburst rested his gaze on the slim gold band on Adrian's ring finger. "Talk it over with your wife. The worst thing a man can do is make major life decisions without including her."

Adrian slid his thumb across the metal band he should have stopped wearing years ago and muttered, "At this point, I can't make things worse."

Perversely, the thought cheered him. He had nothing to lose. His wife didn't need him, but he had a guarantee to spend the night with her. In the hours between now and then, he'd do his damnedest to make sure she wanted him as much as he wanted her.

Ignoring the spread of bagels and donuts against the side wall, he settled at the conference room table. A few minutes later, the love of his life took the seat next to him, her knee bumping his.

"Sorry," she murmured, destroying his hope the contact had been intentional.

"I'm not. You can bump and grind against me anytime."

She shot him a warning glare as the others migrated from the carbohydrate smorgasbord toward them.

"I'm imagining your body rubbing against mine, your softness against my hardness, slowly, back and forth," he whispered. He'd give the appearance of behaving, so only she would know how naughty he wanted to be.

Eyes wide, she shifted her hips on the chair. He attempted to conceal his smirk as she called the meeting to order. Under the table, he settled his hand on her thigh.

"We'll use our new television commercials to demonstrate our customers trusting us to take care of their needs," she said to the group.

"Not only their needs, but we want them to come away with the belief we'll deliver complete satisfaction with no regrets," he added, inching down her skirt to her knee and teasing up the fabric to caress her bare skin.

As the meeting continued, he tangled his leg with hers, spreading her knees and trailing his fingers along her thigh. When she shifted to give him access around the edges of her panties, triumph and desire coursed through him, but he glided back toward her knee, intent on building a slow burn in preparation for the night.

She tilted toward him, her breast sliding over his arm, and clicked on an image on the laptop screen. His libido went wild. He couldn't wait to fill his palms with her softness, to suck her until she moaned and thrashed beneath him. His cock pulsed. The plan for a slow burn was going to send him up in flames.

○3

Marcia stood side by side with Adrian, forearms and occasionally hips brushing as they watched the commercial shoot. The rush of excitement pounding through her veins would disappear for good when he left. The anticipation building in her had to be satisfied by a single night.

"We're going to work through lunch to get these takes exactly right," Mr. Sunburst proclaimed, plopping in the director's chair.

"I better get some sandwiches delivered," she said, breaking contact in order to rearrange her personal appointments. With Rob and Sabrina not arriving until later, she could reschedule during an afternoon lull.

After she returned to Adrian's side, he arched an eyebrow. "Ordering sandwiches requires a lot of calls."

"I might have a hot date tonight I need to get ready for." She winked.

He slid his gaze down to her toes and then up to her face. "You look ready to me."

"Shows what you know." But her breath caught at the approval in his eyes. She wanted so badly to believe she could still please him.

"I'm going to show you everything I know. You can count on it." Despite the harmless flirtation, something stronger lurked in the depths of his sparkling brown eyes.

Her phone rang, cutting off her analysis. "The tech team is meeting with the security consultants, and they'd like you to be part of the discussions on a few concerns," her secretary reported.

"Of course." She brushed her lips over Adrian's cheek. "Keep things running smoothly here. I won't be long."

He squeezed her fingers, the promise in his touch filling her with warmth.

But six hours later, every bit of heat had deserted her. She'd blown off the manicure and pedicure, then her hair appointment, and finally the bikini wax, while the IT department scrambled to patch a malfunctioning server before it disrupted front desk operations and derailed the promises of trust Adrian and his PR team were delivering. If she didn't get a chance to swing by the hotel gift shop to pick up her shapewear, they'd have to have sex in the pitch dark.

At some point during the afternoon, she'd spilled coffee on her white blouse but still managed to get enough inside her for over-caffeinated jitters to set in. On the plus side, Rob and Sabrina had been delayed yet again, so she hadn't missed the filming of their arrival.

Instead of a maître d' leading her and Adrian to their five-star dinner table overlooking the ocean, an administrative assistant brought in stale sandwiches for dinner. While the IT team talked amongst themselves in code lingo, Marcia searched the reservation system until she found the room reserved by Madame Eve. In theory, she could be inside it in under three minutes, but in reality, at least three hours of work loomed before she could consider ducking away from her responsibilities.

Five hours later, the computer server had been repaired to everyone's satisfaction and she stumbled into the hallway. Adrian strode toward her. "Rob and Sabrina are arriving. If you come with me, we'll be just in time to watch their filming in the hotel lobby."

"Great. I'm going there now." But she couldn't force a smile to accompany her words. She'd had one last chance to salvage her marriage and had ruined it by working until she was cross-eyed with exhaustion and the night was half over.

He wrapped his arm around her waist and guided her into the elevator. "You're holding up great. Remember, crisis mode doesn't last forever."

But he wouldn't be by her side when it finally ended, so how could the future hold anything brighter? She leaned on his shoulder, soaking up his strength and comfort until the doors opened. They walked from the office to the hotel building, entering through the side door next to the closed gift shop, where her sexy lingerie and fancy dinner clothes lay hidden somewhere inside.

No wonder she'd failed at marriage when she'd put saving it so far down her priority list.

Chapter Nine

They'd entered the lobby from the side opposite where the camera crew waited. Instead of observing behind them as she'd planned, Marcia had put herself within lens view. Worse, she'd arrived at the same time as Sabrina and Rob.

While Rob chatted with the hotel staff, Sabrina made a beeline for her, her arms wide open. "Marcia!"

Summoning a happy smile, she stepped forward and hugged her friend. "Thank you for coming."

"I'm sorry you got stuck with the company mess, but I'm so glad you handled it so Blake could be with Luciana and little Max." Sabrina lowered her voice. "Don't tell anyone yet, but Rob and I are expecting. I hope Blake's example shows Rob no crisis is too big to leave in someone else's hands when our time comes."

"I'm so happy for you." Despite the sincerity of her congratulations, she floundered under a sea of jealousy and welling tears. Was it too much to ask for some of the perfection everyone else experienced to come her way?

"So who's your friend? Introduce me."

"This is Adrian. He's helping us with PR and—"

Sabrina's eyes widened. "*Your* Adrian?"

Oh hell. Marcia had forgotten how much she'd confided in her friend. "Yeah, but—" Her claim of a work-only relationship fell flat in the face of the one-night stand they'd both committed to.

"So nice to meet you." Sabrina offered him her hand. When he shook it, she covered his hand with her other one. "Marcia has told me so much about you."

He added a second hand to the affectionate shake. "I'd love to hear what she said."

Sabrina eyed their piled appendages, specifically the ring finger on his left hand. "She wears her wedding ring, too. All the time. You should ask her to show it to you."

"I swear, that's the last time I share anything with you in confidence," Marcia said, cheeks burning. At least her embarrassment pushed aside the self-pity that had threatened to overwhelm her.

Her friend laughed. "Adrian, I can't wait to get to know you in person. Marcia, we are going to have a long talk very soon. But, tonight, I have an amazing husband who'd dead on his feet and needs to get to our room before he crashes." She kissed each of them on the cheek and sashayed across the lobby, linking her arm around Rob's. He smiled at her, settling his palm on her stomach.

"Their secret's not going to stay a secret for long with a pose like that," Adrian said.

"Rob knows what he's doing. They can handle the media. We just need to get our footage edited and shared with the appropriate channels." Maybe, after that, they'd still have a couple hours left to fall into bed together where she could at least sleep in Adrian's arms, even if they were too tired for sex.

"Get a good night's sleep everyone, and be ready to work first thing in the morning," her husband called across the lobby. "We're done working for tonight. I don't want to share any more of the time I have left with you," he added in a whisper to Marcia.

The camera crew and PR team cheered and quickly dispersed, leaving them alone with the nighttime hotel staff. After a stop at the front desk, Marcia had their room key but nothing else. She'd left her laptop, her purse, and even her phone in the room where she'd been holed up with the tech team. Not only did she lack the shapewear to mold her figure into some semblance of how Adrian remembered her, she didn't even have a change of clothes for the morning.

"I requested this. You'd think I'd be prepared, but I don't even have condoms," she admitted, bracing against the far wall of the elevator.

He shrugged. "We could try to make a baby."

"Wh—what?" She shoved away from the wall.

He raised his hands. "Just kidding. Mostly. I'm not opposed to babies, but we should make sure our relationship will last longer than a night before we complicate it further."

Not sure if she was relieved or disappointed, she shook her head as the doors opened on their floor. "Someday, I'm going to laugh about everything that's gone wrong today. You go on in the room. I'll go back to the front desk and get condoms."

He squeezed her hand, tugging her away from the elevator. "I have a bunch. Trust me. We'll be covered every time."

She snickered at the double entendre but then sobered as reality crashed down again. "I don't know if I can stay awake for the first time, let alone a repeat."

After unlocking the door, he held it open for her to enter ahead of him. "How about we each take a turn in the bathroom and then we'll see where the night leads?"

If anywhere. She heard the unspoken words loud and clear. Who needed condoms if they didn't bother to have sex?

Making use of the complimentary soaps and shampoos, she washed her body and then her undies and bra, hanging them over the tub to dry. One of her preparations from the morning paid off. A fluffy white robe hung on a hook behind the door. After wrapping herself in it, she emerged from the bathroom.

Adrian lay sprawled across the king-size bed, eyes closed. He'd taken off his suit coat and tie but left his shirt on, half-buttoned, and his pants open. He hadn't been kidding about working out. The man didn't have an ounce of fat on him. Where he'd once been flat and skinny, his body now rippled with muscled texture. The handsome boy she'd married had grown into a gorgeous, ogle-worthy man who deserved a woman every bit as beautiful and perfect.

Resisting the temptation to curl next to him, she continued past the bed to the curtain covering the sliding door to the balcony. She nudged the door open and wandered into the cool night air, the concrete cold under her bare feet.

Gripping the iron railing, she stared over the ocean beyond the city until the tears streaming down her cheeks left her unable to see farther than her hands. She and Adrian had had a long, slow end to their marriage. But they'd finally reached the very end.

∝

Despite his best intentions, Adrian must have dozed off. The bathroom was empty, and the wind blew the curtain where the door to the balcony stood open. He pushed the drape aside, revealing Marcia slumped against the railing. Reaching her in two strides, he wrapped his arms around her from behind. "Why are you out here instead of in bed with me?"

Her shoulders lifted in a helpless shrug. "I had such high hopes if I made this evening special enough we might reconsider how we could save our relationship. But the day has been a disaster, and we've already lost half the night."

"We're together now, which means we've already improved on the past seven years." He didn't care about the trappings, just savoring every moment with her.

"I had dinner reservations at the swankiest restaurant in town." Her voice quavered. "I was supposed to get a manicure and a pedicure and a sexy hairdo. I even planned a bikini wax and ordered new clothes and shapewear to make my curves a little more alluring. None of it happened."

He turned her in his arms to face him, touched by all the trouble and thought she'd put into the evening, even though nothing could have been more enticing than her alone. "I didn't agree to meet you for any of those things. I agreed to meet you because I wanted you. Just you."

He tugged on the cloth belt, until the robe fell open, revealing her lush, naked body. All his blood rushed to his cock. "How the hell are clothes supposed to make you sexier than this?"

"*This* is not sexy." She attempted to pull the lapels together, but he enjoyed the view too much to let her cover up. "Look at yourself in the mirror and compare what you have to me."

Huh? "Hate to break it to you, but I'm not that narcissistic to get turned on by checking myself out."

"Well, I'm not going to turn you on either," she shot back. "I'm rounded where I'm supposed to be flat, and overblown and droopy where I'm supposed to be simply curvy."

"Who says what you're supposed to be?" he demanded, ready to take a swing at whoever had led her to believe she was less than perfect. "I say you're beautiful. If you want to change your shape to maximize your health and self-confidence, I'll go the gym with you every day and support your efforts. But if you're ashamed because you think your body doesn't meet some sort of beauty criteria, then stop right now. From the moment I met you, I wanted you because you're you, Marcia, and *you* turn me on, regardless of the size of your hips or boobs or anything in between."

"That's the most beautiful thing anyone's ever said to me." Her gaze softened, and she released the edges of her robe, wrapping her arms around his neck.

He should have said more beautiful things to her. He should have crafted a speech that encapsulated his feelings and the passion flowing through him. But he hadn't, and her naked flesh against his thin, open shirt left him incapable of coherent thought.

A slim gold chain hanging from her neck and disappearing into her cleavage caught the light. He tugged it, drawing out the end where her wedding band with its pathetically small diamond dangled. "No wonder you don't want other people to see this tiny thing. It should have come with a complimentary magnifying glass."

Marcia shook her head. "The diamond is perfect, but wearing the ring on my finger came with a complication and a double standard I wasn't prepared to deal with. People ask questions for idle conversation." She sighed. "I didn't have any answers about us. I still don't have answers."

"But even though you didn't want to tell people about me, you still wore my ring." Heat spread through his chest. He might not have answers either, but he couldn't help hoping. "Why?"

"Tucked next to my heart, it helped me feel less alone."

Adrian lifted the warm metal circle to his lips. "I like knowing you carried a piece of me with you." But his ring against her skin wouldn't sustain him for another seven years. He needed a real connection.

"But I was deluding myself," she continued. "I didn't have a part of you that really mattered."

Yes, she had. Whether she knew it or not, wherever she went, she'd had his heart. "Well, for tonight, you have every part me, and I get every part of you."

He cupped her breasts and bent to graze his mouth over one nipple. She arched against him, and he teased the band of the ring across the other nipple.

"Yes," she whispered.

Straightening, he lifted her, chest to chest, taking her in his arms.

She stiffened, proof he hadn't erased her insecurities. He pressed his palms to her naked ass, and her rigidity melted and her breath quickened. Better. Then she wrapped her legs around his waist and her arms around his neck. Perfect.

"We're going inside. I don't want anyone peeking at our balcony and sharing in this reunion," he said. With the heat of her core rubbing his bare navel, his cock strained. Damn, he should have gotten naked first, so he could lower her onto him and take her hard and fast all at once.

But hard and fast wasn't the kind of reverence he wanted to show. He intended to love, cherish, and all the other things he'd vowed during their wedding ceremony. And he hoped with all his heart their first time in seven years wouldn't be their last.

Chapter Ten

*A*s Adrian laid her gently on the bed, Marcia wanted to assure him she wouldn't break. But when he left in the morning, she might not only break, she might very well shatter.

He removed the robe from her arms, trailing his fingers along her inner elbow and wrist and finally over her palms, sending shivers racing up her limbs.

"You like that." He smiled and traced her stiff nipples.

"Yes, I like it." She moaned. "In case you've forgotten, I like everything you do to me in bed. What I want most is to feel your weight on top of me and inside me."

"Most? So you want me to skip this?" He leaned over her, kissing first her lips and then her chin and neck. Continuing to work his way down, he sucked her breasts and licked toward her navel.

She should have been self-conscious, desperate to cover her thick torso before she turned him off, but he caressed her with such reverence, the self-doubts silenced in awe and desire. At last, his hot, gorgeous mouth reached the juncture of her thighs.

"Oh." Inviting him to touch and taste her everywhere, she let her legs fall open. "I haven't decided if I want you to skip this or not. Keep trying to convince me your way is better."

Rumbling laughter vibrated her clit. "I'll give it my best shot."

"Please do." She gripped his hair, floating in a haze of pleasure as his lips skimmed along her slit. He turned her to butter, first molding then melting her. "This is so nice."

"Nice?" He lifted his head, disbelief etched in his face and tone. "Don't tell a man his lovemaking is 'nice.'"

But it was, in the very best way. Beautiful. Perfect. Instead of trying to explain, she giggled. "Amazing."

He slipped his tongue inside her.

"Extraordinary." She gasped, too filled with desire to laugh any longer.

Replacing his tongue with a finger, he encircled her clit with his mouth again.

"Exquisite." She wanted to find the perfect adjective to convey the sensations he evoked, but no word was good enough to explain the beauty and pleasure filling her. Her brain splintered and then she could no longer think at all.

He played her higher and higher, encompassing her in amazing sweetness until the pleasure consumed her and she tumbled over the edge. Muscles trembling, she jerked wherever he touched her. "Adrian, please. I need your cock inside me. I want you to come with me."

He rose over her, bringing his face even with hers. Sinking into his kiss, she tasted both her pleasure and his desperate need on his lips. More than anything, she wanted to fulfill his desire as beautifully as he'd fulfilled hers. Without breaking contact, they stripped off his clothes together. Naked, he ripped open a condom and sheathed himself..

She lifted her hips, and he surged into her. His body fit with hers so perfectly, tears sprang in her eyes. "I'd convinced myself the memory of us was too good to be true, but it's too good *not* to be true. Nothing can compare to the reality of you." Wrapping her limbs around him, she hugged him as close as possible. If only she could hold him tight enough, she'd never have to let him go.

He moaned into her neck. "Oh, Marcia, I've missed you so much. You fit with me. You rock my world even when we're lying still. Being with you thrills me and completes me. You are and always have been my other half."

Her body trembled so hard, she couldn't control it. He quaked against her, their alternating spasms pushing each other in a beautiful dance. They approached the pinnacle of desire as one, their tears and shouts of joy mingling together.

ෆ

Daylight filtered around the edges of the curtain, and Marcia started. Oh no. She couldn't have fallen asleep. The last thing she remembered was Adrian collapsing against her chest, their breathing heavy and hearts hammering in unison.

His torso remained half-draped over hers, his arms and legs tangled with hers, as he slept with his lips nestled against the pulse of her neck. Their one-night stand had come to an end far too soon. When he opened his eyes, she'd have to give him the damned divorce he wanted.

They'd lost so many years. Instead of using every second to convince him their relationship deserved another chance, she'd fallen asleep when her entire future rode on their night together.

"Are you awake? Why are you tensing?" he murmured.

Her panic grew. "Because I have things to do before I leave this morning." The words came out testier than she'd intended.

"Like what?" He met her gaze, a hint of wariness in his eyes.

"Like give you something to remember." She couldn't simply fade from his life. She needed to leave her mark. Even if she couldn't have him forever, she needed her memory to have a permanent home with him.

"I'll never forget." He nuzzled her collarbone, and his erection stirred against her pelvis.

If she continued to lie under him, he'd give her another beautiful, amazing recollection. She needed to create a memory for him so he would remember why she had once been special to him.

With a twist of her limbs and torso, Marcia reversed their positions. Adrian lay on his back while she straddled him, her breasts and ring necklace swaying in his face.

"Hell of a view." The last of his sleepy contentment ebbed away. With his arousal springing to life, he lifted his head and captured her nipple with his lips.

She gasped and ground her hot core against his thigh. Then she tugged free of his grasp. "Lie still and don't do anything. Just tell me how you feel."

As she kissed the corner of his mouth, her ring and her breasts glided over his chest, a sweet pendulum that hypnotized his cock into standing straight and tall.

He groaned and fought for the enormous control required not to caress her in return. "I've died and gone to heaven."

"Too cliché. I want you to tell me how you really feel."

"So demands the woman who claimed my lovemaking was 'nice,'" he teased. He hadn't died, but she was his heaven.

A wicked grin lit her face. "I'm not going to be nice."

Scraping her nails over his pectorals and flat nipples, she dragged her body along his pelvis. He reached for her hips, but she swatted his hands away. She stroked the tip of his cock along her hot, wet opening.

Need slammed through him, and he strained for more, desperate to claim the paradise he could never get enough of. Using every last thread of control, he tucked his hands behind his head to keep from thrusting into her.

She pinched his ass, and he jerked, his cock bobbing against her pussy. Before he could beg her to repeat the erotic tease, she kissed and licked her way across his abs, turning him cross-eyed with desire.

"Not only do your morning gym workouts intimidate me, they've transformed you into a different person from the man I remember," she admitted.

"I swear it's the same me," he whispered. "Muscles and physical endurance mean nothing because I turn weak the moment I'm with you. If you don't surround my cock with your sweet pussy now, I'm going to lose control and embarrass myself."

"I would love to surround you and make you come for me." She scooted down the bed and swirled her tongue around the tip of his cock then licked straight to the base.

He dug his fingers into the pillow, trying to hold back the tsunami building inside him. "I want to come inside you. I want you to tremble and fall apart around me."

"Sounds *nice.*" She shot him another wicked grin and opened a condom package. After rolling it down his length, she positioned above him again and glided down, taking him in all at once.

He willed himself not to explode on impact. Addicted to her brand of *nice*, he overdosed on the sheer, unfiltered pleasure from his personal goddess. Marcia rose above him and then plunged down. Again and again. Leaning over him, she captured his mouth with hers and kissed him, still pumping his shaft.

"I'm coming." He gasped, trying to pull back to avoid hitting the peak before she caught up. Grasping her hips, he angled them for maximum pleasure and drove into her with desperation. "Please come with me."

She rocketed apart, her muscles contracting against him. He couldn't contain his orgasm a second longer. Pouring into her, he gave her everything he had, praying it would somehow be enough.

Bliss surrounded him. He'd found his paradise and would never leave.

Marcia's muscles started to relax, but then panic filled her expression and she tensed. She shoved off him and stumbled to the floor.

Already missing her soft, warm body, he reached for her. "What—where are you going?"

She jumped to her feet, her eyes wild and cheeks flushed. "Damn you, Adrian. Damn you for turning my life upside down and then asking for a divorce. I will never forgive you for this."

Bliss dissolved into blind panic, and he grasped for her hand. They'd bypassed all talk of divorce, hadn't they? Surely what they'd just shared had changed everything. "Marcia."

She evaded his touch, slamming into the bathroom.

Disoriented and still weak with post-orgasm tremors, he disposed of the condom and staggered to the closed door. "Marcia, can we talk please?"

He tested the knob, but it wouldn't turn. She'd locked him out, just as she'd locked him out of her life for the past seven years. He still loved her. And he still didn't know how to bridge the gap.

Chapter Eleven

Marcia glared at herself in the bathroom mirror. She would not cry. She'd hang onto her anger and use it to propel her out of the room without shattering.

With movements too jerky to be natural, she picked up the pieces of clothing she'd left hanging on the tub and dressed. Finally, she lifted the necklace with her wedding ring over her head, squared her shoulders, and emerged from the bathroom.

Adrian stood on the other side of the door, still naked, his body sculpted as if from marble, his expression inscrutable. "Before you walk out on me, I have one thing to say."

Say you love me. Say it's all a mistake, and we never should have left each other. Say we should spend every night together forever.

"You need to file for divorce," he said.

Her heart, already bruised and broken, shattered anew. She shook her head, pressed the ring and necklace into his palm, and then raced for the door.

He beat her to it, slamming his back against the door before she could open it. "If you file, I'll agree to anything you want. Alimony, my motorcycle, my 401(k), my membership in the skydiving club. Whatever you want, I'll sign it over to you. But I can't be the person to file because I don't want a divorce."

Her pulse pounded in her ears. She didn't want to take anything from him. The only thing she'd ever wanted was his heart. "I can't either," she whispered.

Reaching out, he stroked his fingers over her cheek. "I want to be your husband. I want to wake up to your smiling face every morning and fall asleep spooned against your back every night. I want to give you a foot rub after you have a lousy day and turn to you for a neck rub when my week sucks."

She opened her mouth and stepped toward him.

But he continued talking. "I love you, Marcia. I loved you from the moment I saw you wandering lost on your first day on campus. I've waited every day for seven years for you to need me as much as you did that day. But you don't need me because you're a strong woman who can handle whatever mess is thrown at you. I love you even more because of your independence and strong will."

Overwhelmed by his beautiful speech, she took a shuddering breath, trying to understand where their confessions left them. "If both of us refuse to take action to officially end our marriage, and you love me and I love you, then what? I don't want to spend another seven years in relationship limbo because neither of us has the guts to make a move."

"I'll make a move." In a flash, he flipped their positions, pressing her back to the door. He dashed across the room and grabbed a condom then returned, slamming his mouth into hers, his kiss demanding and frantic. Pushing up her skirt, he shoved down her underwear and drove his finger straight into her, claiming her with an urgency that turned her instantly wet and wanton.

She grasped his shoulders and wiggled her hips until her panties fell to her ankles while he rolled on the condom. Kicking the garment away, she latched her leg around his waist. He grasped her ass and lifted her as if she weighed nothing.

"Both legs around me," he ordered.

She complied, and he drove into her, desperation leaving no room for sweetness or gentleness. She didn't want it. Abandoning all finesse in the primitive urge to mark him as her own, she squeezed and scratched while he did the same.

"Damn it, Adrian, I love you. I've always loved you." Her body unraveled until she couldn't think or speak.

He continued to pump into her with hard, frenetic strokes. "Promise you'll never leave me again."

"I promise. We'll never use the D-word again."

He thrust harder, faster, deeper. "I swear. Say you love me again."

"I love you," she screamed. The orgasm blasted through her, tearing her apart from every direction. She clung to him as the only thing left in her world. Grasping his head, she whispered in his ear, "I love you so much."

He exploded inside her, a torrential rush that left him trembling.

When the storm subsided, they still clung to each other.

"I never want to lose you again," he whispered, his voice raw. He brushed his lips over her temple in a gesture so tender, tears filled her eyes.

She cupped his jaw. "You won't. I'll live wherever you are. If Sunburst can't transfer me to an East Coast corporate or hotel management position, I'll quit and find something new."

He rested his forehead against hers. "Don't quit right away. My home isn't on the East Coast. My home is with you. Mr. Sunburst suggested I could work for him, but if that's too weird, I can find a position with a California PR firm. I've also toyed with the idea of starting my own company."

She dropped her feet to the ground, standing on her own but still embracing the love of her life. "How about we both open dialogues with our bosses about our job options. Then let's come back together and have a long discussion about those options. After we talk, we need to include some serious bedroom negotiations and then talk some more about what we both really want before either of us takes a new job or prepares to move."

His lips curved in the sweetest smile she'd ever seen. "I love the way you think."

"Good, because I love you." Standing on tiptoe, she kissed him hard.

His cock stirred, and his eyes brightened. "Do you think we'll get fired if I make us late for work?"

"I think we can risk it." She took his hand to lead him toward the bed, but instead of trailing after her, he tugged on her wrist.

As she turned, he knelt in front of her, holding between his thumb and forefinger the ring she'd returned to him. "Marcia Johnson, will you do me the great honor of being my wife forever and ever, till death do us part?"

Happiness swelled inside her, leaving no room for doubts or insecurities. She smiled down at him, the biggest crisis of her life resolved more perfectly than she ever could have predicted. "That's Marcia Torres to you, sir. And seeing as I want more than one night with my husband, my answer is a resounding, love-filled, unequivocal yes."

And they were indeed very late for work.

ONE NIGHT WITH HIS WIFE

A 1Night Stand Story

By
Sara Daniel

Dedication

For my readers.

Chapter One

"The judge refused to approve it."

"What?" Luke Cox jumped to his feet, smacking into the airplane's overhead bin. Fumbling the phone, he shoved it up to his ear again, his lawyer's bombshell too important for him to miss a word.

The passengers on either side shot him dirty looks as the flight attendants started their pre-flight walk through the aisle. Rubbing his aching forehead, he eased into his cursed middle seat, the throbbing almost canceling out the never-ending pain in his hip. Almost.

"What do you mean? Rosalind signed everything without contesting or haggling over the terms. You said this was the easiest divorce you've ever handled. What could have gone wrong?"

Luke had walked out on his marriage, but Rosalind hadn't argued or tried to stop him. After all, who the hell wanted to be tied to a guy with one-and-a-half legs? Fact was, the remaining half pretty much sucked too. She hadn't signed up for that kind of baggage when they'd said their vows, and he'd done the right thing by letting her get out.

A flight attendant leaned next to him. "Sir, please turn off your cell phone and buckle your seatbelt to prepare for takeoff." Instead of the sexy, flirty stereotype, she looked like a linebacker who'd lay him flat in the aisle if he didn't follow protocol.

Nodding, Luke reached for the seatbelt strap but needed to complete the call before he turned off his phone. He'd planned to be single by the time he boarded the plane. Instead, he was coasting away from the gate still a married man.

"In the months since Rosalind signed the agreement, your company net worth has gone from nothing to millions," his lawyer explained. "The judge thinks she's entitled to some of it, or, at the very least, he wants all the papers re-signed with proof that she understands how much she's giving up."

"Then give the money to her." Luke scrubbed his knuckles over his face. He'd never meant to keep anything from her. She could have every penny. She deserved it for worrying through his tours of duty with the Marines, for the baby he'd promised but they'd never made, and for all the other dreams she'd put on hold for the past ten years.

The point of the divorce had been to give her a better life. If his bank account provided the means to improve on the original plan, so much the better.

The flight attendant marched down the aisle toward him again. "Sir, turn your cell phone off now. We're preparing for takeoff."

Luke nodded his understanding and lifted an index finger in a bid for a few more seconds. He needed to ensure the divorce situation would be fixed before the plane landed.

"She's moved a few times since she originally signed the papers," the attorney continued. "My people are trying to locate her. The judge postponed the case until both parties agree to a fair division of assets or she testifies she doesn't want her portion."

"If you can't find her, hire a private investigator ASAP. I want her agreement by this afternoon. No more delays." Call him old-fashioned, but Luke didn't want to be legally married when he met his one-night stand date in a few hours.

He'd never once considered cheating on Rosalind, and she would never have cheated on him. Nor left him, either, so he'd been forced to walk out on her. He'd never forget the hurt and betrayal in her eyes when he had. Even if she never found out about his date, he recoiled at the thought of betraying her a second time by sleeping with someone else before their relationship received the judge's official death knell.

The flight attendant leaned into his field of vision again, her lips a thin line, her eyebrow much thicker but still a single slash across her annoyed face.

"I'll call you as soon as I land in Montana. Have good news for me by then, or I'll be looking for other legal counsel." Luke flipped the phone off before the attendant confiscated his electronics.

Within minutes, the plane accelerated down the runway. Closing his eyes, he tried to sleep, but his mind refused to turn off. The possibility of giving up half of his share of the company's net worth was probably sending his legal staff and accountants into cardiac arrest. However, the money meant nothing to him.

While his best friend and business partner, Alex, had immediately bought a snazzy sports car with his newfound wealth, Luke hadn't spent a penny until he'd signed up for Madame Eve's 1Night Stand service. He'd requested a blind date who didn't care about his missing leg or his brand-new money, only his cock driving into her until she screamed in ecstasy.

The date of his fantasies had better be good because the reality of his life was pretty damned shitty.

ଔ

Luke drove the rental car through the entrance gates of the Alvarado Ranch Resort. Not only did it boast impeccably manicured grounds, the main lodge was a hundred times larger and more impressive than any farmhouse he'd ever seen. An elegant sign directed guests to a spa in one direction, horse stables in another, and an eighteen-hole golf course in yet another. The resort appeared to be the perfect destination for people who wanted to "get away" and still have every comfort and convenience at their fingertips.

Rosalind had always dreamed of working somewhere with large, maintained stables, well-bred horses, and unlimited riding opportunities. If she were with him, she'd consider the Alvarado Ranch Resort a slice of heaven, but she'd want to be working with the horses, not checking in at the front desk. Wherever she'd ended up, he hoped horses played some part in her life. Her expectations had never been lofty enough to include affording a horse of her own, but she wouldn't be happy if she wasn't near at least one.

Although he'd contacted his lawyer every fifteen minutes since stepping off the plane, no one on the legal staff had come any closer to locating Rosalind. He wished he could see her face when she learned she'd have enough money to set up her own little ranch with all the horses she wanted.

He wouldn't be seeing her face again, though, which meant he needed to stop thinking about her. He'd arrived at the Alvarado Ranch Resort to move on and reclaim the manhood his country's never-ending fight against terrorism had stripped from him, not brood over the pieces of his life he'd never get back.

Ignoring the valet option by the front door—missing half a leg didn't make him a cripple, damn it—he parked at the far end of the parking lot and tossed his duffle bag over his shoulder. Gritting his teeth and cursing his throbbing hip, he walked—fine, he limped like a freaking cripple—into the lobby.

The place buzzed with activity. Luke shuffled sideways to avoid getting mowed down by a luggage cart headed straight for him and bumped shoulders with three other people milling around. Muttering apologies, he stumbled to the relative calmness of the long line at the registration desk. After several minutes of waiting, he arrived at the front of the line and gave the cheerful young clerk his name.

"Yes, Mr. Cox." She squinted at her computer monitor. "Welcome to the Alvarado Ranch Resort. As you can see from the commotion around here, we have a big group leaving this morning. Unfortunately, because of this, your room isn't quite ready. Can I set you up with a tour of the resort and some complimentary drink coupons while you wait?"

"I'll take the drinks." His date likely hadn't arrived yet. If the single non-stop flight offered by the airline hadn't departed so early in the day, he could have gone to the courthouse and convinced the judge to finalize the divorce before he'd left. Everyone in the law office had assured him the paperwork would sail through and get rubber-stamped, so his presence wasn't needed. *Ha.*

"I'd rather skip the tour and wander the resort on my own. Do you have a map or something?" he asked the clerk.

"Of course." She set a placemat-size sheet of paper on the counter between them. "If you want to go horseback riding or participate in our 'working-ranch' activities, take this path." She traced a pen along the route. "If you'd like to do some fishing in the lake, take this path. Any of our employees will be happy to help you get set up with everything you need."

"Thanks." After retrieving two condoms from his bag in case he hooked up with his date sooner than planned, Luke tucked them in a hip pocket, left the duffle at the desk then folded the map and shoved it in the other pocket. Winding through the crowded lobby again, he gave the zooming luggage carts wide berth and made his way outside. Once alone, he took a deep breath and shrugged out the tension that had crept into his shoulders from the curious and pitying expressions that always followed his limp.

Fishing had never held his interest, and golf was even worse, so he proceeded toward the stables. Although horses had been Rosalind's passion, he'd come to appreciate them on her behalf. Fifty feet from his destination, he paused as a group on horseback trotted over the hill at the far end of the pasture. Oh yeah, she would think the ranch was heaven.

Despite her small frame, the woman on the lead horse sat tall in the saddle, her black hair arranged in a thick braid over one shoulder, a Stetson on her head. Damn, either the resort or the divorce disaster was messing with his mind, making him hallucinate that was Rosalind riding toward him.

But no wonder he thought of her when even the cowboy hat was the same copper color as the one she'd worn since the day he'd met her. He'd given her shit about that thing from the beginning, but his favorite fantasy involved her wearing nothing but the damned hat and riding him hard and long.

His cock jumped to full salute, and he shuffled behind a fence post so his hard-on wouldn't be obvious to everyone who glanced his way. Once the riders drew close enough for him to see the woman's boobs bouncing, he'd be lucky not to shoot his load in his briefs. The one-night stand couldn't come soon enough to satisfy his long-overdue need for release.

The riding group approached the corral, and surprise derailed his fantasy. The woman didn't just look like Rosalind—it *was* her. He dug his fingernails into the fence post. What the hell?

Coincidence, my ass.

Not when a *coincidence* equaled a setup where bad shit went down.

Chapter Two

*W*ho would have set Luke up to run into her? He'd never heard of the Alvarado Ranch Resort before Madame Eve had booked his one-night stand to take place there. He'd learned about the matchmaking service through his business partner, Alex, who had used it to hook up with the woman he'd ended up marrying. Before that, Alex had hooked his sister up through the same company, and she'd ended up marrying her date, too.

Not that Luke intended to marry the woman he slept with. No way. But Madame Eve ran 1Night Stand, a classy operation, not a sleazy scam outfit. Moreover, Alex had personally recommended it. After carrying Luke's unconscious body a freaking mile in the desert to save his miserable life after bad shit from really bad guys had gone down, Alex wouldn't have set Luke up with the emotional equivalent of a grenade to the heart.

In the corral, Rosalind swung off her horse. After giving the animal an affectionate pat on the neck, a few whispered endearments, and setting it free to roam, she turned to the other members of her group. Holding the bridle of another horse, she calmed both the animal and the older woman in the saddle, talking her through the dismount. Then she high-fived a boy who'd climbed down on his own and propelled him toward the gate, away from the horses.

Finally, she shifted her attention to the last person still sitting astride, the young girl's skinny legs encased in metal braces. "How did you like the ride?"

"I want to keep going."

Rosalind grinned, her face so radiant Luke couldn't breathe. "Every time I get on a horse, I want to ride forever, too. But even though you and I don't need a break, the horses do, and I think some other people in your family might, as well. So, come back tomorrow, and you can ride again."

Luke leaned his head against the fence post. He hadn't seen her so happy since he'd had two working legs, but, even then, the smiles hadn't been genuine. She'd tried to fool him, yet he'd seen her worry the Marines would return him home in a flag-draped box. But the pure happiness on her face while she stood in the corral stroking the horse's neck reminded him of when they were newlyweds.

The enthusiastic rider held out her arms to Rosalind, and she lifted her to the ground with an easy swoop. "Help me walk to the gate, so Daddy doesn't have to bring my wheelchair."

Across the corral, a man froze in the process of maneuvering a wheelchair toward them. He set the chair aside while Rosalind steadied the child, encouraging her without rush her.

Reaching the gate, the girl threw herself into the man's arms, chattering excitedly. Every person, from the older woman, to the parents and the kids, heaped adoration on Rosalind as they said their good-byes. She accepted the compliments graciously, passing on the praise to the horses, the rest of the staff, and even back to the well-mannered family.

After she sent them on their way, she surveyed the mounts still saddled and milling around the lot. One had wandered toward Luke's corner. She took two strides in his direction then her eyes widened and her smile disappeared. Yep, she was better off without him making her life miserable.

Whether a true coincidence or a nasty setup had brought them together, he had to use the opportunity to take care of the loose ends of their relationship. Then he could let Rosalind get on with the happy, fulfilled life she deserved while he met his one-night stand with a clear conscience and a burning libido.

"Luke?" Rosalind could barely speak around the stallion-sized lump in her throat. She advanced across the dusty paddock in a haze of shock and disbelief. Yet, the closer she came, the more real he appeared. His tight charcoal-gray T-shirt showed off his well-defined chest and bulging arm muscles. He might not be an active Marine anymore, but he sure hadn't missed a day of training.

He might have missed a haircut though. His light-brown hair fluttered in the breeze, teasing his ears and forehead the way she once had with her fingertips. The set of his strong jaw assured her such touches would no longer be welcome. Still, he'd come to her for the first time since he'd walked out on her, and she had to count that as a positive sign. Forcing a smile, she stopped on the opposite side of the white shoulder-high wooden fence.

"Luke, what a surprise." She reached through the fence to place her hand on his forearm. Before she made contact, he stepped back, so she gripped a rough fence slat instead. Regardless of the reason he'd come to her, he must not intend to resume their relationship if he evaded her innocuous caress.

He squinted at the horses, the stable building, the pasture—everywhere but at her. "This looks like your kind of place."

"You know me with horses—I'd sleep in the barn for the chance to work with them." When Rosalind had been forced out of the base housing she'd shared with him, she hadn't thought she'd ever find a place to call home. Maybe her heart would never consider any other place her real home, but she'd found the next best thing.

"So, if I go in the barn, will I find a bedroll and pillow in one of the stalls?"

Not only had Luke shown up out of the blue, he teased her with sweet familiarity. The gentle banter combined with his evasion of her touch likely proved he was a figment of her imagination.

Georgina, the mare waiting to be unsaddled, moseyed over and nuzzled her. Luke might be a mirage, but the horse, at least, was real. "No sleeping in the stalls. My boss doesn't allow it." Stroking the animal's velvety nose, Rosalind smiled. "Tell me, Luke, did you come to my stable looking for a ride?" His eyebrows shot up, showcasing his beautiful brown eyes. Suddenly, the words she'd meant so innocently took on an inappropriate and intimate meaning. "On a horse, I mean."

Not that she wouldn't love to straddle him and ride him, hard and wet. Cheeks burning, she tipped her hat over her eyes so he wouldn't guess the need he inspired, the same need that kept her awake at night while the rest of the ranch slept.

"No rides—of any kind. We need to finalize a couple of things before the divorce can go through."

"Oh." The sucker punch landed dead center in her gut. She wrapped her arms around her stomach, trying not to double over with the pain. She was such a fool, assuming his presence meant they'd pick up where they'd left off, as if nothing had changed. He'd told her their marriage was over. He'd looked her in the eye and stated he no longer wanted to try to make a baby. He'd wanted her out of his life permanently.

He hadn't changed his mind.

Georgina nudged her shoulder, and Rosalind buried her face in the mare's neck, taking the support the sweet animal offered until she was steady enough to face Luke without collapsing. "Give me a few minutes to unsaddle the horses and get them settled. I think I have some free time before my next riders are scheduled. You can meet me on the other side of the stables."

As he meandered down the fence line, she hugged the mare again. Why the hell had *Luke* come to see her about the divorce? He'd never contacted her again after he'd walked out. His lawyers had chased her down. The military had chased her out. But he had never, ever, taken one step in her direction. If he had, he would have discovered she was the easiest thing he'd ever tried to catch.

She kept her palm on Georgina's neck and strode toward the stable. Rosalind could have simply clicked her tongue, and the horse would have followed her, but Rosalind needed the extra contact to fortify her for whatever Luke wanted to discuss.

Inside the barn, she removed the tack and brushed her flanks then rewarded her with both an apple and a sugar cube before moving toward the entrance to the corral for the next mount.

"You're spoiling my horses," her cousin and boss, Javier, teased, wagging a finger at her as he walked down the aisle between the stalls. Six feet away, he stopped, the smile lines on his deep-brown skin disappearing. "Whoa, Rosalind, I was joking. What's the matter?"

Apparently, her poker face sucked. She shook her head, not ready to talk but too much of an emotional mess to fake any semblance of normalcy.

"Did one of the guests do something to you? Did something happen on the ride?" Javier expected employees to treat guests with utmost respect, but he also expected the guests to treat the employees and animals with respect in return.

"No, the family this morning was an absolute joy. I expect they'll make reservations for another ride tomorrow."

"But they left you with all the cleanup work."

Despite his indignation, she relaxed. Javier liked the guests to handle the chores that came with riding, part of his "working-ranch" concept, but she preferred to send the others on their way so she could, as he claimed, spoil her babies.

"They weren't ready for that part, and I like taking care of the horses on my own."

"So, why do you look like you're going to fall apart? I haven't seen you this shaken since the day you arrived."

Trust her cousin to get to the heart of the matter and refuse to let it go. She fidgeted with the brim of her hat then whistled out the corral entrance. Another horse would come so she could occupy her hands.

"Luke showed up," she admitted. "He wants to talk about the divorce."

"It's not final yet?" Javier demanded.

She shrugged and unbuckled the saddle of the new horse, heaving it off. "I don't know. I guess not. I'm going to talk to him after I finish here."

He took the saddle from her hands before she could put it away and crossed the stable to hang it up. "I'll finish with the horses. You take the afternoon off."

"I don't need the whole afternoon." Rosalind didn't want it and couldn't stand the thought of hashing out their breakup for hours. What could they haggle over? They had no kids, no property. The only thing she'd taken had been her wedding band.

"Use the rest of the time to take care of yourself, Rosalind. You need it. Contact Madame Eve and pressure her to find you a date. I don't know why she's taken so long. I filled out the 1Night Stand application for you the week you arrived here. You have been checking your e-mail, right?" Returning to her side, he wrapped his arm around her in a comforting hug.

For a moment, she savored the protection and care he offered, but she had to stand on her own. Javier had given her a reason to roll out of bed each morning with her dream job at his resort, but he couldn't fix her personal life. She had no interest in keeping up with any electronic messages and less interest in the one-night stand fix he'd attempted to set up. She pulled away and turned.

Luke stood across the stable, glowering at her. "Well, I see how you got a job here."

Chapter Three

*I*f Rosalind had stopped caring about Luke's opinion, his knee-jerk conclusion would have been funny. "Yes, connections are valuable in any profession. But before you make assumptions, you might want to hear what the exact connection is."

"Or don't, so you can act like an ass and embarrass yourself more," Javier said, bunching his fists and drawing his lean wrangler's body into a fighting stance.

Rosalind rolled her eyes.

Luke continued to glare.

"I had to leave the base housing, since, of course, I didn't qualify to stay there without you. My aunt let me move in with her while I figured out what to do." She focused on Georgina leaning her head out of her stall, since the sympathy and regret softening Luke's gaze threatened to derail her thoughts. "My aunt had been tracking down long-lost relatives for some big reunion. Long story short, Javier Alvarado and I are second cousins or something. He was gracious enough to offer me a job on his ranch based on my shoestring-relative qualifications."

"I offered it to you based on that, but you'd be cleaning toilets or sorting mail, not touching my horses or taking care of my guests if you hadn't proven you had real qualifications," Javier said.

Before she could respond, he switched his attention to Luke. "Mr.

Cox, I don't know you from shit, and I don't care to become acquainted with anyone who treats Rosalind the way you did. However, if you hurt her again, you'll get to know me in an extremely unpleasant way. Understand?"

Luke continued to stand implacably, his gaze hard again.

She had no desire to instigate a stable brawl, especially between two stubborn people she cared too much for. Javier had the height advantage and the agility from training horses every day, but Luke had more muscle mass, along with his military training. She strode toward her estranged husband, calling over her shoulder to Javier, "We're going to Mac's to talk over a glass of lemonade." She gripped Luke's sculpted forearm. "Come on."

He didn't move, instead staring down at his arm like she'd violated his personal space by daring to lay a hand on him. And, of course, he was right. She had no right to touch him.

But his distaste didn't prevent heat from seeping up her arm. Her body hadn't gotten the message she could no longer claim him. Unfortunately, he seemed intent on reiterating the facts until she was forced to accept he no longer wanted her.

Rosalind touched him without hesitation, as if the expression were completely natural and not something that caused his world to stop and then crash down around him. Sucking in a breath, he tried to control his cock, which had no concept of "down." Rosalind's cousin continued to glare at him, looking like he wanted to throw a punch and could probably land a decent one.

Luke might let the guy get in a couple of freebie swings, but he would absolutely not reopen the door on the irrational jealousy that had spurted through him when he'd first seen Rosalind hugging the guy. Whether she hooked up with a coworker or embraced a relative, he'd given up his claim on her. He'd done it so she could move on and find a guy who could give her the things she needed.

Removing her hand from his flesh, she folded her arms across her chest, pushing her breasts against the soft fabric of the red Western shirt embroidered with her name and the resort's logo. A horse poked its muzzle over a stall door a few paces away and snorted. The stiffness melted from her posture, and Rosalind stepped toward the animal, patting its nose and murmuring nonsense. Then, without glancing at Luke, she marched out of the stable.

If she'd looked back, she would have caught him ogling her ass. Worse, she would have noticed his limp hadn't improved and had probably even worsened. But at least he hadn't given in to using the cane yet.

With him following a couple of paces behind, she strode down a wide concrete path toward a wooden, ranch house-style building. A rough-hewn sign in front had been etched with the words, *Mac's Bar*. Large rocking chairs on the front porch served as outdoor seating.

Bypassing them, she opened the door, holding it for him. He didn't need anyone to do so, but no doubt she remembered those first weeks out of the hospital when he had needed assistance with everything. He grasped the edge of the door and motioned her in first.

She waved to the burly lumberjack of a man behind the bar.

"Rosalind." His crinkled face lit up, and he shuffled out from behind the counter toward her. "How did I get so lucky to have you visit me this early in the day?"

"Hey, Mac." She hugged him and kissed his cheek. "I'm the lucky one to get the afternoon off to spend with you, and you can tell Carmela I said so."

He chuckled and tapped the brim of her hat. "Oh, you better believe I will, and I'll tell her you gave me a lip-smackin' kiss to boot. What can I get for you, darling?"

"Lemonade, please. And whatever Luke wants, as well." She tipped her head in his direction, including him in their cozy reunion.

"Whiskey. Neat." The upcoming conversation definitely warranted a drink to get through.

"Bring an extra lemonade for Luke too. No one can step in here without giving your homemade specialty a try," Rosalind said.

"Do you want a whiskey for yourself?" he asked her.

"Absolutely not." She patted the bartender's arm. "I can't afford to have anything cloud my judgment. Excuse me. I need to wash my hands before I sit down."

Luke found himself in the crosshairs of a steely glare. Mac may not have said a word, but he'd delivered the same message Javier had sent. Rosalind's friends were lining up for a turn at ripping him apart, not exactly the way Luke had planned for the day to go when he'd boarded the plane.

With her out of the room, he took his time arranging his leg into a comfortable position under the table. As the bartender brought their drinks, she emerged from the bathroom, the edges of her hair damp around her face. She set her hat on an empty chair, and Mac squeezed her shoulder. Before marching away, he shot Luke another deadly scowl.

Rosalind settled onto the empty chair across from him. "So, uh—" She unwrapped a straw and swirled it in her lemonade. "What things need to be finalized? I thought I'd signed everything the lawyers needed."

He clenched his jaws. Her rushing to finish the last of the business tying them together shouldn't have ticked him off, but it did. "I thought so, too. The judge was supposed to rubber-stamp it this morning. Unfortunately, the identity theft app I'd been working on that just seemed to eat our money—"

"And Alex's money," she added.

"Yeah." Of course, she knew. He didn't have to explain the past to her. She'd been by his side the whole time, supporting him every second until he'd turned his back on her. "Well, it suddenly took off. We stopped bleeding money, and it started pouring in instead. The company's worth more than I ever dreamed, way more than when you signed all those papers that gave me the company and its debt without giving you anything in return."

She shook her head, her braid whipping with the ferocity of the movement. "I don't want your money, Luke. I never wanted your money."

Never having doubted the assertion, he lifted his whiskey.

"Your baby, yes, but not your money," she said, her solemn gaze boring into him.

He tossed back the liquor. If only the path burning down his throat would make him forget his dreams of having a baby with her. "Without a lawyer representing your interests, the judge believed you were getting ripped off with the settlement we'd agreed on. The truth is, you would have gotten ripped off by that agreement, so I'm glad we have a chance to make it fair."

Once again, her braid whipped back and forth with her emphatic denial. "The company is yours and Alex's. I didn't do anything except cook dinner and give you space to work. I came into our marriage with nothing, and I left with nothing, so I came out even."

The whiskey burned in his gut without taking the edge off his nerves. He slapped the empty glass on the table. "You wasted ten years of your life with me. I don't call that even."

"I don't call it a waste," she shot back. "If we'd had a kid, then, yes, I'd take your money and put it in an account for his or her future, but that never happened. I don't need or want anything for myself."

He closed his eyes. "You should be thankful we don't have a kid."

"We had a deal, Luke. When you retired from the Marines, we'd start a family."

"I got my leg blown off," he shouted, opening his eyes to glare at her, hating the sorrow in her voice and himself for not being able to deliver on her dream. "We never took that scenario into account."

She shoved her drink away. "Your leg is not the same piece of anatomy as your dick. Maybe you hadn't noticed because you've been too busy *being* a dick."

Yes, yell at me. Take your anger out on me. He wanted her hate and resentment, not her sorrow and disappointment. Luke reached for the extra lemonade and slammed back half of it before saying, "You're right. I was a dick. I don't deserve you. I never did. I want you to have the chance to find someone better than me, to get something better from him than what you got from our relationship."

"Well, money won't make that happen." She slumped her shoulders, her voice little more than a whisper. "You don't have to pay me to go away, Luke. I'll just go."

The lemonade turned sour in his stomach, and he pushed aside the half-empty glass. Every divorce he'd witnessed from the sidelines or heard tales of later, the couple had fought over money, with each party claiming as much of the pie as he or she could get away with. But Rosalind offered him everything. He hated the possibility that someone down the road might take advantage of her generosity. She needed to look out for herself first, not him.

Perhaps, he could make her do so by convincing her to hate him and then take his money in revenge. "Look, I didn't come here with the intention of tracking you down."

Her soulful brown eyes widened, and she lifted her glass again. "You just happened to be wandering around Montana, and here I was?"

"I signed up for a blind-date one-night stand at this resort, and I ran into you by accident while I was waiting for my date to arrive. But I'm sitting with you now because I really don't want to be married to you when I sleep with someone else tonight."

Chapter Four

The drink slipped through Rosalind's fingers. Pale-yellow liquid and ice cubes spilled down her shirt before the heavy glass shattered on the floor.

Ever a man of action, Luke shoved away from the table and called to Mac. But she remained frozen, unable to care about the drama of the spill. She'd been keeping her shit together over Luke seeking her out to finalize their divorce. But the admission that he wanted to have sex with someone else paralyzed her. It destroyed her.

He'd moved beyond their relationship, beyond fixating on ending it. He was ready to start a new chapter of his life. But she couldn't move on. Body, heart and soul, she'd loved him and still did. A divorce wouldn't change her feelings, and neither would seeing him with another woman. But it sure as hell would hurt.

From the direction of the bar, a towel flew toward them. Stretching upward, Luke snagged it from the air with quick reflexes and a gorgeous display of biceps and washboard abs. "Here. Use this to dry your shirt." He held it toward her.

After fumbling for it, she pressed it to her chest. His hand still tangled in the cloth ended up covering her breast, his palm rubbing her beaded nipple.

He hissed and squeezed his eyes closed. But instead of yanking his hand away, he became immobile, warming her through the wet fabric until the reaction of her breast to the cold morphed to one of desire. Desire he no longer returned.

Breaking contact, she pushed back her chair, her cowboy boots crunching on the broken glass. Broom and dust pan in hand, Mac joined her, and she reached to take the equipment from him. "I made the mess. I'll clean it."

"I'll take care of it," he said. "You worry about changing your shirt."

Glancing down, she took in the outline of her bra on clear display through the clinging red fabric. As soon as Luke had told her he planned to sleep with someone else, she'd poured a drink on herself to get a classic, "wet T-shirt contest" reaction. She'd crossed the line from desperate into pathetic. "Guess I'd better. Sorry for the trouble, Mac."

"You're no trouble." He cut a harsh glower toward Luke. "He, on the other hand, needs to get the hell out of my bar if he values his life."

With the jukebox off and no one else around to distract him, Mac had likely heard the entire conversation. She couldn't defend Luke when his intentions had cut her so deeply.

Hugging the towel across her chest, she pivoted toward her not-quite ex-husband. "The main resort building has a business center on the second floor. You can use it to print out whatever papers you need me to sign to release my claim on your business and your money. While you start on that, I'll swing by my room and change clothes. I'll meet you over there."

Luke's gaze lingered on her chest. "I'll walk you to your place, or your car, or where you need to go. The lawyer will have to send me the documents, and that'll take a couple of minutes. But, once I get it, it should print in no time."

She shrugged, too cold, vulnerable, and beaten to argue. Besides, she wouldn't refuse a final chance to have him walk alongside her.

Outside, the sun nearly blinded her after the darkness inside the bar. Two ranch hands drove along the path on a golf cart. The bright light and her desperate imagination combined to create the illusion of Luke stepping in front of her to purposely block anyone from glimpsing her wet chest.

"So, how far away is your place? Do you have a house or an apartment nearby?" he asked after the cart had passed.

"Employee housing is down this path." She led the way along a narrow road behind the bar. "Most older employees, or those with families, live in town or out in the country. But the younger, single kids stay in the dorm-like, on-site housing. I'm the old woman of my dorm." She tried to force a laugh. Being old didn't bother her nearly as much as being single. "Can't beat the convenience, and I don't have to worry about transportation."

"I'll make sure the settlement gives you at least enough money to buy a house and a car," Luke said.

The idea of a place for herself alone left her cold. "I'd buy my own horses before I bought either of those things."

"Then do that. Or all three."

"No." She glared at him. "I'm working my dream job with all the horses I could want. For the last time, I don't need or want your money, Luke. Stop insulting me by throwing it in my face."

"I wasn't insulting you," he muttered.

Anger being preferable to pain, she stomped the rest of the way into the dorm.

Most everyone was working in the middle of the day, but nineteen-year-old Hank lay sprawled on the couch in the common room. He half-turned and waved then swung around and leaned over the edge of the couch, staring from her to Luke. "*You* brought a guy back with you? No way."

Heat crept up her cheeks. Her time of sexual experimentation had ended as soon as she'd laid eyes on Luke. Once he'd left, she'd had no interest in opening her bedroom door to anyone else. And Luke certainly hadn't followed her with the intention of getting it on in her ridiculously small bedroom. He had a much better offer lined up for the night.

Without the sun casting any illusions, he stepped between her and Hank, and Rosalind offered hasty introductions then said, "You two can hang out together while I shower and change."

Hank opened his mouth, but before he could embarrass her with another smart-ass comment, she added, "And, Hank, Luke is a Marine. He could take you down using only his pinkies."

"Former Marine," Luke corrected, his right hand balling into a fist.

"Always a Marine," she shot back.

After Rosalind disappeared down the hall, Luke limped to the nearest chair. For her sake, he'd pretended not to favor his shitty hip on the walk. To pay for it, he'd spend the rest of the day limping twice as badly.

The kid on the couch eyed him, probably wanting to kick his ass, too, although, compared to Javier and Mac, his glare didn't inspire much concern. "How'd you meet Rosalind?" Hank asked.

Luke closed his eyes and rested his head on the back of the chair. "Horse trailer with a flat tire. You know how to change a tire, kid?"

"Never tried. I hope I don't have to find out."

"Learn how," Luke advised. "It could be the best thing that ever happens to you."

She'd been giving horseback rides to soldiers' kids through some volunteer program on base, and her trailer had ended up with a flat. He'd been acting like a smartass during training all day, so while everyone else got the evening off, he'd been pegged to go out and change her tire. Within seconds of catching a glimpse of her face beneath her cowboy hat, he'd been smitten. For reasons Luke had never understood, the feeling had been mutual. Six weeks later, they'd married and begun their happily ever after.

Fairy tale endings were nothing but a pack of lies.

"Luke, if you want to, you can come back," Rosalind called from down the hall.

He opened his eyes. Hank gawked at him like he was the luckiest bastard ever. He stared down the kid with enough lethalness to ensure the boy thought twice before putting the moves on Rosalind. Then he limped down the hall, stopping at the open bedroom door.

Dressed in a turquoise Western shirt, jeans, and cowboy boots, Rosalind stood in front of a small mirror, brushing out her wet hair. She glanced at him but didn't smile.

"So, this is home?" Luke glanced around the room. A twin bed, small nightstand, and simple chest consumed most of the floor space. She could have so much more if she took his money. Even the modest base housing had provided more comforts.

"The stable is home," she corrected. "This is where I sleep." She set the brush on top of the chest and spun away from the mirror to the nightstand. Her hand trembled as she lifted a gold band from a small, clear tray. Holding the ring between her thumb and index finger, she twisted toward him. "I don't wear this. It just sits on my nightstand. If we're over, you should take it back."

Facing down a flurry of fists from her overprotective friends didn't make him flinch, but the tiny metal circle did. He warded it away with his palm. "I don't want it."

"Take it anyway." She pushed it into the center of his palm and closed his fingers around it. "Maybe I'll be able to move on if I don't stare at your ring every night before I go to bed and when I wake up every morning. Makes me sound kind of creepy, huh?" Her lips quavered.

"You need to step up your game if you want to creep me out." He thumped his chest. "Marine, remember?"

A smile blossomed on her face, and he grinned in return, relieved he'd avoided causing more pain. The cold band in his palm, though, erased any temporary relief. Of course, he had hurt her when he'd left her, but he'd believed she would bounce back and get over him quickly. In some ways, she had. She'd moved away and poured herself into a job she obviously loved. But, if he interpreted the other clues right, she seemed to have no interest in moving on from a relationship standpoint.

Maybe returning his ring signaled a start. Good for her. Unfortunately, its presence had the opposite effect on him. He dropped the band into his pocket, afraid he would spend the upcoming months staring at it, unable to continue to his plan to get over her and on with his life.

Rosalind's limbs trembled so much she nearly abandoned the braid she could normally form in her sleep. At last, she secured the hairband around the scraggly end and plopped her hat on her head. Good enough. Fussing over her appearance wouldn't stop their relationship from ending, and it wouldn't make Luke look any less gorgeous while he ended it.

Refusing to glance at the empty tray on her nightstand that mirrored the emptiness in her heart, she squared her shoulders and faced him. "Do your lawyers have everything ready?"

"They should, by the time we get to the business center."

Unable to speak, she nodded. No delay then. They'd reached the end. Leading him out of the room and down the hall, she prayed Hank would ignore them.

Of course, nothing had gone the way she'd wanted so far. Hank gawked over the back of the couch. "Damn, I think you broke a record for the fastest quickie ever in this dorm."

Luke opened his mouth, but she didn't give him a chance to speak. "We don't always get to control how long things last," she called to Hank, and then slammed out the door.

If she had her way, she and Luke would last forever. Why did he have to come to end their relationship in person in the most painful way possible? Oh yeah, because he had a date to sleep with someone else and needed to check Rosalind off his list of things to do first.

Lengthening her strides to stay ahead of him, she swiped at her cheeks to keep them dry. She could cry on the inside. She could cry later. But she would not let him see her pain.

As she approached the stables, she slowed. A couple of horses were grazing on the other side of the fence, and she called to the closest stallion. He perked up his ears and trotted over, nuzzling for sugar cubes. Dang, her pockets were empty.

"Hang on, Smokey. I'll grab one from my stash."

Luke had caught up, and she called, "This will just take a minute," as she headed for the stable. He grunted, but she hadn't been asking permission.

She slipped around the corner, took a sugar cube from her locker, and then returned, offering the treat to her eager friend. After stroking Smokey's face for a moment, she reluctantly swung her attention to Luke.

With his back against the sturdy rails of the fence and his face tipped to the blue sky, he appeared in no hurry to continue their torturous march to the hotel. Maybe she could stall and earn a few more minutes of treasured memories before the inevitable end. "Do you want to go for a ride?"

"On a horse?" Luke's expression was incredulous. "Have you forgotten about my leg?"

Of course, she hadn't forgotten, but she didn't see why it mattered. "A prosthetic shouldn't stop you from riding."

"I'm not some little kid you can lift on and off the saddle," he snapped.

"You can get on another way. Don't use it as an excuse."

"An excuse?" His eyes bulged, along with a vein on his neck. "It's not a freaking excuse. It's real. I lost half my left leg, and the remaining half is a pretty shitty. I'm going to need a hip replacement in the next couple of years. Instead of getting better, my limp's getting worse."

After all he'd been through, she hated to think of him continuing to suffer and enduring more medical procedures. She hated even more that he didn't want her by his side to help him through his new trials. "I'm sorry your limp hasn't improved. I'm sorry your hip causes you pain and discomfort. Mostly, I'm sorry you haven't accepted your injury is a permanent fact of your life."

"I don't want you to feel sorry for me," he gritted out.

Sudden fury engulfed her. She stomped so close the brim of her hat bumped his forehead. "Oh no, you wouldn't want me to feel sorry for you. You want to keep your monopoly on feeling sorry for yourself, so you can just wallow in it and use it to push people away."

His eyes narrowed, but she wasn't done.

"I see people on this ranch with far more debilitating injuries, diseases, and disabilities than you have, and they climb, crawl, and wrestle their way onto my horses. But more than just riding, they *try* to keep living, instead of cutting out every part of their lives that existed before their injury or illness."

His jaw tightened. "I'm still living. I didn't cut out my past life."

"You cut *me* out," she whispered, retreating. Pain coated her anger. Worse, he was still trying to cut her out.

He rubbed the spot where her hat had touched him. "I didn't have a choice whether to live with my injury. You did."

Anger surging past the pain, she shoved his chest. "I never got to have a choice. You made the choice for me." And she never, ever would have chosen to turn her back on him.

Chapter Five

"What would you do if you had the choice?" Luke demanded.

Not leave you, God damn it. If she told him what she wanted, he would stop her. So, she simply did it, molding the length of her body to his as she kissed him. His lips were warm and moist, contrasting with his hardness everywhere else, and Rosalind glided over their lushness, savoring their exquisite shape and texture.

She explored each corner of his mouth and sucked his lower lip. Then she kissed him full on again, clutching his face in her hands. Her hat dislodged and slid off, but she didn't stop to retrieve it. Skating her tongue along the seam, she teased him until he opened and allowed her inside.

He tasted like whiskey and lemonade and pure, masculine, one hundred percent Luke. Like an addict, she couldn't get enough. When at last he rubbed his tongue with hers, a sob escaped her. She missed his kisses, his affection, him. She missed him so much. If only she could hold him forever. But she had to let him go. She should have already let him go.

Rosalind shoved away from him, picked up her hat from the ground, tipped it low over her face, and paced away. Luke closed his eyes and leaned on the fence, grateful for the sturdy construction. If it collapsed, he would go down with it. His unsteadiness, though, had nothing to do with his crap leg and everything to do with his wife.

He wanted her to continue kissing him forever. He wanted her choices to guide them because hers were a hell of a lot more enjoyable than any he'd made since he'd returned to the States on a gurney.

"What the hell did you do to her?"

Luke's eyes popped open. Fists bunched, Javier strode toward him from the direction of the stable. Glancing at Rosalind to see if she would attempt to soothe the situation or let him take the punch he deserved, Luke blinked in shock. Doubled over in the grass across the sidewalk, she held her hat over her face, shoulders shaking as strangled sobs spilled from her.

Rosalind never cried. Never. Not when he'd been deployed to a war zone. Not when she'd sat by his side in the hospital. Not even when he'd told her their relationship was over. The sight punched through him harder than any fist her cousin could land.

Lodging her hat into place, she straightened and swiveled toward her cousin. "He didn't do anything. I'm the one to blame."

"Then why are you crying and he's not?" Javier demanded.

Instead of answering, she turned to Luke, her face blotchy, tears streaming. In that moment, he would have given her the world, cut off his other leg for her, anything she wanted in exchange for holding her in his arms again and taking away her pain.

"I need some time to myself," she said, blowing out an unsteady breath. "How about I meet you in the business center in an hour? The staff can help you print out whatever you need, and they have plenty of pens."

Pens? Why were they discussing pens instead of the fact that kissing him had made her cry?

"If you get everything ready, I'll sign whatever you put in front of me," she continued. "Then I'll be out of your life, and you'll be free to do whatever you can't do as long as I'm in the way."

She wasn't in his way. With his half-assed leg, physical therapy needs, and perpetual limp, he would be in her way, and he couldn't stand burdening her with his problems. But he'd also been wrong to make the choice for her. In trying to save them both heartache, he'd created more.

He needed to better explain the reasons he'd pushed her away and prove they had nothing to do with her or how he felt about her. Hopefully, then she would come to the same conclusion he had, without resenting or crying over him.

Before he could put his disjointed thoughts into words, Rosalind traipsed into the stable. With another glare that promised a brain bashing for him, Javier followed her.

A few minutes later, Luke continued to support his weight on the wooden railing. Not only had the kiss left him reeling, sick dread from her promise to get out of his life coiled within him. Something clattered, and he twisted toward the corral.

Perched on the back of a horse, her cowboy hat straight on her head, Rosalind galloped across the pasture, her figure growing smaller, and the hole in his chest growing larger. After she crested the hill and disappeared from sight, he studied the remaining horses. The one she'd fed the sugar cube to was gone.

When he looked away from the corral, he found Javier watching him. Since the guy hadn't started beating him to a pulp yet, maybe Luke still had a chance. "Can you help me get my ass up on a horse, so I can go talk to her?"

"You've said more than enough already."

"What I've said has made it worse."

Javier slapped his black cowboy hat against his thigh. "No shit."

"Look, I didn't realize how much I'd hurt her by leaving. I thought she'd be long over me by now. I want to give her whatever closure she needs. Finalizing the divorce is the best thing I can do for her."

"You expect me to believe making her sign something your lawyers have drawn up is really having her best interests at heart?"

"I don't expect you to believe anything I tell you, but you heard her agree to sign. I'm not 'making her' do it."

"Oh yeah, I could definitely tell she agreed of her own free will," Javier said with heavy sarcasm.

Luke shoved away from the fence and limped toward the other man. "I'm trying to give her more money. The judge overseeing our case wants her to have more money. If you have any influence over her and can convince her to take me to the cleaners, I'd love for her to sign something that will set her up for life. God knows she deserves it for putting up with me."

Javier glowered at him, but Luke refused to blink first.

Finally, her cousin said, "You're not the complete asshole I expected. I'll make you a deal. I'll put you on a horse and send you out toward Rosalind on the condition that she signs none of your documents until the lawyers in my legal department have looked them over for her first."

Relief hit him so hard and fast, Luke nearly swayed. Extending his right hand, he said, "Deal."

ఴ

Tucked off the main trail, Rosalind lay on a blanket on her favorite knoll. Hidden from view by trees and the natural rise of the ground, she could keep the real world at bay and pretend Luke hadn't shown up insisting they put an immediate end to their already-dead marriage.

But, perhaps because it felt like a fantasy rather than reality, she couldn't pretend she hadn't kissed him. The wellspring of emotion when she'd done so had led to the most amazing, beautiful sensations she'd experienced since the last time they'd made love. While caressing him, she'd memorized each of his features to play over and over in her mind for the rest of eternity.

After closing herself off from all emotion for so many months, she'd become overwhelmed by the sudden overload, sobbing the way she'd promised herself she would never do in front of him. Well, she'd done it, revealing her weakness and how badly he'd hurt her.

Grazing close enough for her to hear the crunch of field grass between his molars, Smokey nickered, a tone usually reserved as a welcome to other horses. More horses, she could deal with. Human riders, she could not.

She twisted to look. A single horse and rider crested the hill and turned down the side path toward her. Her breath caught. Rather than a real-world intrusion, the gorgeous man approaching embodied her deepest fantasy.

Although she'd been tough on Luke for refusing to try to mount a horse, some people couldn't and shouldn't attempt to ride. She wasn't a doctor, and hadn't been privy to his medical information for over a year. She no longer knew the extent of his capabilities. But that hadn't stopped her from unleashing a tirade on him.

Georgina whinnied a greeting, and Rosalind stood on shaky legs to greet the team. "What are you doing out here?"

Luke's crooked smile nearly sent her fragile heart into cardiac arrest. "You said I should stop making excuses and try to ride, so I did."

"Nice. I guess it would be rude to say 'I told you so.'" Maybe if Rosalind played it cool, the act would keep her from throwing herself at him again.

"How about I'll let you say it if you help me dismount?"

She helped grown men dismount on a regular basis, but wasn't so naive she assumed she'd be as unaffected by his closeness as she was with the resort guests. Still, she wouldn't deprive either of them because of her weakness. She moved to the left side of the horse and took control of the reins.

"Put some of your weight on my shoulder and back as you climb down. You can also hang onto the saddle horn while you swing your right leg over to keep the weight off your left leg until you have your right side under you to support you. How did you get on Georgina?"

"Your cousin tossed my sorry ass up here. Although, I ended up riding for so long I thought maybe he'd sent me out in hopes I'd never return and archeologists would find my skeleton in a fifty years or something." Luke chuckled, the rumbling tone sending shivers through her belly. Using the horse's strong back to support his weight, he maneuvered down, avoiding putting pressure on his left side.

Javier. *Interesting.* The guys must have worked through their macho posturing and moved on to male bonding. She almost wished she'd stuck around to witness the transition. Maybe Javier would tell his wife Caroline, about the exchange, and Rosalind could convince her to share her insight.

"I can't vouch for Javier's intentions toward you, but I know he'd send out a search party for Georgina if the two of you didn't return by dark."

Luke snorted. "You might have mentioned that before I got off the horse."

She grinned. "This is my favorite spot on the ranch, besides the stables, of course. I won't let you die and ruin the atmosphere with a decaying body."

Releasing the horse, he placed his hand on her shoulder. "Keep talking like that, and I might get the impression you care what happens to me."

His banter lifted her heart. What a relief to have a conversation without every word between them launching an emotion-packed grenade.

She motioned him toward the frayed quilt. "I don't have a chair for you to sit on, but you can share my blanket."

After he released her and stepped away, she loosened Georgina's saddle and tucked up the reins, allowing her to graze freely next to Smokey.

Luke sank to the ground with an awkward shuffle, stretching out first his injured left leg, then the right. For some yet-to-be-determined reason, he'd followed her rather than accept her request for alone time. Thankfully, he hadn't brought any papers that she could see, so impatience didn't appear to be the cause.

In the relatively short time she'd had to think, Rosalind had already gained some perspective. She would be alone for the rest of her life with years to regret not taking advantage of every moment with Luke. So, she tugged off her boots and lined them up in the grass at the edge of the blanket, balancing her hat on top of them. Then she lay back next to him and stared up at the impossibly blue sky.

A few puffy white clouds passed over. Luke shifted, the denim of his jeans rustling, a sound that shouldn't have been sexy but was.

"I need to apologize for making you cry," he said.

She turned her head toward him. Lying on his right side, he faced her, torso propped up by his elbow, his cheek resting on his open palm.

She could have wept simply from the gorgeousness of his pose.

Instead, she said, "No apology necessary. It's not the first time I've cried over you. I'm sure it won't be the last."

His eyes clouded. "I hadn't witnessed it before, and I hate knowing I hurt you that much."

Hated it, maybe, but not enough to change his mind about pushing her out of his life. She angled toward him. "I didn't mean for my crying comment to sound so pathetic. I don't cry over you all the time. I have a good life here, and I love what I do. I'm going to be fine when you leave."

Of course, she would be heartbroken, but she could live a pretty good life with a broken heart.

He tucked a stray hair behind her ear. "You are an amazing woman."

Skin tingling from his gentle touch, she blinked at the unexpected compliment. She obviously hadn't been amazing enough for him, but she still appreciated the affirmation. "Thanks. I'm glad the app you worked so hard on became a success. I've talked to some guests who use it, and they are delighted to have the extra financial and identity protection."

"You don't use it?"

"As soon as you figure out how to integrate an app into a bridle or a saddle, I'll be first in line. Until then, I'm about as low-tech as you can get."

"Still no cell phone?"

"I always thought the last holdout on a technology should get some sort of prize." She grinned, working hard to keep the conversation light despite her intense curiosity about his life without her. "Are you still doing all the techy stuff with the app?"

"I've hired a couple of guys who keep up with the daily maintenance, so I can focus on long-term development and investor relations."

"Investor relations? You?" She'd had to stop him from punching the poor bank officer who'd turned down his loan application. Thankfully, Alex had believed in him enough to back his dream and help him launch his post-military career.

He grinned. "Yeah, I knew you'd see the humor in that, but I can schmooze when I have to."

"I know you can." She tipped her face toward the clouds again. Luke had the charisma to win anyone over whenever he chose to turn it on. Having a wife who preferred the company of horses over people wouldn't win any converts. From a business standpoint, dumping her made sense.

Warm lips pressed to hers, and her eyes popped open. Luke skimmed his mouth over hers with such delicious perfection. She lifted her arms and encircled his neck. Nothing could be more heavenly than lying under a clear blue sky and kissing the man she loved.

He caressed her cheek, each stroke so tender and sweet. Instead of crying for the experience they would never repeat, she savored every second in his arms. He kissed a trail along her jaw and then teased her earlobe until she shivered.

As he chuckled against her ear, she captured his still-smiling lips with her own. Dragging her fingers through his hair, she massaged his scalp the way he'd always enjoyed when his hair had been shorter. The strands had grown long enough to sift between her fingers, but the same groan of pleasure spilled from his lips.

He slipped his tongue between her teeth, increasing the fervor of the kiss. She wanted to continue watching the passion and intensity blossom on his face, but, unable to keep her eyes open, she let her other senses take over. Managing to cherish and ravish her at once, he explored her neck and throat with gentle caresses.

When he cupped her breast, she arched, hating her clothing for preventing skin-on-skin contact. Kissing him harder, she tugged his T-shirt from his waistband until she could drag her hands underneath and knead his warm, smooth back.

His sinewy muscles rippling in intriguing ways as he shifted, Luke tugged apart the first snap on her shirt. "How far do you want to take this, Rosalind?"

"Further than you want to go."

Chapter Six

*I*f Luke hoped she'd be the one to jerk the reins of common sense on the runaway horse of desire, he was mistaken. Rosalind pulled his shirt over his head and tossed it away from the blanket.

"If you believe that, you don't know me as well as you think you do." He captured her hand with his own and pressed it on the fly of his jeans.

Oh Lord. Her mouth dried, and her stomach flipped at the thick, hard evidence of his desire. She'd been prepared for his size, but not Luke's visceral reaction to her. Regardless of the questionable status of their relationship, he still wanted her. Desperate not to throw away her final chance, she opened his jeans. "Yes. I want you inside me."

"Promise?"

Till death do us part. She swallowed the vow from years ago so she wouldn't scare him into changing his mind. She'd take as much as he offered. Somehow, it would have to be enough to last her until death.

"Yes." She tugged on his neck and kissed him again, letting her lips and tongue converse with his in the one language where he'd always agreed with her.

He ripped apart the rest of the snaps then raised her above the blanket to peel the shirt away and unhook her bra. Once he'd bared her chest, he laid her back again and lifted his mouth from hers. "You are so beautiful."

"You make me feel beautiful," she whispered, drifting her fingers through his hair again.

With a brush of his mouth across her chin, he trailed lower, resting his face in the center of her chest, his hands cupping the sides of her breasts. Contentment radiated off him, an emotion she hadn't felt from him since he'd lost his leg.

Despite her core pulsing with desire and her breasts aching for his attention, Rosalind would have happily ignored her needs to lie unmoving, basking in his tenderness, for the rest of her life.

Capturing her nipple with his mouth, Luke swirled his tongue around it and tugged with his lips. No longer able to lie there and let him control every aspect of the encounter, she arched. He continued to play with her nipple, enrapturing her, while unbuttoning her jeans. Eager to help him shed her unwanted clothes, she elevated her hips.

Moving lower, Luke kissed the underside of her breast then journeyed down her navel. He dragged her jeans and panties down together before rolling to his side. Drawing his hands along each leg, he chucked her jeans next to her boots in the grass.

He sat up and freed his cock from his open pants. It bobbed as he ogled her from top to bottom, his gaze searing her nerve endings and melting her core.

"Touch me," she begged.

"Where?"

"Everywhere."

He smiled and glided his tongue along her inner elbow. She jerked in surprise, the emotion immediately replaced by another shot of desire. Moaning her need, she opened her legs in invitation. He propped her foot on his shoulder, caressing her thigh then skimming his lips across the sensitive inner skin.

"Trace your finger along my slit." She'd meant to issue an order, but instead she begged her desperation for his intimate touch.

"If it's what you want." He drew the digit down her aching clit and along her soaked slit, spreading her wetness from front to back and then to her clit again.

"Luke, again, please." The leg propped on his shoulder shook uncontrollably. Perilously close to coming from the way he watched her with heavy-lidded eyes, mouth half open, chest rising and falling, she tumbled to the razor edge of pleasure from his glorious touch.

Grasping her hips, he lifted her to his face. With one long stroke, he licked her from top to bottom then teased her clit with quick flicks of his tongue.

Rosalind clenched the blanket in her fists, needing to scream but not wanting to let the pleasure culminate and end so quickly. He thrust his tongue inside her, and she couldn't hold back. Waves of pleasure slammed through her, and she convulsed, yelling his name.

Damn, she'd come so hard and fast. She'd never whipped so far out of control with so little warning, and she couldn't bear if Luke mocked her for doing so. But when she peered up at him, the intensity on his face never wavered. He lowered her slowly and then took a condom from his pocket. As soon as he'd sheathed himself, he reached for her again.

Of course, he would never mock her performance. Shame from thinking so filled her. She knew him better than that. He intended to continue to draw out her pleasure and his own, as well.

Gathering her strength, she pulled her boneless body to a sitting position. She didn't want to just come again. She wanted to connect, to make love, to become one.

Straddling his lap, she sank down, driving his thick, full cock inside her. "Luke."

"Oh yeah, baby. You feel so good."

She kissed him, tasting her pleasure. While she hurtled toward another climax, guaranteed to leave a permanent imprint on her, he called out with a generic *baby*, as if he didn't know the name of the person who made him *feel so good*. She couldn't let their encounter continue in a one-sided vein.

"Say my name," she whispered. "The version you only use when we make love."

Instead of speaking, he gripped her hips more firmly, plunging with long, sure deliberation. Needing him to see who he made love to, she bit his lip hard enough to force him to open his eyes. He drove his tongue into her mouth while pumping with hard, frantic tenacity.

Whether he purposely held back on giving her the personal nod she desired or had simply moved beyond speech, she couldn't tell. She could barely conjure her own name as she squeezed his waist with her thighs, drawing him in deeper, determined to show him how unforgettable he was to her.

"Rosie," he gasped.

Any triumph dissolved in the swirling vortex of longing. She'd missed him so much, missed the hot, desperate need, missed the perfect melding of bodies.

"Ah, God, Rosie. You are so sweet, so perfect."

She kissed him hard, cutting off the words she'd wanted so badly to hear, but could no longer handle without succumbing to tears. She would not break down in front of him again.

"Oh fuck, I'm coming. I can't hold it back." He stiffened, his hands digging into her ass cheeks. "Come with me, Rosie, please."

Luke never lost control. Never. And because he did, she spiraled out of control. His desperate command rocketed her over the edge. She clung to his torso and buried her face in his neck, rubbing his thundering pulse. She had everything she wanted. If only she could hang on to it and never let it end.

If Luke had his way, he would have stayed buried inside Rosalind forever. But he hadn't had his way since those assholes around the world had showed their love for him with a not-so-friendly grenade.

He held her for as long as he could stay still, but, finally, his hip became too twitchy. He lifted her to ease the pressure on his leg, and she shifted off his lap, ending their connection.

While she reached for her clothes and began dressing in silence, he cleaned up and tucked his cock in his pants then lay back on the quilt and stretched his hip.

They hadn't talked about the reasons he'd ended their relationship, as he'd intended when he set out to find her. He couldn't regret what had happened, but he also couldn't marshal the insensitivity to bring up a list of reasons he couldn't stay with her in the aftermath of such incredible sex.

Luke waited for Rosalind to finish dressing and cuddle against him. Instead, she tugged on her boots, affixed her cowboy hat on her head, and stood. With a single whistle, she garnered both horses' attention. He sighed. Not only had the time for talking passed, their peaceful interlude had come to an end, as well.

While she commandeered the animals, adjusted their gear, and murmured to each one, Luke reluctantly stood. A few tentative paces assured him his leg wouldn't give out, but he still limped like a pathetic old man. If he couldn't get back on the horse, he'd have to reconsider the scenario of future archeologists digging up the remains of his body. He'd never accomplish the return trip to the resort on foot.

"Georgina's ready for you if you're ready for her," Rosalind called.

"And how's that going to happen? You as my stepping stool is not an option." He wouldn't risk injuring her by making her bear more of his weight than she could handle.

"But this stump over here is, and you'll be able to do the rest, as long as your arm and core muscles are as strong as they used to be." She gestured toward a wide, flat, two-foot tall tree stump.

"Bring it," he challenged.

Her lips curled, and her approval stirred his cock and heated his blood. "Great, but I can't bring the stump to you. You have to come to it."

He grinned, almost not minding that she tracked his progress he approached.

"You can grip the horn of the saddle and push on Georgina's back to get on the stump. Then you should be high enough to climb on from there," Rosalind said, holding the horse's bridle with one hand and stroking the animal's face with the other.

Her confidence in him inspired him to prove her right. Luke didn't need to ask if the mare would cooperate. Rosalind's bond with it would keep it from bolting or turning on him.

In less than two minutes, he sat astride the horse. His wife crooned her praise to Georgina, but her eyes glittered up at him with an admiration he could have gotten lost in. Hell, before things had gone so wrong, he often had.

The return ride to the stables provided a helluva better view than the ride out. He got the pleasure of ogling Rosalind's firm ass encased in tight denim and her strong, straight back. By the time they entered the corral, he was in dire need of adjusting himself.

A plethora of stools and handles abounded at the stable to make dismounting almost too easy. Rosalind waved away his offer to help with the horses, so he shuffled over to the wall, out of her way, letting her do what she did best. He could have watched her work all day, but how quickly he'd fallen under her spell in the pasture scared the crap out of him. He needed to refocus on his real life.

Two text message notifications blinked at him from his phone. His lawyer delivered the first. *Great news. We've been contacted by your wife's lawyers and are negotiating. I expect the details to be hammered out quickly, so we can expedite the agreement through the system.*

The man had told Luke exactly what'd he wanted to hear on the plane at the beginning of the day, so why didn't it feel like great news anymore?

Not wanting to acknowledge the answer to his question, he clicked on the second text. *I hope you enjoyed your one-night stand. It's been a pleasure working with you. –Madame Eve.*

Enjoyed. Past tense. What the hell? He clicked reply, and typed, *I haven't had my one-night stand yet.* Hell, he hadn't even gotten into his hotel room yet.

After he shot off the retort, Luke realized Madame probably sent automated messages to all her clients, and his just happened to arrive in his inbox a bit early. The thought of going up to a hotel room to meet someone turned his stomach. He had to contact Madame again and postpone the hookup.

He'd offer to reimburse his date for her trouble. Whoever he'd been matched with would never compare to Rosalind. Going ahead with the date wouldn't be fair to the other woman, and he couldn't contemplate touching anyone else.

Before he could formulate the first sentence, another text from Madame Eve lit up the screen. *Rosalind Cox wanted exactly what you requested. She didn't care about your injuries or wealth. She just wanted you. I matched you with her.*

Regardless of Alex's stellar experience with the service, 1Night Stand was a crock of shit. He pounded his thumbs over the screen again. *Rosalind's my wife.*

In less than three seconds, another reply arrived. *Then your pairing is even more perfect.*

He stared at the message. Madame Eve had purposely set him up with Rosalind. Nothing about him running into his wife had been a coincidence after all.

Chapter Seven

"*I*s everything okay?" Rosalind approached him, concern on her face. She lifted her hand toward his shoulder but dropped it to her side before touching him.

"Yeah. Everything's great." He shoved the phone in his back pocket but couldn't meet her gaze.

She continued to stand in front of him, waiting.

He scrubbed his knuckles over his forehead, unable to imagine how she'd react to the news. Keeping the truth from her, though, would only make the situation worse. "I got a text from Madame Eve. Turns out you were the one-night stand date I traveled all this way for."

"Oh." She bit her lip. "Madame Eve's 1Night Stand service is the same one Javier used when he bought me a one-night stand date after I came to work here. I never planned to use it, but it was easier to go along with him than refuse."

"You never got a notification of our date?" Luke wanted to be angry but couldn't work up any steam. Rosalind had been far too shocked by his presence to have had any part in tricking him.

She shrugged. "I don't know. I haven't checked my e-mail in a couple of weeks. I can log in when we head to the business center and see if I missed any messages."

"A little late now."

She winced. "So, our quick tumble out in the pasture—that was what you came all this way for?"

"I guess so." Too bad she'd been resourceful enough find a way to get him back on the horse. They could have been stuck in the field for hours or maybe days, making love until her cousin finally sent a search party out to find them.

Rosalind fidgeted with the brim of her hat, tugging it over her eyes. "You must feel like you wasted a trip. I'm sorry."

Oh hell. He hadn't meant to shower her with guilt. Maybe he should have felt that the journey hadn't been worth it, but he didn't. Not a bit.

He pried her fingers off her hat and tipped it up so he could look into her eyes again. "I don't want you to be sorry. This is so unexpected, I don't know what to think, but I'm not sorry. I didn't waste a trip. I guess Madame Eve couldn't find anyone who was a better match for me than you. And if that's the case, my biggest disappointment is that I don't want our time to be over yet."

A brightness flickered in her gaze. "How long are you staying at the resort?"

"Until tomorrow."

She nodded and inhaled. "Invite me to your hotel room tonight."

His cock leapt, but, even more troubling, his heart did too. She offered him the opportunity to get the most out of his one-night stand date, and of course he would take it. But he'd never wanted just one night with his wife.

However, a single grenade had taught him he didn't get to have everything he wanted. Rosalind had carved out a life on the ranch. His life remained on the East Coast. Plus, his leg needed more surgery.

Nothing had changed since he'd left her. He couldn't offer her the happily-ever-after fairy tale they thought they were living after they'd said their vows.

Rosalind could read the misgivings on Luke's face, but he met her gaze and said dutifully, "Will you spend the night with me?"

"I thought you'd never ask." She winked and brushed her lips over his cheek. Whatever it cost her, she'd give him a light and easy, no-strings good time. She wouldn't ruin it with tears and emotion. Luke wanted a one-night stand, not a wife. And for one night, she'd be exactly that.

She tucked her hand around the crook of his elbow and led him out of the stable. In silence, they continued across the resort grounds to the hotel building.

"I still need to pick up the key to my room." He turned toward the check-in desk.

Across the lobby, Javier's wife Caroline—president of operations of the resort—motioned to her.

"Take your time. I need to talk to someone." Rosalind brushed her fingers over his bicep and then self-consciously walked toward the beautiful blonde who looked like she belonged on Rodeo Drive, not in the middle of rodeo country.

"I've been talking with Javier," Caroline began. "He's worried about the documents you've been asked to sign. Our legal department is looking them over for you, so, for your own protection, don't sign anything until they've finished their review."

Rosalind glanced toward the front desk where Luke already had his key card in hand. "I appreciate the concern and the trouble you've gone to for me, but I don't need your lawyers to make him bleed a bunch of money for me. I just want to give Luke what he wants, so he can have the life he wants."

Caroline followed her gaze. "He's the one, huh?"

He'd been The One since the moment he'd approached her, laughing that he was her roadside-assistance knight in non-shining, camouflage armor. Until he'd been injured overseas, he'd loved playing hero for whatever everyday rescue she'd required, but afterward, he'd rejected all labels that pegged him as her personal hero. However, he'd given her one more night. She would treasure the precious hours and minutes together before he left her for good.

He approached and pressed a key into her palm. "Room 503. Join me whenever you're ready."

"I was born ready," she quipped.

He tipped her hat to the side and sauntered toward the elevator without looking back.

As soon as he disappeared inside, she returned her attention to Caroline, but left her hat at the odd angle. The other woman watched her far too closely.

"Luke's not going to take advantage of me, either physically or in what he's asking me to sign," Rosalind assured her.

"All the same, the legal department wants to meet with you as soon as possible, so they can better understand your interests and help you get what you want."

"I appreciate the effort everyone's going to on my behalf, but it's not necessary. The only thing I'd like returned to me is my heart, and your lawyers can't draw up a contract to make that happen."

Caroline's expression softened, and she placed a manicured hand on Rosalind's arm. "You're part of the Alvarado family. Our legal counsel may not be able to give you what you want, but Javier and I will always be here for you, no matter what."

Tears filled Rosalind's eyes, and she hugged the woman who'd become both sister and friend to her, despite their opposite fashions and interests. "Thank you. I appreciate everything you've done for me. Truly. I'll meet with the lawyers as soon as Luke checks out tomorrow."

"And you'll have dinner with Javier and me tomorrow evening," Caroline decreed.

She nodded, welcoming all the family and support she could get. Although Luke would soon be gone from her life, he'd still be fresh in her heart and would remain there forever.

After she left the lobby, Rosalind stopped in the restroom to wipe all traces of despair from her face. With a wide smile fixed in place, she entered Luke's room and secured the door behind her. Although the room appeared empty, she spotted a box of condoms on the nightstand and a light shining from under the bathroom door.

Perfect.

Her smile became genuine, and she stripped off her clothes. Naked, she adjusted the cowboy hat on her head and approached the bed. After tossing aside the sheets, she sat with her back against the wall, knees raised and legs spread.

"Hey, you sexy Marine," she called. "I hear you're looking for a good time tonight, and that's exactly what I'm here for."

No strings. Nothing to make him feel guilty for leaving her in the morning.

Thank goodness Luke's heart had been given a clean bill of health at his last checkup. If it had been in anything less than top condition, he would have gone into cardiac arrest when he stepped out of the bathroom. His number-one fantasy lounged on his bed with a come-hither smile, a cowboy hat, and nothing else.

Holding his gaze, she trailed her hand down her chest, over her slightly rounded stomach, and into her pussy.

"Oh God, Rosie." His cock strained, trying to drive its way out of his jeans and into her. He ached to lick her sweetness from her fingers. He wanted to devour her.

Unfortunately, he couldn't make his legs move toward her. Not because of all the things wrong with his crap leg, but because he feared the fantasy would dissolve if he moved closer. A Marine didn't show fear, but, for a moment, it paralyzed him.

Still staring at him, she lifted her hand and licked each digit. Then she tipped her hat just low enough to break eye contact with him and dropped her feet off the mattress. Standing on the carpet, she sauntered toward him, hips and breasts swaying. "You didn't invite me to your room so you could stand all the way over here by your lonesome, did you?"

He gathered what remained of his wits. "Of course not. I was just enjoying the view."

"Good. I have some close-ups to show you, too."

His brain cell deserted him again, but his cock nodded its eagerness.

Rosalind sashayed behind him. Grazing his back, she slid his shirt up and over his head. After tossing it aside, she brushed her lips between his shoulder blades and encircled him with her arms, gliding her palms over his chest, her breasts pressing against his back.

The sweetness surrounding him teased him with so many possibilities, yet didn't allow him to act on any of them. Needing to act and explore the body she'd so willingly bared for him, he reached around and palmed her ass. Before he could enjoy the delightful curve of it, his leg wobbled.

Taking a step forward, he caught his balance but propelled out of her embrace. *Shit.* He'd hoped to avoid such a pathetic move. Slowly, he turned toward her, unable to dodge her reaction. "If my leg wouldn't give out, I'd take you against the wall over and over while you screamed for more."

Her neutral expression didn't waver. "Good thing your leg isn't cooperating because I have other plans for you tonight."

He blinked. Neither desire nor disappointment for the fantasy he could never fulfill flared in her eyes. Instead, she jiggled her assets and stalked him, backing him toward the bed. She had plans for him? He'd taken the lead in the vast majority of their past sexual encounters and had assumed he would again.

Just before he bumped the edge of the bed, Rosalind grasped the waistband of his jeans and tugged his pelvis toward her. Her knuckles teased his navel while she worked his button free and lowered his zipper.

"How far are you planning to take this seduction?" he asked while he could still manage to push words through his lips.

"All the way." She stroked her palm over the bulge in his briefs. "You got a problem with that?"

"Hell, no." Not as long as she kept up the barrage of attention on his greedy sex organ.

"Good." She dropped his jeans down his hips then followed them with his briefs. His cock sprang free, and she rubbed a palm across the head.

Pleasure and need swamped him. Hissing, he eased into a sitting position on the bed before he fell. Rosalind leaned over him, trailing kisses down the length of his shaft.

Wanting to pleasure her, too, but lacking the discipline to shift away from her heavenly mouth, he circled his palm around her breast and teased the nipple with his thumb.

To his disappointment, she abandoned his cock and knelt, giving her full attention to working his jeans farther down his hips. "Can I take your prosthetic off, or do you want to unfasten it, so we can get you out of these jeans?"

Detaching the device from his knee was the most expedient way to get out of his clothes, but no one saw him without his prosthetic except his doctor, and occasionally his physical therapist. He wouldn't return to being the helpless man who needed his wife to attach his limb and dress him. "No. Nothing comes off. The jeans are low enough for everything we want to do."

Rosalind released him and stood, fisting her hands on her hips and pursing her lips. "No way am I spending the entire night with a man who won't make the effort to take his pants off to be with me. I'm not having a half-assed one-night stand, Luke. I want you as naked as I am."

Chapter Eight

*H*aving accepted her as his date, Luke shuddered at the possibility she might bail on him. But remove the prosthetic—no. He would not compromise on that point. He refused to showcase the reminder of exactly how much he lacked being a full man. Rosalind deserved a whole man at her side.

"I'll take off my shoes and then I'll be able to get my jeans off." Normally, he never removed the shoe from his prosthetic foot. Removing the appendage, as she'd suggested, proved much easier. But even though his hip hurt like hell when he leaned from the waist, and his physical therapist warned him against such action, he reached down to begin.

Rosalind knelt again and brushed his hands away. After removing the shoe and sock from his right foot, she worked the much-tighter shoe loose from the prosthetic foot.

Back rigid, he gritted his teeth and stared across the room. Her actions didn't hurt—he couldn't feel a thing—but he hated that he needed her help. He would not be relationship dead weight, forcing her to take care of both his needs and her own.

Finally, she wrenched the shoe free then kissed the top of first his prosthetic foot, then his right foot. "Now we can strip those jeans off."

The fabric peeled off his right leg, but, on the left side, the cuff tangled around the junction of the leg's metal pylon and the foot appendage. More humiliation, damn it. He could have avoided it all by simply wearing shorts or lying naked in bed with the sheet covering his lower half when she walked in. Better yet, he should have convinced her that even if his pants hung around his knees all night, nothing about the pleasure he planned to bring to her would be half-assed.

"You know, you can have such a thing as a 'too authentic' prosthetic. No one needs to keep the problem of pants tangling around their ankle if they no longer have said ankle," she teased, straightening the denim and casting it away.

Although he appreciated her attempt to lessen his humiliation, it arrived too late. His cock had softened to half-mast, and he simply wanted her to leave before he became even more pathetic in her eyes. "I appreciate your patience, but this isn't going to work."

"Why not? All your important parts worked fine earlier." She tossed his briefs aside then slid her hands up his legs, one hand caressing the metal pole on his left side, and the other, his right calf. She paused just below the knee on his left leg. "Is the stump still tender?"

"Not usually." Not as long he didn't overdo it during the day and took the prosthetic off at night. He didn't intend to follow either guideline.

Rosalind didn't push him for a more accurate response. Instead, she massaged his thigh muscles and stroked his inner thighs. Adding her lips to the mix, she feathered light kisses along his sensitive skin, the brim of her hat grazing his stomach. His cock sprang to life, begging for her special brand of attention. Running her tongue along its length, she appeased him and made him desperate for more all at once.

"Lie down, and turn so you're not hanging off the bed," she ordered.

He shifted to the center of the mattress and reclined but remained propped on his elbows on the pillows so he could watch her.

"You follow directions nicely." She winked. "Now we can get this rodeo started." Imitating a lasso routine, she whipped her arm in the air and twirled it in a circle.

Luke started to laugh, but her jiggling breasts and hips caused the humor to stick in his throat. She enticed him more with her natural expression than any seductive routine could have. "I might want you to repeat that dance once you're on top of me. You'll be closer, and I'll be able to study you and make sure I didn't miss an important move."

"Oh yeah? You think you need to study up on my moves?" She smirked.

"A lot of studying." He added as much gravity to his voice as his dry throat would permit. "Hours and hours. I'm a slow student. I'll probably need special tutoring."

She crept onto the mattress then directly over him, straddling him with one foot on each side of his hips. Her newly-emerged aggressor side turned him harder than the steel pole attached to his left leg. After dropping to her knees, she bent down and pressed her mouth to his. Her soft, deliciously persuasive lips nudged him until he succumbed to lying flat.

His cock jerked, brushing the wet heat of her pussy. Oh, yes. He wanted to sink in and drench himself in that wetness. He gripped her hips, needing to fill her so damned bad. The tip of his cock slickened, her desire mixing with his pre-cum.

Shit. "I forgot to put on a condom," he muttered.

Instead of pulling her toward him, he braced his arms to keep her from taking him inside. She made him lose his mind. He longed to skip the protection and give her the baby she'd always wanted, the baby he'd promised her before his gait had become less steady than a toddler's.

"Got you covered." She snagged a packet from the box on the nightstand and gave him a naughty smile, her pussy once again teasing the tip of his unsheathed cock.

"Not yet, you don't," he ground out, his common sense and desperate need for her warring within him.

She laughed and kissed him again, the brim of her hat brushing his forehead. Then she shifted down his thighs and blew gently across his cock.

He jolted, too far along to be teased, and stroked her soft breasts, hoping his touch would entice her to hurry. "Are you trying to make me come without touching me?"

"Not trying to, but if you do, we'll start over, and you can come for me a second time." She grinned and wiggled her hips, causing her breasts to bounce.

Sweet Jesus, she was going to kill him. He'd beg her. Not only would he promise her the world, he'd deliver on it, too. But he couldn't endure her putting off his trip to heaven a moment longer. "Rosie, get a condom on me. We can repeat as many times as you want, but I need to be inside you now."

"I'll hold you to that." She rolled the condom down his length then positioned over him. Lowering her body, she took him all in, like in the pasture.

But, unlike the last time, she didn't give him a chance to set the pace. She thrust down and lifted, riding him with as much ease and perfection as she did the horses earlier, her glorious, ripe breasts and hat bouncing.

Her hat shifted over her eyes, and although the cowgirl fantasy had been hot, Rosalind didn't need any enhancements to increase the heat she generated in him. Plus, he wanted to see her face. He tossed the hat across the room. "Unbraid your hair."

Confusion streaked across her face, and then her eyes widened. "Now?" Her legs trembled at his sides, and her core muscles pulsed around him.

"Now." He grasped her hips and picked up the rhythm.

Within seconds, the wavy strands from the braid cascaded down her shoulders, curling around her breasts, and his hot cowgirl morphed into a rumpled woman in the throes of passion. Damn, he loved the transformation.

"Luke." She pumped her hips, lips parted and eyes half-closed. She cupped his balls while he trailed his fingers down her navel, nestled them in her pubic hair and found her clit.

Her muscles spasmed, and her legs tensed. Slamming down on him one last time, she collapsed onto his chest, shaking and clinging to him.

Unable to hold back any longer, he shot his ecstasy into her, giving her everything he had. It had been hers from the start, anyway.

"Rosie." He rubbed his hand over her damp spine, savoring the continued tremors beneath her skin.

With his wife in his arms, he had no idea how he'd ever leave her again. But to give her the full life she deserved, the life his presence would keep her from achieving, he had to let her go.

As Rosalind attempted to rise off Luke, he hugged her tighter. "Going somewhere?"

"Just rolling over." She pushed her messy hair out of her face and brushed a kiss over his cheek. If he didn't let her go, she'd blow her resolution to keep their interactions light. In the midst of sex, she could get away with more passion and clinginess, but she'd convert the "afterglow" into an "after-scared-off" if she didn't create some space between them.

"Tired of being on top and want a turn on the bottom?" he teased.

Yes, please. Not that she'd get tired of any position with him, but her desire for him was insatiable. "I'm going to order some room service. If we're planning to keep this pace all night, I need sustenance. Unlike a certain sexy Marine, I'm not superhuman."

"It's plenty obvious I'm not superhuman," he muttered.

His arms around her slackened, and she took the opportunity to roll off and out of bed against her instinct to prove how the loss of his limb hadn't weakened him in her eyes. She'd tried plenty of times, and he still refused to believe. Whipping his T-shirt over her head, she padded across the room and placed the order.

"Tell them the tip doubles if they leave it outside the door," Luke instructed.

She shouldn't have been surprised he refused to give strangers the opportunity to check out his leg or quickly avert their gaze from his prosthetic. He hadn't wanted her to check it out, and she'd seen every piece of it before. In the past, she'd tried to assure him people didn't mean any insult by their fascination or discomfort, and only his feelings and response mattered. Apparently, he still wasn't ready to let others' reactions roll off him.

After hanging up, she bent over to gather the clothing strewn across the floor.

From the bed, Luke groaned. "Oh, baby, you have to put on more clothes than just my shirt before you step into the hall, or I'll have to fight off every guy in Montana for you."

She wiggled her bare ass in the air and shot him a cheeky grin. "You could take them."

He threw back the sheet and strode to her, tugging her hips to his pelvis, his cock demanding entry.

Desire flooded her. "Or, you could, you know, take me instead," she gasped, grinding her ass against him.

"My thoughts exactly." He snagged a condom from the box on the nightstand, the box falling to the floor. Ignoring it, he rotated her toward the bed, positioning her on her knees, facedown on the mattress.

Her new position left her more vulnerable than she could tolerate, and the light-heartedness she'd been trying to project deserted her.

"You can tell me to stop anytime," Luke assured her. "I'll never hurt you."

No, he wouldn't hurt her physically. But emotionally he'd already hurt her so much, and every time she opened up to him, she let him in to hurt her again.

Standing behind her, he glided his sheathed cock along her wet slit and tantalized her clit until she moaned. Spreading her legs wider, she pushed back into him, so desperate to draw him inside she no longer cared about the defenseless position. When she couldn't take another second of the delicious teasing, he, at last, drove into her. She cried his name, taking every bit of pleasure he offered. But no matter how much she tried to stockpile the memories for the future, she only had tonight.

Later, she retrieved the food from outside the door, and they ate naked on the bed. She told him stories of the resort guests she'd met and the young adults who shared her dorm. He talked about the success of his company and his missteps going from an action-oriented Marine to an administrative businessman.

Then he ended all conversation by flipping her onto her back and demonstrating the best way to eat dessert, while she writhed in ecstasy beneath his clever fingers and delicious tongue.

The perfect evening emulated the way she wanted to spend the rest of her life with Luke. Unfortunately, she could only enjoy each moment because he had no intention of being part of the rest of her life.

Chapter Nine

Luke awoke to the nightstand light illuminating the hotel room, darkness behind the shades outside, and his stump throbbing like an SOB. He glanced at Rosalind. Lips parted, she sprawled naked, beautiful and exhausted on the bed, sleeping in the same position where they'd finished making love.

She slept so deeply, she wouldn't notice if he removed his prosthetic to relieve the pain. When she started to stir, he'd put it back on before she awoke. He set the device on the floor next to his side of the bed then pulled up the sheet and wrapped his arm around his wife.

She snuggled against him, and he drifted off, more content than he could ever remember. All his life, he'd looked ahead, preparing for what came next—the next deployment with the Marines, how to take the next step toward improving his identity theft app and attracting more potential customers, and how to prepare for life after his next leg surgery. But, that night, nothing mattered but holding Rosalind in his arms.

When he opened his eyes again, streaks of light peeked around the edges of the curtains, and Rosalind faced him, stroking his scruffy cheek, her brown eyes serious.

He slid his hand down her smooth, naked body, cupping the

delectable curve of her ass, and then dipped between her legs. God, he loved how she was already wet for him. He sank his fingers deeper, thrilling when her eyes dilated and her breath stuttered.

His desire mirroring hers, he rolled her onto her back and shifted on top of her. As he threw his leg over hers, his stump brushed her calf.

Shit.

He'd taken off his prosthetic and forgotten to reattach it. No way did he want to remind her he wasn't whole, especially after he'd spent all night proving just how well his parts worked. He brushed his lips over her cheek and shifted away.

She lifted her head. "What happened? Why are you leaving?"

Too ashamed to meet her confused gaze, he stared, unseeing, at the wall. "I'm not up for another round right now."

He felt her attention shift to his erect cock. "How much more up do you need to get?"

Before he could gather his thoughts for an explanation she would understand, she sat up and tossed the sheet aside. He grabbed for it but missed, and his stump lay exposed on the bed before he could shield it from view.

"You've got to be kidding me." Instead of looking at his leg, she grasped his chin and jerked his face to meet her narrowed eyes.

"I took the prosthetic off, okay? I can't sleep while I'm wearing it." Damn, she had no right to be angry. He was angry with her for seeing him as less than whole. Precisely why he didn't want anyone in his life, so he didn't have to defend removing his crap leg whenever he felt like it.

"You can't sleep while wearing it, but you can't have sex without it?" she demanded.

He swallowed. "Of course I can have sex without it."

"But not good, hard sex? Only a pity fuck or a blowjob where you can lie there feeling helpless while I service your baser needs?" If it had been possible, her eyes would have shot mortar fire at him.

"I don't want anyone's pity, especially yours."

"Good, because I've never given it to you, and I'm sure not going to start now." She dug her nails into his shoulders. "Get on top of me,

Luke, and push your cock into me. I want you to make love to me so hard the people in the next room will complain to the front desk about how loud I'm screaming."

She couldn't mean it. She couldn't want him with his permanent deformity. But he shifted toward her anyway, unable to resist the invitation and the challenge. As he pressed her shoulders into the mattress, satisfaction suffused her face.

Her approval turned him so hot and, at the same time, made him want to wipe away her contentment and replace it with pure passion. Shifting above her, he hooked one arm under her knee and elevated her leg. Her lips slackened, and her breath hitched. He massaged the head of his cock along her opening, and the passion he longed to see returned in full force.

"Yes." She raised her hips for him.

He hooked his other arm under her opposite leg, lifting her higher and spreading her wider. She tried to move her hips, but he'd taken away her leverage. She moaned, a sound caught between frustration and desperation.

"You wanted *me* to take *you*," he reminded her.

"So, do it, please. I'm empty without you."

And he'd been empty since the moment he'd left her. He plunged in, filling them both.

She gasped. "Luke, oh, Luke. More, please more."

He thrust, desperate to give her everything she wanted. She clutched his back while he plunged over and over, crying out with more desperation and greater need. Pure emotions played across her face—not an ounce of pity, only ecstasy, passion, and love.

The truth was etched across her face. She loved him. She'd always loved him. Even though he'd cast her aside, her love hadn't dimmed.

Sure, after his injury, she'd sometimes looked at him with sympathy and concern, especially during those moments when he'd been suffering the most. But, most of the time, she'd delivered tough love. And above all, she delivered real love—everlasting love.

He'd been stupid to throw away her acceptance and partnership. Although he couldn't promise never to be stupid again, he'd never be idiotic enough to leave her again.

Convulsing around him, she screamed her orgasm as promised. He kissed her, swallowing her cries, keeping her passion for himself alone. When her tremors subsided, he pulled back.

She opened her eyes, confusion settling in their depths. "You haven't—"

Flooded with love, he kissed her lips gently. "I'll get to it in a minute. Don't move."

He stepped to the floor and hopped two steps to where his jeans hung over the desk chair.

"Oh, a condom. I forgot." She flopped on the pillow.

He hadn't even thought of protection, but raising a child he might not be able to keep up with, although still a scary prospect, no longer terrified him into pushing her away. Taking what he needed from the pocket, he returned to the bed.

"Not a condom. If you want a baby, I'll try twenty-four hours a day with you to make it happen. This is what I couldn't make love to you without." He held up the gold band that she'd returned to him a few hours ago.

Rosie's jaw gaped as she stared at it.

Kneeling between her legs, he took her left hand from the mattress. "Give me a second chance to be your husband. I can't promise I won't still be an ass and make stupid decisions, but I'll never leave you again. I do promise that I'll love you forever."

Before she could say a word, he pressed an index finger to her lips, needing her to hear everything in his heart first. "Wherever you want to live—in your dorm room, this hotel, a house in the nearest town—I can live anywhere, as long as I'm with you. I'll never push you away again. Have your lawyers draw up a contract to strip me of everything I own if I hurt you. I'll sign whatever you want. I'm yours, Rosie."

He slid the wedding band on her finger, where it fit every bit as perfectly as the first time he'd placed it there. Switching his gaze to her face, he focused on the tears glittering on her lashes.

"Damn it, I promised I wouldn't cry around you again, no matter what."

Before she could swipe at the tears, he caught her hand, and then kissed her tears as they escaped. "I'm hoping these are happy tears, but, either way, you don't have to hide them from me."

"Very happy," she whispered, wrapping her arms around his neck and her legs around his waist until his cock lodged at her opening.

"Can you tell me you love me again?" He knew it, but still needed to hear the words from her lips.

"I love you, Luke, always and forever, my husband." She took him in, body, heart, and soul, completing his life more permanently than any amputation could sever. "You are in for a hell of a lot more than one night with your wife."

Which was exactly what he wanted. "I'm all in. For a lifetime."

~A Note from Sara~

Dear Reader,

I hope you've enjoyed the journey and watching the storylines in the One Night with the Bridal Party series develop.

I love to hear from all my readers, whether you want to chat about one night stands, marriage, characters who need their own stories, or something crazy and quirky like squirrels. Drop me an email at sarashafer@rocketmail.com and share whatever's on your mind. Also, subscribe to my newsletter to stay up-to-date on my book releases and other author news: http://eepurl.com/rx_AL

Sara Daniel
www.SaraDaniel.com

www.ingramcontent.com/pod-product-compliance
Lightning Source LLC
Chambersburg PA
CBHW061932170626
46813CB00006B/2374